HER HUSBAND'S LIES

An unputdownable psychological thriller with
a breathtaking twist

T.J. BREARTON

Joffe Books, London
www.joffebooks.com

First published in Great Britain in 2022

© T.J. Brearton

Cover art by Nick Castle

ISBN: 978-1-80405-672-1

For Stuart

It's good you're out there, man.
No, you don't have to dedicate one to me now.

PROLOGUE

The man said he knew her, that they had friends in common. He named the friends.

He was good-looking; that was one thing. But there was something in his eyes that Kerry couldn't quite place. Most men looked at her like they wanted her. They'd always been around, since she was young, dissecting her with their eyes. Men who mooched off her mother for what little she had. The small piece of land her mother owned, the modest livestock. The booze and the drugs.

Kerry didn't know her father. Didn't even know who he was. There were three candidates, but none willing to take the paternity test.

The man was probably lying about their mutual friends. All men were liars. It was part of their nature. They were opportunists.

But he seemed to have a secret. And when he looked at her, Kerry felt like she shared that secret. So when he asked her to come with him, she went.

She wasn't stupid; she was a senior in high school. She knew some men were craftier than others. They weren't all the bumbling drunks of her experience, looking for her in the dark after her mother went to bed. This man was red-blooded, straight, with the same hormones as the rest of them. The thing was, sex didn't seem the biggest priority on his list. And that was intriguing. He wanted her, but he was in control of his desire. And maybe that was the secret. He had some kind of poise the other men didn't, some knowledge about his future.

Intriguing. Attractive.

They never texted, only met at the house. There were a number of buildings on the property, including a bunkhouse. With her mother drunk and passed out, and with Stan off in town (probably at the bar), Kerry met up with the man.

The bunkhouse was where she spent time when she wanted to be alone, away from her mother. Or with her friends when they wanted to get a little drink on, a little smoke on. She'd done her best to chase away the smells of mice poop and mildew; she'd made it nice.

She was a little bit proud when he saw it.

"This was actually the original camp," she told him. "It was built by my grandfather — my mom's dad — when he first bought the land."

"It's nice."

"Then he had the trailer delivered." She meant the single-wide where her mother spent most of her time. "He wanted a place for his family but didn't want to build anymore. That's where my mom grew up." Kerry regretted mentioning her mother. But she was a little nervous, chatty.

The man stepped toward her. The floor creaked under his weight. He gazed at her in a non-threatening way that was nevertheless powerful. She'd never had this reaction before, not to any boy at school. Not even to Moses. Maybe she was wrong in generalizing about all men.

He didn't touch her, just stood in front of her, looking down into her eyes. She felt like she was melting, like her legs were going numb.

He did remind her of the past. The way her mother's boyfriends and semi-boyfriends over the years hit on her, touched her. The one who'd forced himself all the way. She'd hated all that, but it was mixing together now, blending with these new feelings, this attraction. Was something wrong with her?

"Come on," he said. "Come with me. I want to show you something."

She hesitated, then took his outstretched hand. She blew out the candle on the table as he led her out the door and into the cold night. They walked down the driveway, right in sight of the trailer. The TV light flickered in the windows. Blue-and-white flashes. She pictured her mother unconscious in the recliner. Usually, Kerry checked to make sure there was no lit cigarette smoldering. She might turn off the TV and put away the beer cans.

But not tonight.

At the end of the driveway, they turned onto the road. His vehicle sat in the dark. The lights were off, but it was running.

The stars were out above. Kerry's breath rose toward them as he opened the car door for her.

He waited. She looked into his eyes, the bit of light she could see reflected. He was smiling, just barely. His tongue poked out of his pursed lips.

"Have you done this before or what?" she asked. It was meant to be coy. Cute.

"Yes," he said.

Was it wrong to trust him? She wasn't even sure trust was a factor.

She slipped into the warm car, and he shut the door.

CHAPTER ONE

FRIDAY, FEBRUARY 24

It had never felt right to her. Her husband's crash, where he'd been when it happened, none of it. For six weeks, she'd been left wondering.

At least the media had stopped coming around.

Everyone knew that novelists were introverts, and Callie was no exception. It was why she lived here: quiet anonymity in the rural northeast. A few people knew who she was, but not many.

The people of Hawkins — population 989 — weren't focused on fiction writers. They tended to their dairy farms, stabled their horses, worked at the school, prison, or in the local government. They eked out a living working service-retail in a county that ranked the most dependent in the state. *Oh, there's a semi-famous novelist living nearby? Hold my beer while I don't give a shit.*

She didn't resent their indifference; she appreciated it. Living a regular life, left alone on her ten-acre property with her husband — this was the dream.

Until six weeks ago, when the dream became a nightmare.

Yes, the media had stopped coming around, stopped lurking at the end of her driveway, hoping for a glimpse of the reclusive writer. Normally, a single-car highway accident would merit a mention in the local news police blotter and that would be it, but Callie's semi-celebrity and the fact that her husband was in a coma had drummed up a little more interest. Not much else happened in rural upstate New York in mid-winter.

The reporters had finally given up, though, drawn off by other scents. She wondered if they'd come back. Abel could wake up any day. At least, that was the hope. And when he did, the reporters might come looking for the full story, wanting to know what he remembered.

Just like she would.

Six weeks ago, Abel had driven off the road and into an icy lake. Before plunging into the frigid water, his truck had hit a tree. Though the vehicle glanced off and kept going, he'd cracked his skull.

That was what the police had said, but the details of the accident had always been murky.

Whether he'd hit black ice or swerved to avoid a deer, they didn't know. It had happened in the middle of nowhere at dusk. No one had seen anything, no one had heard anything, and Abel's old truck was too beat up to tell the accident investigators much about the story of the crash. So they'd called it a terrible accident and closed the case.

It was a long time to be without your partner. But it might be only the tip of the iceberg. As she put herself together that morning, getting ready for her regular trip to the hospital, she was reminded of a statistic that two to four weeks was the typical length of a coma. After that, things looked bleak, with some patients staying that way for years. The longest had been gone for twenty-seven.

Callie couldn't imagine it. It already seemed like her husband didn't exist, and that felt bad enough. As frequently as she visited him, six weeks was still a long time not to talk to your spouse. To look into their eyes, or be looked at in return.

My poor, sweet man.

Six weeks, and this once-vital forty-three-year-old who didn't smoke, didn't drink, had already wasted away. This formerly bearded carpenter in his corpse-like repose. Surrounded by beeping machines and the hushed rumble of the persistent vegetative ward at Pearl Medical Center in Burlington, Vermont.

All because he'd lost control of his vehicle and swerved off the road.

All because, for some reason, he'd been an hour away from home, in a region where he had no clients she was aware of.

It had never felt right to her. Not in her gut. Abel was just too reliable, too good a driver. He'd spent his life navigating snowy back roads in the North Country. And Lake Clear was a place he rarely ventured, with nothing showing up in his appointment book to explain his trip there.

So she dreamed of him. About his being in trouble. About a hit-and-run. About him being trapped inside his truck, the water pouring in, and she was trying to get to him, to pull him out, but the door was stuck.

When she wasn't lying awake with insomnia, she dreamed about faceless men surrounding him, dragging him into the water, pulling him under to finish him off.

CHAPTER TWO

It was seventy miles to Burlington — longer if Callie took the bridge and avoided the expensive ferry.

In the beginning, her trips to see Abel had been daily. Then five days a week. Now three or four, depending. The guilt of that gnawed at her as she drove. Normally she could rationalize it away, but today she was distracted by a car that seemed to be following her.

She kept checking the rear view — the roads to the ferry were small backcountry roads, not a lot of intersections, so it made sense that a car behind you stayed there for some time. But the vehicle seemed to be keeping the perfect distance: a good ten car lengths back, the distance you'd keep if you were tailing somebody and didn't want to be conspicuous.

And when she *did* make turns, the vehicle followed suit.

It was a sedan, maybe gray or light green. Not the cross-over SUVs that populated the region. Not a pickup truck, either. A Corolla or an old Honda Accord, maybe, with a lone figure at the wheel. Callie kept checking the mirror until she got to the ferry.

As she pulled up to the gate, she checked behind her, but the vehicle had finally stopped following. She caught a glimpse of it moving north up Route 9, and then it was gone.

Callie exhaled. She paid the fare and rolled aboard when the ferry arrived.

She shook off the sense of being followed — obviously she hadn't been — and reminded herself why she did this, why she made these trips. It was to be with her husband. To comfort him and love him. And, hopefully, to remind him of the life he was missing.

Abel didn't have anyone else but her. His brother lived on the other side of the country; his parents were deceased. Callie and Abel had one son, Cormac, a sophomore in college. And Callie's parents had retired out of the country, in Costa Rica.

They'd come north once since Abel's accident, and Callie's mother was hinting at another visit. She'd been hinting for weeks, really, but Callie continued to pooh-pooh it, and her mother continued to stall on buying the plane tickets. Which was as it should be. Callie loved her parents, but it was so much better not to be around them.

Her last trip to see them, three years before, had been ill-advised. She'd thought she'd get two birds with one stone: spend quality time with Mom and Dad, and kick-start a new book with the change of scenery. Neither had worked. The "quality time" was mostly spent listening to her mother's monologue on the decline of Western civilization, and the book had been scrapped a month later.

No, her mother didn't really want to come back to the States. Wendy Baker-Pavlis was uncomfortable here already. A former college professor, she'd left because she'd decided there was no more redemption possible for American culture: *We've devolved into a mindless consumer society, arguing over whatever hot topic the media serves up on any given day.*

Callie disagreed. She thought there was always the possibility of redemption.

But Wendy didn't relish the prospect of spending more time in her daughter's home, either. Not while her daughter's husband developed bedsores seventy miles away. While his muscles atrophied and his skin paled and hair thinned. They didn't tell you that about coma patients. That some of them, like Abel, started losing their hair.

Wendy would wonder aloud if he had any interior life. If — despite the conventional wisdom that a coma patient felt nothing, saw nothing, heard nothing — if there *was* something. Some connection to the outside world. Or at least some interior activity. Some dream, some thought.

Callie didn't know. But she *did* know that Abel didn't need her mother around, henpecking and questioning everything. He didn't need anyone but Callie. So she read to him, and she spoke to him, and she tried to comfort him.

One thing her mother was right about: he'd lost weight. Twelve pounds, to be exact.

Callie tried to remain upbeat. But on her bad days, she shared her mother's pessimism. It felt like Abel was gradually disappearing, and soon there would be nothing left.

* * *

When the door was shut and she was alone in the room with him, Callie took Abel's hand. She studied him in the soft light. The hospital had allowed her to make the room nicer, so she'd brought a lamp. Plus books, a couple of framed photos, and red-and-black-checked fleece blanket. It was warm in the hospital, but the blanket was a familiar thing.

She talked, as she usually did, about their lives. Hoping that other familiar things — the subject of their son, for instance — would have an effect. "I sometimes think, what if Mac was little again? You know? What if this had happened to us back then? Little Mac running around, Breezy chasing him, and you're gone." She was referring to their dog, now passed on, called Breezy.

"I don't think I could have handled it," she said. "Having to explain to Mac where you were. Having to do it all without you. So I'm grateful for that." She watched the shallow rise and fall of Abel's chest. "Mac's doing good, though. I talked to him last night. He says everything's okay. He's staying focused."

She thought a moment and added, "It *is* Mac, though . . . He could be totally bullshitting me."

Their son was nineteen and had been away at college for two years. Cormac was a great kid — bright and kind. They were fortunate. They'd agonized for a couple of years about having more kids, to give Cormac a sibling, but once they'd decided, it turned out they were unable.

Cormac didn't seem any worse for it. He had a knack for being grateful, for feeling fortunate, as if he felt lucky to be here. Lucky to have made it before his parents lost the ability, apparently, to conceive.

The way Cormac had put it: "It's like that scene in the Indiana Jones movie. You know the one? When he just makes it out of the room, before that big stone door rolls down with a thud."

"When did you watch Indiana Jones?" Callie had asked.

"I saw a meme."

"You're saying my womb is a cave?"

"And I made it out just in time."

"That's great, kid. Thank you." But she'd laughed. And she'd known what he meant; he was truly — and, given his age, preternaturally — grateful for his existence.

It had been a couple of days past New Year's when his father's car had skidded from the road into icy water. Cormac had just returned to school from his holiday break. As soon as he'd heard about it, he'd raced home. Visiting his father in the ICU, he'd vowed to drop out of college. "Absolutely not," Callie had said. "Your father is getting everything he needs — and he needs you to stay in school. Everything is going to be fine."

Cormac had grudgingly agreed and returned to school days later, but since then, Callie had checked regularly. Despite his verbal reports that all was well, she knew her son. Already easily distracted, he was struggling to stay focused. And who could blame him? But this, too, was the way things needed to be. Her parents needed to remain in Costa Rica; her son needed to remain studying law and justice at St Lawrence.

She let go of Abel's hand. "I'll be right back."

Pulling the door gently shut behind her, she left Abel's room. She knew all of the nurses on the ward, every staff member from the orderlies to the neurology specialists.

She waved at the nurse currently seated at the nurses' station, Brie. She was thirty and blonde and had tattoos. Brie waved back and smiled and snapped the gum she was chewing.

Callie continued to the small coffee area off the hallway, between the nurses' station and the restroom. The rooms were all on the opposite side, each with a view. Views for the visitors, of course. Not the patients.

It wasn't cheap.

All in all, it was costing over seven hundred dollars a day for Abel to be here. To have the machines feeding him, the nurses bathing him, the physical therapists exercising him. The world's most expensive spa facility.

Over seven hundred dollars a day, for six weeks and counting. Between the hospital, the initial emergency services, the ambulance rides and all the rest, the bill was approaching forty thousand. It was everything they had saved.

Going without health insurance was not one of the best decisions she and Abel had made. Well, it hadn't really *been* a decision, but a perpetual kicking of the can down the road. Something they'd talked about dealing with for years and then avoided. *Over a thousand dollars a month? On the off-off chance something might happen?* Callie was a novelist — nothing to worry about there. Death by over-caffeination, secondary to writer's block, as a coroner might say.

But Abel was a caretaker and a carpenter. He worked with power tools. He climbed onto roofs. They should have known better.

It was a cliché, really. *You never think it's going to happen to you.* It felt unlikely. And then, it did happen. Your husband went careening off the road in his old pickup truck and plunged into a freezing lake.

But, she reminded herself as she fixed her coffee, she was lucky. Thousands of people lost their loved ones every day to vehicle crashes. Abel wasn't lost; he was still here. One day, they'd be back together again.

And if she ran out of money before then? She would tap her parents and friends, create a GoFundMe, exhaust every option.

There was only one scenario she worried about. One thing that could change and make matters worse.

It was her friend Annie, a radiation tech at another hospital, who'd brought it up.

"If his brain activity changes, it's not good."

"Why? Change like what?"

"If he becomes unresponsive. Fixed pupils, things like that. Have you seen the charts? His brain activity chart?"

"They showed me all of that. Everything is good. And I'm his spouse, and I have medical power of attorney, so . . . ."

"Good. And even if you have trouble paying, they'll keep treating him. As long as all that's good. But . . . ."

"What?"

"Did Abel ever sign a DNR?"

It had given Callie pause. "That's a Do Not Resuscitate?"

"Yeah."

"No. I don't know. I don't think so. I would know, right? I mean, he never told me anything like that. We never really . . . we didn't talk about this stuff much."

"No one usually does."

"How can I find out?"

"I don't think you can. He would have done it through his PCP." She meant his primary care provider, his doctor. "And they can't share that, even with a spouse," Annie said. "Honestly, I think the only way you'd know is if the hospital admin came down one day and said they had a problem."

Callie had tried to find out, and Annie had been correct: Abel's doctor couldn't share the information.

It had left her in terror for a few days. The thought that if Abel took a turn for the worse, it could result in tragedy. They would have to unplug him. Callie would have to let him go.

She didn't like to think about it, but there it was. Like a cliff at the end of the road. She didn't know if she could ever recover from something like that. She was an independent person, always had been — always worked for herself, or gigged, never had a nine-to-five. But she'd always craved a partner and never liked being alone. Abel was her rock.

"What if something happened?" Callie had asked Annie. She couldn't help but wonder if the circumstances of the crash could affect the DNR.

"What do you mean?"

"What if it wasn't an accident? The state police reconstructed the crash, but they were never exactly sure. They'd basically guessed that he just lost control of the vehicle. The weather was bad, a mix of precipitation, the plows were slow to react, *blah blah blah*. But what if it was a hit-and-run? What if somebody else was responsible?"

Annie had thought about it. "I don't know that it would matter. I mean, maybe it could. That's really bioethics. And cop stuff. Above my pay grade, hon."

So Callie had hunted around. They knew one lawyer, and she called him.

"It wouldn't change anything about his DNR," the lawyer said. "If he was the victim of a crime, his DNR would be carried out just the same. But, if evidence of a crime was proven, yeah . . . a successful lawsuit might be able to get all of your money back."

CHAPTER THREE

Her phone buzzed in her bag, on the floor against the wall.

"Hang on, honey." Callie set the book she was reading to Abel down on the hospital bed and went to her bag.

An unfamiliar number. A 315 area code. Spam was a constant problem. *Hello, we're trying to reach you about your car's extended warranty* . . .

She dropped the phone back into the bag and returned to his bedside to resume reading. But for a moment, she merely sipped her coffee — a bit bitter, a bit bland — and studied her husband. His beard was gone and he was clean-shaven. His closed eyes seemed to be receding into his skull. She dabbed his dry lips with a wet paper towel.

"What happened to you?"

It was a whisper.

"Why were you in Lake Clear?"

Abel had grown up in the North Country. He owned a tractor and a small excavator. He rode a motorcycle in the summer. If it had an engine, he could drive it. How many times had they come across people on the side of the road — tourists, typically — who'd miscalculated a turn and slipped into the ditch?

Abel even kept a winch and chain in his truck; he'd haul people out and save them the expense of a tow truck, or jumpstart their dead batteries with his portable charger.

He was the helper. *He* was the capable one. Not someone who gets into accidents. At least, not someone who loses control on a slippery turn. He knew better. He could judge the road in inclement weather. Never the daredevil, always the responsible driver.

In the early days, just after the accident, the state police investigator, who was nice in an avuncular way and seemed capable and interested, suggested why Abel had been in Lake Clear: "Maybe he'd been meeting with a new client? There are a lot of second homes out there on Upper Saranac. Places to care for through the winter."

"It's possible," she'd said. "But all the caretaking he does is close to home. He likes to be able to respond quickly in case of emergency."

"Right, right. What about the carpentry work?"

"It ranges a little further. He's just so meticulous, though. He writes it all down. I almost always know where he is, what he's working on. And this was just . . . there's nothing."

Two weeks later, the investigator, whose name was Footman, had closed the case. Abel had been in a car accident, no foul play. The roads had been unquestionably treacherous — multiple accidents had occurred in the region that day. He'd been knocked unconscious when the truck jumped from the road and hit a tree — the old vehicle lacked an air bag, and he'd slammed his head against the glass of the windshield.

After the tree, the momentum had carried him farther out over the frozen lake beside the road, where the truck's weight punctured the thin ice.

By the time the emergency services pulled him out, he'd been partly submerged for over twenty minutes. Only his upper chest and head had remained above the surface. If he had rolled just a few inches farther, he would have drowned.

A motorist passing by had seen Abel approximately four minutes after he'd gone in. It had taken Rory Harper, a local, thirteen more minutes to wade in and, using Abel's own winch and towrope, pull the vehicle out.

Harper was able to drag Abel's truck backward through the ice and muck, enough that the EMTs could access the cab when the first responders arrived another nine minutes after that.

Despite Harper's noble efforts, Abel was hypothermic by then. Between that and the head trauma, his brain had swollen. And gone into hibernation.

Callie watched him now and decided — at least for the moment — not to think anymore about why. Cosmically, there was no answer. Or, there were non-answers. *The Lord works in mysterious ways. These things happen.* But practically, reasonably, there were no answers. Just questions.

Finally, she returned to the book they'd been reading. *Crow Killer: The Saga of Liver-Eating Johnson.* It wasn't her cup of tea — a real-life story about a wife and unborn child killed by Crow braves — but Abel liked historical nonfiction.

* * *

On the way home that afternoon, she checked to see if anyone was following her. Maybe in a gray-green early model sedan. But no one was.

Her phone rang.

The roads were wintry but plowed and salted; she risked a quick glance. Same number as before.

She ignored it.

* * *

Fifteen minutes after she'd arrived home, the phone rang again.

Callie hurried from the bathroom, where she'd been just finishing a shower. She was always eager to pick up the phone these days, in case it was Cormac. Or the hospital with that magical phrase: *Mrs Sanderson, a wonderful thing — your husband is awake.*

But no. It was the same 315 area code.

Callie gave up and answered. Maybe it really was important. "Hello?"

No one spoke. Just breathing.

"Hello?" Callie repeated. "Excuse me, who is calling?"

Finally, a voice:

"I know what happened to your husband."

CHAPTER FOUR

Callie's stomach tightened. Her skin felt electrified, the fine hairs standing on end. "Excuse me — I'm sorry — what? Who are you?"

The voice was soft but not meek. A young woman. "I'm nobody. I mean, my identity isn't important. Just what I know."

"Are you a reporter?"

"No." The caller didn't elaborate.

"What do you mean, you know what happened to my husband?"

"I don't know everything." The voice was still soft, calm. "I only know some things. But I want to help you."

Callie stood at the kitchen counter in her towel. The house was drafty and the evaporating shower water chilled her skin. But she didn't want to lose this call. She hurried to the woodstove in the corner of the living room and opened the flue. Flames took the smoldering wood.

"Who are you? What's your name?"

More breathing. Then: "Althea."

"Okay, Althea . . . Like what? What do you know?"

Thoughts flooded Callie's mind. *What would a cop do?* Question the caller's motives: *what is she selling?* Maybe wait

18

vehicle in various places, yes. Including some scratches from when the motorist — I think his name was Rory Harper — pulled it out."

Harper flashed into her thoughts for a moment. She'd met him just once at the police station in the hazy days following the crash. Wild hair and a gnarly beard. A shy quasi-hermit who lived in the Lake Clear area. He'd been polite and tolerant of her effusive thanks — from what she remembered — and then went quickly on his way.

Footman said, "So we had Harper's efforts to winch it out doing damage to the rear bumper. We had all the damage done going into the water, hitting trees. And the fact that your husband drove an old truck that was already in rough shape."

It was true. Abel had kept using the old Toyota for most of his work, despite owning a brand-new Chevy. The Toyota was dinged and dented, with rust spots and splatters of paint.

"So what exactly does that mean?"

"Well, one thing — I'm remembering those scratches, but because they came from Harper, they weren't in the accident report. So that information was not accessible anywhere. The only people who know about it are myself, Harper, maybe a handful of first responders who might've noticed, but doubtful."

"There are pictures, though?"

"Yeah. You had the vehicle scrapped, correct?"

"You told me I could. Three weeks ago. It was totaled."

"Yes. Right. And everything was concluded."

She pieced it all together. "So you're saying the vehicle could have been struck from behind. And no one knew that except you and a couple of others. That's why you reacted just now."

"Mrs Sanderson, like I said, the forensics just couldn't make a real determination. They weren't confident saying yes or no. I'm only reacting to—"

"Abel was never in any accidents."

"Yes, I remember that was something you told us at the time. You were adamant he was a safe driver. That he never

— you know — that nothing had ever happened. Was Althea Cooper specific? You said she mentioned a doctor, and bears. That was it?"

"That was it." Callie chewed on her bottom lip. *My God. If Abel was hit from behind . . .*

"Mrs Sanderson, is it possible Cooper is someone who knows you, or at least knows you were skeptical about your husband's accident?"

"No. I've never really said anything to anyone. Just . . . sometimes I think about it."

"Sure. You never know, though. A conversation with a friend, maybe an email. Have you had any hacking incidents?"

She'd considered the very same thing. "No."

"Well, just check your cyber security. To be on the safe side. This kind of thing — if it is a scam — the way they work is to have someone in the background, while someone else does the performance. She might not seem the hacker type, but maybe she's got some computer genius boyfriend. That kind of thing."

Maybe her brother, Callie thought for a second.

Footman went quiet again, with that soft din of voices and office phones burbling in the background. She felt like she was on a roller coaster. One minute she had convinced herself everything was settled: her husband was recovering from an accident, and nothing more. He would be fine; there were no riddles to solve. At least, nothing she could figure out. The next moment, clairvoyants and cops were saying the same things — he could have been the victim of a hit-and-run.

Or even purposely injured.

A line rang in the distance. Footman covered the phone so that his voice was low and muffled as he spoke to someone.

Callie went back to her tea, set aside the saucer she'd been covering it with, removed the bag and set it on the saucer.

She considered, for a moment, the way she was dressed, the fact she was drinking caffeine at this hour . . .

Something her mother had told her years ago came to mind: *We make our decisions in an instant, then spend the rest of the time trying to justify them.*

Callie already knew what she was going to do this evening — a kind of low-grade clairvoyance of her own at work.

Footman came back one the line. "All right, Mrs Sanderson. I hope that you—"

"Mr Footman, one more thing. What do you think about the vehicle she described?"

"Sorry? Oh. You said a . . ."

"Green SUV. That's all she said." Callie almost mentioned the car from earlier but decided to keep that quiet for now.

"Yeah, I don't know. Huh. There wasn't any, ah . . . Well, as you may recall, Mrs Sanderson, that area — that section of Lake Clear — there's nothing around. There's the campgrounds a couple of miles away. And there are the homes on Upper Saranac Lake. But we spoke with those owners, and there was nothing — no eyewitnesses, no cameras . . ." Footman covered the phone again. *Be right there. Just another minute.*

"That's fine," Callie said, making a decision to end the call. "I remember. Okay, Mr Footman. Thank you."

"If there's anything else I can do for you, don't hesitate . . ."

Five minutes later, she was backing the brand-new Chevy down the driveway. It was almost three in the afternoon, but in late February it wouldn't be dark until six, so she had time.

Lake Clear was just about an hour away.

CHAPTER SIX

The weather called for flurries, but the snow was profuse, the kind that stacked up fast. Spicules of ice crackled against the windshield as Callie hugged the turns and tapped the brakes.

Easy, easy, she told the truck. Told herself, really. She was anxious but also excited. For six weeks she'd been idling. Visiting Abel, checking in on Cormac. Eating and drinking enough to stay alive. Keeping herself distracted from her husband's worsening condition. Being a mother to her son.

It had been a time in her life she'd come to think of as the Great Pause.

The early days had been tough, sure. The shock of Abel's crash, of his sudden absence. But it had been busy. Her life had exploded. She was used to long cups of coffee while staring at the laptop in her home office, and suddenly her days were all doctors and hospitals, police and press. Kind-hearted strangers leaving casseroles on her doorstep. Her days were full.

Until they weren't.

Because that was what happened in every tragedy. In death, certainly, the well-wishes and the casseroles stopped coming. When your spouse was in a coma, it was the same thing — only, you weren't supposed to grieve. And you couldn't move on.

The Great Pause. As if a divine hand had pressed the button on the remote. Everything froze. Life kept going, in a weird way — bodily functions kept happening, people went to work, church, and school. But for Callie, there were no more plans. The future was held in abeyance.

She couldn't move on, and she couldn't give up.

You're not allowed the "giving up" kinds of thoughts until about two years in, she thought.

Right. Not until time had ground to a halt. When, every day, all they did was move him a little, so the sores didn't spread. When his muscles had wasted away to limp slabs of meat beneath parchment skin . . .

It was terrible to put a time limit on something like your husband's life, on the amount of time you could withstand the Great Pause and the Great Wasting Away of the man you'd previously spent over two decades with, had raised a child with, had experienced every conceivable emotion with. A man who knew you, sometimes better than you knew yourself.

Even if he didn't know everything. Even if there were still mysteries.

Callie tapped the brakes again and then touched the gas pedal, leaning into the latest curve. Always better to accelerate slightly into the turns — something her father had taught her years ago. Or had it been a friend's father? It might've been. Considering how absent Dad really was.

The trees blurred past. Evergreens, coated thickly in white. The snow dove for the windshield as she gained ground. She was through Saranac Lake and out the other side. Then she was past the tiny blip of Lake Clear — just one general store closed for the winter, a tiny airport no one ever used (no one she'd ever met, anyway), the local landfill, a few houses, bookended by a Presbyterian church and a Roman Catholic church — and then nothing again but winding road, the whack of the wipers, the powerful thrum of the engine.

The daylight was waning as four o'clock came on. Callie hunched over the steering wheel, clutching it with both hands as she peered out.

Close now.

She hadn't been here for a month and a half. It was a blurry memory, mostly of Footman's smooth voice and the silver sides to his high-top haircut. The smell of aftershave in his unmarked police car. The sense that the whole thing was some strange dream.

Footman had shown her the crash site, pointing out a tree nearly cracked in half. Other, smaller trees near the water's edge — just saplings — that had been mown down completely.

She slowed as she reached the spot. She saw the bent tree as she pulled over and parked the Chevy on the shoulder of the road.

The cold hunted the gaps in her jacket, and she pulled her winter hat down a little more around her ears as she walked toward the trees near the water's edge.

There should've been a guardrail out here.

She'd had the thought many times. She'd voiced it once to Footman. But it wasn't that kind of a spot. Guardrails were for steep embankments, deep ditches. It was flat through here. The route was old, and over the years, the lake edge, which was shallow and swampy, had encroached.

Still. It's not safe for people.

Well, apparently it was.

Unless you were being followed, maybe. And someone ran you off the road.

She pictured Abel that night, just a few days into the new year. Had he been followed? Had he known it? Had he only realized it after it was too late?

Boom. She imagined the impact. The stranger rear-ending Abel, sending his truck into a fishtail. He pumps the brakes, but it's too late. He'd been needing new tires, she remembered — the Toyota's were getting bald . . .

Back end loose with slick tires spinning, the momentum carries him off the road, where he hits the beech tree and cracks his head against the glass. It sends him careening through more small trees and out onto the ice.

Nearing the deep end, he breaks through. The nose of the truck goes down until the tires hit lake bottom. Water pours into the cab, submerging him up to his chest.

Her vision starred with tears as she imagined it: Abel is suspended by the seat belt, his arms afloat in the frigid water. His breathing is rapid and shallow.

For seventeen minutes, his brain slowly swells, shutting down, and his lungs fill the cab with clouds of air, the breath freezing against the windshield.

Icicles form on his eyelashes as his face turns blue.

Rory Harper arrives and winches him out, and EMTs extract him from the vehicle. But seventeen minutes have elapsed. *Seventeen minutes* — an eternity when floating in the dark and cold, utterly alone. A void in which he remained.

Callie walked toward the lake. The road and the lake curved in. Two U-shapes that came together like a couple of parabolas, almost meeting at the vertices, but not quite. That gap, between one vertex and another, was about twenty yards. Twenty yards of scrub and sapling trees growing right out of the water. A swampy area that had been frozen over then, as it was now, but shallow, just inches deep.

Her feet sank into the snow, and she was careful of the ice beneath it. She was confident it was frozen solid in late February, but she still wasn't taking any chances, not venturing farther than the shallow area.

Just far enough to get a good look at the houses close by. The silent witnesses to the night her husband — for all intents and purposes — disappeared.

Three houses. Three that she could see through the white haze of snowfall, anyway. One just barely.

Footman had said police talked to the neighbors, the owners of those stately homes. But had they really gone to every door? Down every private drive? She doubted it.

Somebody had to have seen something.

Somebody had to *know* something.

There was a reason Abel had been out here. He wasn't just joyriding. Abel Sanderson was a man of purpose.

She stood a moment looking, and the wind came through, chapping her exposed face. She huddled deeper into her jacket and turned back for the Chevy, trudged up to it, and got inside, where she opened her phone. The cell coverage was limited out here, just one bar showing, and no 5G. GPS would likely work, since it used different satellites, but she'd already looked up the area and taken screenshots just in case.

Upper Saranac was one of three lakes in a chain. Lower Saranac was almost entirely state preserve, and so was Middle. Upper was the least publicly accessible because it bordered the most private land. Here, the elite made their second homes. Bordering the lake were the Great Camps the owners might call cabins but anyone else would call mansions.

Porch railings made from red birch. Furniture carved from maple and oak. Clerestory ceilings with antler chandeliers, exposed beams and bear skin rugs. Deer heads hanging on the walls — some of them. The Great Camp owners weren't all hunters. But the ones that were liked their trophies.

You couldn't hunt black bears in the Adirondacks, but that didn't stop them from being a decorative favorite. From small figurines to sculptures built to scale, people loved their bears.

Bears everywhere.

Callie rolled forward in the Chevy, going slow now.

The Great Camps and second homes were accessible by water, most of them, but they were reachable by land, too. By private roads. She had her map showing these roads — pictures she'd taken of that map — and she was going to try them, one by one. Follow each one to the house at the end. See if there were any green cars parked there.

CHAPTER SEVEN

Most of the private roads were dirt. Narrow and rooty. A dense canopy of pines let in scant light or snow. Some roads were short — driveways, really, with a twist here or there — but the longest reached almost a mile. Some led to more than one home. Wooden signs marked the forks, often hand-carved and painted. *The Malones. The St Bonaventures. The Scanlons.* Some roads started paved and turned to dirt later. Only one was asphalt all the way up to the garage — *The Deiffenbachs.*

Callie didn't recognize any of the names. Maybe one or two sounded vaguely familiar, but no one Abel had ever mentioned. And this was a different world, too, culturally speaking. Callie was a working-class writer. Abel was a carpenter. They cobbled together their living.

The people here hailed from cities and suburbs, from the corporate world. Some of them made six figures before the end of first quarter.

Most of the roads led to empty, dark homes. Callie would drive in, discover the place still and quiet, no vehicles. If there was a garage, she'd quickly get out of the Chevy and have a peek inside. Twice, so far, she'd encountered people at home. Parked vehicles, lighted windows, other signs of life like footprints in the snow or shoveled walkways. At one massive home, a silhouette darkened a front window.

But she'd seen no one up close. Very few signs of life. Secondary vehicles, mostly. The occasional pick-up truck or weather-beaten sedan. Four-wheelers and snowmobiles. One mud-splattered Jeep.

Some of these — like the white pickup with the ladder rack and the *J. Emmons Contractor* decal on the side — were signs of caretakers. People like Abel.

Caretaking was something he did on the side, for a select few. It typically started with an introduction, a reference. The very first job he'd gotten, some ten years ago, had evolved out of a house renovation. He'd redone the kitchen of a sizable cabin in Keene Valley, and the owners had asked him if he would consider looking after the place for the winter. It basically entailed snow removal, pipe insulation, pest control. People who left their cabins alone too long returned to collapsed roofs, frozen pipes, and raccoons-in-residence. His business had built up to five customers over the past decade, and she thought she'd known them all.

None were here, in Lake Clear.

She could have been wrong. Or this could have been the start of a new relationship. Maybe one of Abel's existing customers had referred him, and he'd driven out for a meeting.

If so, the police had never uncovered it. Or had they really looked? Maybe that should be her move, instead of this. Instead of driving in and out of the damn woods, bouncing over roots and rocks, startling the few people who were home, she should call Footman back and ask him. If he didn't know, she could look through Abel's contacts, make some calls herself.

The day was turning to dusk, the woods darkening. She'd probably covered most of the places to check anyway. She'd stitched her way along Route 30, weaving in and out of the shorter driveways, and been going up and down the private roads branching off of it since 4 p.m. It was now 5:30. Her bold action had fulfilled its promise the best way it could: she had an idea how to proceed. She could head home for the night.

But then she saw the figure standing at the head of the next drive.

A black bear, carved from wood, erect on its hind legs. About three feet tall, the statue held a mailbox on its head.

The Marshes.

Callie swallowed over the anxiety collecting in her chest and started down the road.

* * *

Seeing the black bear statue felt like confirmation. Althea Cooper wasn't just shooting in the dark; she really knew something. But who was she? Was she messing with Callie or truly trying to help? Who was she connected to, and what did it have to do with Abel?

Feeling more frustrated than fearful now, Callie bumped over the uneven road. When a house came into view after about three quarters of a mile, she slowed.

The vehicle parked in front of the attached garage was a mid-sized SUV. It wasn't until her headlights hit it that the color reflected back: dark green.

More confirmation.

Callie rolled to a stop, engine softly grumbling. She didn't move for a moment, just sat with her hands on the steering wheel, engine idling.

At least the vehicle didn't match the style she'd thought might be following her. But still, the fact that Cooper had mentioned a green SUV was discomfiting.

Finally: the house was big. Three stories, sided with rustic cedar shakes and fitted with an enormous wrap-around deck pocketed with a covered hot tub. Lots of shadows and hard angles. It was, just as Cooper had described it, *kind of boxy.*

Way too many coincidences to be chance.

She has to be from here, Callie said to herself about Cooper. *Or know these people.*

A long row of stone steps, making one turn halfway to the top, climbed to a deep, dark porch. The main floor, it seemed, was the second story.

The windows were dark, but smoke drifted from a high, narrow chimney. Barely discernible against the dusky, overcast sky, it could have been from a hot new fire or the embers of an old one.

She checked the vehicle again. The emblem above the rear bumper labeled it a Nissan Pathfinder. A coil of mountain climber's rope sat in a metal roof basket. Snow coated the vehicle, including the hood, suggesting it hadn't been driven for at least a couple of hours.

The snow was still coming down, but the flakes were larger now, sparser, twirling to the ground. The brunt of the storm seemed to have passed while she'd been bumping down private driveways.

Turn around.

Turn around? After coming all this way? She'd driven up to more than a dozen houses at this point. This was number fifteen. And a bear marked the entrance, a dark green SUV sat in the driveway — what was she afraid of?

Some woman you never met called you up and implicated this vehicle — and whoever owns this house — in Abel's accident. That's what. Everything about this is wrong. Every part of it.

Okay. Callie checked her phone, momentarily seizing on the idea of calling Footman. But the coverage was even worse here, this close to the lake. In the Adirondacks, many places still offered no standard cell service, not even for the rich.

Inside was likely Wi-Fi — there were electric and cable lines running in from the main road, connecting all these houses to the grid — but out here, sitting in the Chevy, she was cut off.

She waited, watching the house. Surely, whoever was inside had heard her pull up. There was nothing around but trees — the forest grew right up to the house, thick with Douglas firs and balsams at the ground level, big oaks and maples soaring above. It would be quiet with all the vegetation and the blanket of snow. Enough for someone to hear the noise of her big, grumbly truck.

The daylight was just about gone. Only a faint, salmon light glowed in the trees. She'd been here almost a minute by now, and no one had come to the window or snapped on a porch light. Maybe whoever was inside was asleep? Or perhaps there was another vehicle, and whoever was staying here had gone out?

Slowly, she opened the Chevy's door and climbed down. Leaving it running, she walked to the Pathfinder, parked with the front toward the house.

As she got closer, her anxiety increased. That jittery sense of adrenaline. She felt more like a trespasser now than ever, but she couldn't stop. She'd come this far. She neared the front of the Pathfinder. It had been pulled up close to the garage door; between that arrangement and the lack of light, it was hard to get a good look at the bumper. She estimated the vehicle's age around fifteen years, similar to Abel's pickup.

The bumper was chrome and looked rusty. Was it dented? Maybe a little. It could have been worse before now and been buffed out. She'd seen Abel pop dents on vehicles; even if the result wasn't good as new, it mostly worked. You could also buy replacement parts online. So, did the green SUV appear to have recently struck another vehicle? Hard to say. Maybe if you wanted it to.

Footprints led from the Pathfinder to the steps. Probably an hour old, given the rate of snowfall. She followed them to the steps rising toward the large porch. Quite a few steps, maybe thirty, with a slight turn halfway up.

Stopped at the bottom, Callie could now see something at the top. Two somethings.

More bears.

Statues on each side of the staircase. Each on its hind legs, paws hanging in front, eyes shining.

She let out a deep breath, watched her exhalation rise, and decided. In movies and books — not so different from the ones she wrote — characters were always making questionable decisions. The right choice here was simple: leave. Get back within cell-service range and report to the police that she'd seen a green SUV, the same color as reported by a witness, with potential signs of damage. And that there were indications Abel had visited this very house just prior to his wreck. His possible hit-and-run.

Maybe even his attempted murder.

The thought was chilling — she hadn't quite let the idea take full shape before this moment. It was sickening, scary and grossly foreign. Why would someone want to kill her husband?

An affair. Drugs. Money.

Some secret life gone awry.

But her plan to call the cops was stymied by a question: what would she say about how she'd *found* the green Pathfinder?

It was bad enough her lead had come from a psychic, but for the past hour she'd been essentially trespassing, going in and out of private roads to homes owned by the rich. And wealthy or not, people generally didn't like strangers snooping around their properties. Neither did the police.

"Hello?" The sound of her own voice unnerved her. Part of that was the echo in the trees.

She watched the windows of the house. Was someone inside being as cautious as she was? Keeping out of sight, waiting to see what she was up to?

There was no answer.

Enough. It's time to get out of here.

Heeding the inner voice, she climbed back into the truck. She put her hands against the blower, warming her cold fingers. It was frigid out there — the dashboard display indicated 11 degrees Fahrenheit. She'd dressed warm in her blue parka with the fur-lined hood, but she'd left her gloves in the cab when she'd gotten out.

Fingers sufficiently warmed, Callie gave the house one last look before backing away. She made a three-point turn so she was headed the other direction.

One last look in the mirrors at those bear statues atop the stairs. Kind of creepy, the way they stood there.

They, too, were frozen in time. Suffering from the Great Pause.

She sloughed it off. They were just statues.

"You see that, honey?" she whispered to an imaginary Abel. "Some rich guy couldn't choose between tasteful rustic and North Country kitsch, so he went with both."

Abel didn't answer.

Callie and her husband were by no means classists and didn't begrudge anyone their station in life, rich or poor. But taste, that was fair game.

There were so many things she missed talking to him about. When they weren't poking soft fun at some woman's high-waist jeans, or some dude's hedge-like beard, they were discussing current events, hot-button issues. Movies, books, music. It was better, they'd decided, to build their lives as an oasis. A shelter from the storm. So they'd focused on each other. *Do you want support or solutions?* It was their go-to question when either of them was having a problem. Because sometimes you wanted help solving it, other times you just wanted—

Callie instinctively tapped the brakes when she saw the headlights. She'd gotten less than an eighth of a mile back down the private drive.

The other vehicle was headed her way, its lights stuttering through the trees, going up and down over the uneven terrain. Coming closer.

CHAPTER EIGHT

She came to a complete stop and rolled down the window, listening for the engine. Just to be sure. The rumble came back, reverberating through the woods.

Another truck. Big, from the sound of it.

The private drive was one lane, thick forest crowding either side. A vehicle coming this way would find it impassable with her in the way.

What to do?

In her sudden embarrassment, the fear dissolved. This wasn't scary; this was awkward. There was about to be a conversation: *Hi, who are you? What are you doing here?*

Oh, checking on what a psychic told me about possible foul play in my husband's car crash.

Callie put the Chevy in reverse, flung her arm over the backseat, twisted around, and started backing up.

"Fuck."

* * *

The man was older — maybe sixty, all white hair. He seemed fit beneath his large down parka. His vehicle was a brand-new-looking RAM 1500. He'd just gotten out of it and was walking toward her, a tentative smile on his lips.

Callie rolled down the window as he walked up to the Chevy. She'd had a few seconds to consider how better to begin the conversation. "Hi. I'm so sorry. You must be wondering what I'm doing here. My husband had a car accident in January, just a mile from here."

The man slowed, his smile fading to a look of concern. "Oh no, I'm so sorry."

"It's okay, I just . . . I came out to have a look. I haven't been out here since it happened. Well, right after."

"Sure, sure." He reached the truck.

Callie said, "So, that's, you know . . ."

She trailed off, unable to form the rest. Did she really want to tell this person why she was here? Did she have a choice?

You could just leave it at that and go.

The man gazed up, a faint smile playing on his lips. She could see the collar of a green-and-black flannel beneath his winter coat. "So what brings you *here*?" he asked.

Fine.

"Well . . . There are some gray areas about the accident." She paused, gauging his reaction. He seemed genuinely concerned and interested. "Basically, we don't entirely know what happened," she went on. "The police asked a few of the local residents if they saw anything, and no one did. But I just . . . My husband's been in a coma for six weeks. I suppose it seems a little crazy, me being out here. And this is a private road . . . Is this your place?"

"It is."

"Okay. Again, I'm sorry. Our son — he's nineteen — he's away at college. And it's just me in the house. And I'm just . . ." She pulled a breath, knowing she hadn't exactly answered his question as to why she was here.

He guessed, instead. "So you're asking people if they saw anything? Or heard anything?"

"Yes. And actually, I'm wondering why my husband was out this way. It's not exactly clear to me if he had business, or he was visiting a friend, or what."

Leave it there.

"Anyway, again, I shouldn't be bothering you. Or on your property."

"It doesn't bother me." He glanced away, as if assessing the region. "I can't imagine there's many people home this time of year."

"No, not really." She was feeling relieved.

His eyes came back. "I guess, a little bit, you have to worry about feisty homeowners? I imagine there's a few . . . you know . . . 'law and order' types out here."

"It did cross my mind." Barreling down private roads and snooping around private residences could get you a shotgun in your face. But, she'd decided — and maybe this was wrong — the wealthier types that owned these homes tended to rely more on cameras and calling 911 for home defense.

"Well, we like our privacy out here," the man said, "but it seems like you have a good reason. And I'll tell you what — I remember hearing about the accident."

"You do?"

"Yeah. I felt terrible. The roads in this area can be treacherous." He reached up his hand. "I'm Nathan Marsh."

"Callie Sanderson." She leaned out and they shook.

"Nice to meet you," he said.

As she withdrew her hand, she looked into his eyes and saw he was guarded. Not unkind, but cautious. A poker face. A man who'd be good at keeping confidences.

"How did you hear?" she asked.

"My son Eric told me. We're from downstate, but he's up here a bit . . . Listen, would you like to come inside?"

"Oh no. I don't want to keep you."

"It's no trouble, but . . . okay." He smiled fully, his lips splitting to reveal straight white teeth, a pleasant expression that almost touched his eyes. At the same time, the wind picked up and blew snow from the house.

"You have a beautiful place," she said, as the snow dusted over them.

"Been ours going on five years now. So, yes, Eric mentioned the accident. I went online, and I read about it. Terrible wreck. I'm so sorry. What a tragedy."

"It's okay, thank you."

"And you're . . . a writer? Is that right? A novelist? I think I remember reading that."

"Yes. I am."

"What do you write? What sort of stuff?"

"Well, crime mostly . . . Listen, again, I'm so sorry to have just shown up like this. And I really don't want to keep you. But your son — does he stay here? You said he was here at the time of the accident?"

Marsh was nodding. "He's spent a bit of time here since he graduated. You said your son is nineteen?"

"A sophomore at St Lawrence."

"Eric is twenty-three." Marsh sighed. "He's trying to figure out next moves."

"Ah," she said, picking up on the parental angst. "Yeah . . . it took a while to get Cormac dialed in on what he wanted to study. What college he wanted to attend. We even considered a gap year, for a while."

"We thought about that for Eric, too."

"Did he . . . say anything else about the accident? About that night? That he heard anything, or saw anything? You know, if he was out, coming back, getting groceries . . ."

Marsh's eyes acquired a strange light — there one moment, gone the next. "I think he just read about it in the paper the next day. Or two days, whatever it was. But you can ask him."

"He's here?"

"I assume so. That's his vehicle right there beside you."

She glanced at the green Pathfinder.

Nathan Marsh said, "And he was here when I left a little over an hour ago, to run into town."

47

"Oh," Callie said, bemused. "Because I came to the house. I didn't see any lights on; I didn't see anyone come to the door . . ."

"He's probably in the back, downstairs."

"Okay, sure." It still didn't seem right. "I called out — didn't seem like anyone heard me."

Marsh got that look again. But the smile was disarming. "He wouldn't have heard you. He's deaf."

CHAPTER NINE

Nathan Marsh returned to his vehicle and killed the engine. He retrieved two full grocery bags — the reusable kind. A bottle of wine poked out from one, a baguette the other.

Callie had climbed down from the Chevy but remained indecisive.

With his bags in hand, he regarded her. "Well, Mrs Sanderson, I'd be more than happy for you to come in. It's just me and my son at the moment, so things aren't as presentable as I'd like. But we can talk with Eric and find out if he remembers anything."

Callie glanced at the house one more time, half-expecting the son to be standing in the window, watching.

Marsh said, "If I can't persuade you . . . Well, I hope you have a good night. Come back if you need to. We're here for a couple of days — I plan to get in some cross-country skiing. This snow tonight was just what the doctor ordered."

Just what the doctor ordered.

It punched up a memory, something Althea Cooper had said: *He was at a house nearby. Talking to someone. I think he was a doctor.*

"Yes," Callie said about the snow. "Delightful." She made a distracted grab for the door handle. "Are you on a vacation?"

"Ah, sort of. I'm starting my retirement, in a way. This is what we call 'phase one.'"

She smiled at it. "What do you do?"

"I'm a neurosurgeon."

Bingo, Callie thought. But the minor thrill was quickly replaced with more anxiety. How did Cooper know these people?

"Wow," Callie said, about Marsh's career.

"Well, I focus mostly on prevention now. I'd love to talk to you about it — actually I'm much more interested in the life of a writer — but these bags are getting heavy. So I'll offer a third and final time. If you'd like to come inside . . ."

At last, a decision. "I really need to get going. But you've been so understanding, and I appreciate it."

"All right, then." He stepped back and seemed to regard the layout of the parking area. "You should be able to get around me there. I pulled forward as far as I could. That truck is a monster. And my garage is filled."

"Thank you," Callie said, a bit clumsily, and finally got the door open. Once she climbed back into the cab, she thought Marsh might still be there, bags in hand, to see her off. But he was already partway up the steps.

Bear statues. A doctor.

And a green car.

Like the beginning of an obscure joke.

She let off the brake and the Chevy rolled forward. She was able to get around the RAM 1500, big as it was. She caught a glimpse of Marsh in the rear-view mirror as she continued down the private drive — he was now almost to the top.

My garage is filled.

With what?

Her mind was split. She felt ridiculous, an overreacting teenager from a horror movie. Here was this nice man — a brain doctor, no less — inviting her inside after she'd been trespassing on his property, and after she'd provided the thinnest of motivations for why she was even there in the first place. He'd been gracious and hospitable, and she'd reacted like a scared mouse.

So what if he'd been a little guarded? City people were different. They lived among more humans. And as a medical professional, he had to keep certain information private. He came from a world of etiquette and reasoned social boundaries. You got to thinking that life in rural America was the same as everywhere else; it wasn't.

Yeah, it made you paranoid.

Well, cautious. Skeptical.

She carefully piloted the Chevy along the narrow drive, at one point veering too close to one side, where a bare branch shrieked against the truck. But within minutes, she was back out on a wider road, more level and even. She took this to the main route, then she was headed back toward home, the last bear and its mailbox fading in the rear-view mirror.

* * *

She drove a bit absent-mindedly at first, but when the Chevy's back end lurched to the side, she slowed down. Still, it was impossible to solely focus on the road, slippery as it was.

She was caught by a dilemma: if there was any truth to what Althea Cooper had said, then Abel had been out here meeting a new client. But Nathan Marsh had made no indication of knowing Abel beyond what he'd read in the paper, let alone been prepared to hire him for caretaking or carpentry. The Marshes might not even *need* a caretaker if their twenty-something son was around so often.

So who was lying? In a game of reason, it wasn't any dilemma at all: Althea Cooper was making up stories for unknown reasons. She might be mentally troubled. Or there was some scam. Callie just didn't know what yet.

Then why had she been so put off? Why flee the scene, tongue-tied and nerves chattering?

Because you're an introvert. You've barely spoken to anyone besides Cormac and hospital staff for six weeks. You haven't been writing, either. Not writing makes you go nuts.

It sounded like a poor excuse. No — it was more than social awkwardness that'd caused her to run from Marsh, more than the unbalanced feeling she had from not working. She just couldn't put her finger on what, exactly.

As she approached the crash site again, this time from the other direction, she noticed a single headlight.

Someone was there, right where Abel had gone into the water. As she closed in it became clearer: the source of the light was a snowmobile, the driver standing nearby.

The driver, wearing a full-body snowsuit and a helmet, appeared to be right about where Callie had been, and he was looking down at something. Almost like he was examining her footprints from earlier. Then he lifted his head.

Callie felt his eyes on her. She'd been slowing as she approached; now she pressed the accelerator.

The driver watched for another second, then mounted his snowmobile.

Callie heard an engine behind her. She checked the mirrors and saw another headlight coming her way. The light became brighter and the engine louder as a second snowmobile neared, then caught her. For a few terrorizing seconds, it buzzed along with her on the right, between the road and the lake.

Callie cried out inadvertently: "Jesus, go away!"

Just as she reached the crash site, the second snowmobile joined the first and stopped. They both looked at her as she passed in the Chevy.

She could only see them clearly for a second: one of them wore a distinctive suit, the one who'd been there first — black with yellow stripes on the arms and legs. The other was dressed in black. Definitely two men, and watching her go.

After she was down the road a ways, they took off as a pair. They crossed the road behind her and disappeared into the woods on the other side.

She realized she was trembling all over. Not wanting to get into an accident herself, she brought the Chevy to a stop and took a few shaky breaths.

It took a full minute for the sounds of their engines to fade completely. And for her nerves to recover.

What the hell is going on?

Gradually, carefully, she let off the brake and the Chevy rolled forward.

CHAPTER TEN

ALTHEA

I can read your mind.

Well, no, not exactly. That's not the point — ESP. The point is that I can know things I shouldn't have any reason to know.

Things that just pop into my head, unbidden.

In the end, my mind sort of *becomes* your mind.

Like this one: I was in the shower on one of the nights I wash my hair. Fully lathered up, my thoughts carried on as usual. Linked together like cars in a train.

Except, among them, a stowaway. So here's how it goes:

Casey wants corned beef on rye for lunch tomorrow

Maybe when I bring it to his work, I'll wear that white shirt from Darcy with the opal necklace

Funny things, opals

95 percent are produced in Australia. G'day, mate!

Isn't it the start of winter, there? The opposite of here

Here it's still green and warm

A warm summer night

And the chickens are roosting, the mule is standing asleep

And the man takes me out and away from here, under the stars and I'm happy to go with him

Deep into the woods, to this quaint little cabin

And when his hands close around my neck, I realize I knew this was going to happen

And I let it

And the days grow short and winter returns.

Just like that, a random memory that wasn't mine, becomes mine. I can see it just like it happened to me. That's the visual part.

His eyes on me. The way his lips slightly parted as he breathed out — a soft hiss, like his soul escaping.

If there are words, I can remember them, too. But there weren't many words to this one.

Just feelings, mostly. Just fear.

Something at first that isn't quite trust, but enough excitement to make trust possible.

A dark sort of excitement. The kind that I know is bad, that Mom would disapprove of.

But that makes it all the more tantalizing.

I am young, after all. I am only sixteen. Hey — I may not have had the best role models. I was ruined at a young age, if you want to know the truth. What did you expect?

And now I'm out here in the dark woods, alone.

Can anyone find me?

Althea, can you?

CHAPTER ELEVEN

With distance, Callie's anxiety faded. By the time she was almost home, she decided the snowmobiles were coincidental — a pair of enthusiasts out riding, who noticed tire tracks and footprints in a peculiar spot. One of them had paused to investigate. Nothing more.

As for Nathan Marsh, she'd blown the chance to get information. She'd acted like a panicky lunatic. Here was someone who fit the vague description provided by Althea Cooper — further conversation might've revealed the secret of that relationship. Althea could've been a distant relative. A former patient.

Of course, if that were the case, Marsh wouldn't be able to admit it, but Callie might've been able to spot the brief flash of recognition. He seemed to have a solid poker face, but nobody's made of stone.

Or, better yet — Marsh had claimed the home was theirs for going on five years — perhaps Althea knew the former owners. The bears could have come with the house.

Maybe it had nothing to do with him, directly, at all.

The point was, any number and manner of connections were possible. But Callie hadn't stuck around to find out.

Instead, she'd fled from Dr Nathan Marsh and his expensive home like a bat out of hell.

And now she didn't have any answers. Just more questions.

She sighed and slowed for her turn onto Route 9N. This was the last stretch; she'd be home in ten minutes.

Her thoughts swung back to Althea Cooper, the mystery woman behind it all. Something Footman had said, after Callie had called to report Cooper's phone call.

She actually called a woman a couple of years ago to tell her about her runaway daughter.

Who was this person that called up random strangers and claimed to know things? Who *did* that sort of thing?

She knew where the girl had gone, Footman had said. *She described a cabin in the woods . . .*

Althea Cooper had this knack for teasing, it seemed. For giving just enough information that it registered as possible. This was how charlatans operated, Callie thought. She'd once considered writing a book about a televangelist, fascinated by the trickery of the whole "healing the sick" on stage, how it often relied on people unknowingly giving up information in advance, which the so-called healer then pretended to spontaneously access. As if by miracle.

But it wasn't a miracle. It was prayer cards guests had filled out before they took their seats, with all kinds of personal information.

Anyway, she hadn't gone through with the book. The subject matter would be too touchy for her readers.

The woman got all upset and called us, Footman had said. *We even contacted DEC, and they formed a search team.*

Well, TV preachers aside, the world was full of scams. Healers and mystics and mediums. Maybe there was some truth, somewhere, to some of it. As in, maybe they worked with some truth, something they were privy to, and they embellished using their bag of tricks . . .

So what was that kernel of truth here?

Curiosity had her gripped. As soon as she arrived home, Callie yanked off her boots, got online and ran a Google search. *Runaway girl, missing girl, cabin in the woods.* For good measure, she added *DEC.* The Department of Environmental Conservation was a state agency. Google would automatically filter the results through her internet service provider — it knew her general vicinity — but including DEC would help delimit the search.

The results popped up. Leaning in, she read down the list.

The top story was about a young woman, seventeen, who had gone missing from her Shelter Falls home last June.

Shelter Falls . . .

Callie knew where it was but did a quick check to determine the distance. Just about a half hour away, near Plattsburgh, a small city to the north.

The girl, whose name was Kerry Mullins, had last been seen by her mother on a Sunday evening. By Monday afternoon, after she hadn't returned home, and none of her friends having seen her, the mother called the cops. The search began later that evening, with police interviewing family and friends, knocking on neighborhood doors. By Wednesday, it had expanded into the surrounding towns.

Callie had to jump between articles to get the rest of the story. Some of the papers originally covering it seemed to just drop the thread, but one brought it to some closure: *Six weeks after search began for missing teenager,* it read, *officials call it quits.*

Six weeks, Callie thought. Her mind flashed to Abel, the length of time he'd lain unresponsive.

She put a hand over her mouth, noting the coincidence and imagining the anguish of the girl's mother, Louise Mullins.

Callie hunted some more, looking across the dozen or so articles she'd found for any mention of a cabin in the woods. A couple of articles noted that the search included a number of structures, among them decommissioned ranger cabins. But there was no trace of the young woman at any of these places.

"Nothing like you'd expect to see," said Sheriff Robert Tuggey, who had helped organize the search along with DEC and the New York State Police. "No signs of a person there, no attempt at communication, no use of fire, no SOS, no food wrappers — nothing."

As far as Callie could tell, none of the articles mentioned Althea Cooper, or an "anonymous tip." Yet Footman said *they'd* been the ones to contact DEC. The police. Which made it sound like Cooper's call had prompted the search.

Of course, any hunt for a missing girl in the Adirondacks would include searching the woods, wouldn't it? So maybe Footman had meant that Cooper's call had gotten the ball rolling ahead of time? If so, it was strange to attribute to her what would've been standard procedure anyway.

Kerry Mullins.

Callie sat back a moment, wringing her hands together. Her skin was dry.

According to Google, the girl was still missing. Six weeks had become six months.

Maybe it wasn't Footman's jurisdiction. The state police were divided up into different troops, and investigators like Footman were assigned to work one or another. Callie didn't know if Shelter Falls was in the same troop as Hawkins. Or, really, Lake Clear, since that was where Abel's car wreck had occurred. But if it wasn't Footman's case directly, he might've not been thinking about it very much.

She would call him in the morning and find out.

In fact, maybe she would call Cooper herself.

CHAPTER TWELVE

"Please leave a message."

It wasn't very inspiring. Especially because it was a computer voice, not something Althea Cooper had recorded herself.

After the beep, Callie hung up. She'd considered leaving her message and information, but what if Cooper had been using someone else's phone? With the automated voice, it was impossible to know.

She sat drinking her coffee at her desk. The house was a three-bedroom, and they'd converted this one into her writing den. She'd gotten a good seven hours of sleep and had been feeling good; failing to reach Cooper felt like a setback.

Now what?

She studied a picture of Abel and Cormac on the wall. The two of them stood arm-in-arm on a beach, lush jungle in the background. It was from four years ago, in Costa Rica. Cormac had yet to hit his growth spurt and came only up to his father's shoulder. They wore sunglasses and grinned in the bright day. Callie remembered taking the picture, the Caribbean at her back.

If memory served, her parents hadn't even come to the beach that day. No — her father had gone into the small town in proximity, Parismina. Her mother had stayed home to clean house and make dinner for that evening. Early in their retirement, they'd been as restless as the monkeys in the trees outside their bungalow-style home.

Callie picked up the squeeze ball she sometimes used when thinking through a story idea; her parents stressed her out, no matter how far away.

Her gaze drifted to another photo. Cormac was even younger in this one, kneeling next to Breezy, their white Lab. Meister, their cat at the time, was also in the shot (though just her fluffy tail as she walked away, unimpressed).

Did Althea Cooper ever have a family pet? She was a foster child, so who had adopted her? How in the hell did she know anything about Abel?

This was ridiculous; Callie needed to call her back, leave a message this time. There was no point sitting here. She could keep trying the number until someone answered, but that was sort of crazy.

She spent a moment revising what she wanted to say. When Cooper's voicemail beeped this time, Callie was ready: "Hi. You called me yesterday and we spoke about my husband. I'd like to meet with you, if possible. Just need your address. I don't mind making the trip — I'd like to talk to you in person, if that's all right. Thank you."

There. That felt good. No names, nothing specific. If the phone was someone else's, the message was vague enough to keep matters private. But if it was Cooper's phone, she'd understand every word.

The good feeling lasted a while, but after half an hour puttering around the house, checking her phone more than once in case she hadn't heard the call, Callie was restless. She sat in the kitchen, at the L-shaped counter with the three bar-stools. The spot where Abel would sit and read the morning paper — on his phone. He liked to shake his head and cluck his tongue, saying, "The world is going to hell, Cal," like he was some old-timey husband with an actual newspaper in his hand. But he'd be grinning when he said it, because Abel was one of those perennial optimists. It had aggravated her sometimes — okay, a lot of the time — but she missed it now, of course. Like she missed everything else.

He didn't really think the world was going to hell. He thought people were inherently good and trying their best, figuring it out. "We're in an era of unprecedented peace and prosperity," he said once. "Sometimes we just forget it, because we're so used to struggling."

She could have given him an earful about unequally distributed resources, certain world nations lording it over others, bad attitudes about race and gender that persisted even in this "era of peace," but she would've sounded just like her mother. And he already knew all of those things, anyway. He just focused on the bright side.

What a jerk.

The worst kind of person to get themselves into a coma, because here she was, weeping about it. Like some bereft character in one of her own novels. The broken heroine who needs her man back to make her whole again.

* * *

Footman was next on the list. And he answered.

"Mrs Sanderson?"

"Hi. Me again."

He hesitated. "Is everything all right?"

"Yes," she said, perhaps a bit too eagerly. "Yeah — everything's fine. I just, ah . . . I had a couple of questions. Is now a good time?"

Once more, she picked up the background sounds. This time it was the clink of cutlery — forks and knives against ceramic plates. Footman sounded like he was at breakfast. "It's fine. What can I do for you?"

"I'm really sorry to interrupt. I just . . . I had a question about the woman you mentioned. The one that Althea Cooper called. About her daughter. The one who ran away."

The investigator was quiet.

Callie said, "Louise Mullins. I looked her up." She tried to sound guiltless but felt sheepish anyway. Police investigators were probably always dealing with people who thought they could do the job better.

After a brief moment: "What about her?"

"I was just wondering — why up here? That's one thing. Meaning, ah, Althea Cooper lives in Syracuse, four hours away. But she's calling up here to me about my husband, who had an accident in Lake Clear. And she's calling Louise Mullins about her missing daughter, and Mullins lives thirty minutes farther north. So that's one thing."

Footman cleared his throat. The background came through again — the murmur of voices, the lilt of classical music. If he was having breakfast, it wasn't at IHOP.

When he didn't speak, Callie hurried on. "The other thing I was wondering — you said that the search got started when Althea Cooper called you. Am I remembering that right? So you definitely took her seriously then. Did you have anything to do with the search directly?"

He grunted a second time before he spoke. His tone, while not unkind, was flatly authoritative. "Mrs Sanderson, I'll caution you here. Like I said to you before, it's understandable you want answers. Not everything about your husband's accident was as perfectly clear as we'd like. But people like Althea Cooper, whether intentionally or not, can exploit that uncertainty, no matter how minor. This — what you're doing right now, digging all of this up — this is part of that. This is what—"

"But isn't it odd that she's calling people who live four hours away? She's got to be connected somehow, don't you think? Does she have family up here?"

"I think maybe we should continue this conversation another time. I'm actually off-the-clock right now . . ."

"I'm sorry. Yes. Of course. You have a life."

"I try to. Something that looks like one, anyway." He chuckled a little, breaking the tension.

"I just — I appreciate you talking to me."

"It's easy to let this stuff go to your head, Mrs Sanderson. Trust me. And for you, it's especially hard because it *is* your life. I understand that. We can talk again on Monday, okay?"

"Sure, of course. Thank you."

"All right."

They ended it. Callie sat staring into space a moment, her mind going back to when they'd first met. It had been a couple of days since Abel's accident, and up until then she'd been dealing with uniformed officers, state troopers in their gray outfits and Stetson hats. Footman was from "the back room," which he'd explained meant the BCI division of the state police — Bureau of Criminal Investigation. Each trooper barracks, or station, had a couple of investigators assigned. He'd stepped in and been the one she'd contacted about Abel's case for the duration. There hadn't been much — just those first couple of times meeting in person. He'd been polite, patient.

Just as he had been now.

Almost like he'd handled her.

Oh stop. You're reading too much into it.

Maybe. Just like she'd been reading too much into Nathan Marsh's behavior. Or the fact of his deaf son.

Maybe it was that analytical-observer mind at work. Footman was right: she wanted answers. And without a writing project — or any other semblance of her normal life, really — perhaps she was being obsessive. But she didn't believe she was making up things that weren't there.

These things were there, all right. She just needed to connect them.

But, starting Monday. When people weren't trying to enjoy some personal time, trying to forget the world and their troubles.

She made one more call for now, this time to Cormac. She didn't like to distract him at school — weekends were better. But he didn't answer.

"Hi, honey. Just checking in. Nothing special. Hope you're doing well. Christmas really feels like a long time ago. I miss you."

After ending the call, she looked around her empty home, once full of life. An active, hardworking man; their talkative, good-natured son; a boundlessly energetic dog. The weeping started again.

Time for a walk.

* * *

Their property was ten acres, which was big, as far as she was concerned. Unlike Abel, she hadn't grown up with these wide open spaces. In White Plains, they'd had a small fenced-in backyard. Her father, occasionally, used it to fire up the grill.

In her blue parka, with a woolen hat and gloves, and her warmest boots on, she walked the land down to the river. A steep bank formed the back of the property. Huge boulders piled against it, forming caves and dens. Abel told her they were glacial, deposited thousands of years prior by retreating sheets of ice. Now they were home to foxes and other critters. Those dark caves gave her the willies, really.

But the river was nice. Really, "river" was generous. It was a creek, branching off from one of the local main rivers and reconnecting with it farther east. Narrow enough to cross in places, but pretty fast and frothy in the spring. Now it was mostly frozen, with rivulets of crystalline water streaming between humps of snow-covered rocks.

By the time she climbed her way back up the escarpment — Abel had used the tractor to carve a switchback trail, but it was still steep in places — her heart rate was raised and her breath was coming fast. Breezy's marked grave was at the tree line, and she paused there, getting her wind back.

It was three years ago he'd died, between Cormac's junior and senior years of high school. They'd always suspected — given the average life expectancy of Labradors was twelve years — that he would live his final days right around the time Cormac left the nest. And since they'd brought the puppy home when Cormac was just five, it had worked out that way, with Breezy finally passing peacefully of old age while Cormac was eyeing colleges and deciding what to do with the rest of his life.

Anticipated or not, Breezy's death had devastated them all. Cormac had wept that day, when Abel came back from the vet. Not at first — he'd kept it together and helped his father dig the grave behind the house. Callie had brought lemonade to them as they'd worked their way through roots and shrubs in order to make the grave wide and deep enough, sweat pouring from them, Cormac working non-stop until it was done. He'd remained stoic as they'd lowered Breezy into the hole, wrapped in old blankets — hand-me-downs from her mother, some of them. The familiar buttercup yellow with scalloped edges, plus a faded baby-blue twin sheet with clouds from Cormac's boyhood. They'd thrown the dirt on and stacked it up, shovelful after shovelful, and then Cormac had added the rock he'd selected for the headstone. Upon placing it, he had bent forward, shaking with emotion.

His sobs echoed in her mind, then faded as she brushed snow from the rock. The red heart painted on it blurred as her own eyes filled with tears.

"All right," she said, and snuffed. She found a tissue in her parka and blew her nose. "Enough."

Inside, she took a hot bath and read, and tried to focus on what she was reading, though her eyes kept skimming, her mind wandering from the missing Mullins girl, to the cool smile of Nathan Marsh, and the subtle way she felt gaslit by Detective Footman, as if she were just another busybody who thought they were going to crack a case that didn't need any cracking.

Well, she thought, setting her book aside and submerging a moment beneath the hot water, *we'll see.*

CHAPTER THIRTEEN

SUNDAY, FEBRUARY 26

The phone woke Callie up. She'd been dreaming. Breezy was alive again, a puppy; Cormac a young boy. They'd been riding in a large truck, sitting in the passenger seat. Driving was a man that could have been Abel, at moments, but was also a stranger. She was there too, somehow, a disembodied observer, floating both inside and out of the oversized truck as it barreled down a snowy road. In the near distance, around a blind corner, a vehicle sat crosswise in the road. At the rate they were going, the sometimes-Abel driver wouldn't be able to stop in time. He'd take the sharp corner before seeing the vehicle. By then it would be too late.

She tried to warn them. *Stop! There's something in the road!* But Cormac only petted the puppy that sat in his lap. He spoke to it: *You're a good boy. What a good boy.* The driver, wearing the green-checked flannel she'd seen beneath Nathan Marsh's parka, but his face featureless and dark, downshifted for the curve, then tapped the gas.

Better traction to accelerate around a corner, he said. Only it wasn't a voice she recognized, not even human — but stereophonic in her head, deep and distorted.

Around a cornerrrr

She screamed for them to brake, to see the vehicle in the road, the man holding up his palm as if he could stop what was coming, blood already trickling from his ears, and then her phone was ringing, and she was groping for it in the dark, and answering, "Cormac? Honey?"

For a moment, no one responded. Then, "Mrs Sanderson?" A woman's voice. Familiar.

Callie was still partly caught up in the dream. If she could just make them listen to her . . .

"Mrs Sanderson, it's Althea Cooper. Is this a bad time?"

"No — no, Althea. Thank you for calling back." Callie sat up and swung her legs out of bed. The woodstove had gone out in the night — the cold floor brought her fully back to reality, and the dream faded.

"It sounded like you were sleeping. I could call back another time."

"No, this is good. I should be up anyway. It's okay." She quickly pulled her phone from her ear. Not quite 7 a.m. Althea Cooper was an early riser.

She said, "I got your message . . ."

"Yes, thank you — hold on." Callie found one slipper and toed into it. The other was missing. She checked the area, found it just beneath the bed. "It's cold," she rambled. "My husband used to stoke the woodstove in the morning. He was always up early. I still haven't gotten used to it." She found her long sweater, her favorite, with the hood — one of the few items of clothing Abel had ever bought for her.

Once she had pulled on some sweatpants, she continued: "So you got my message. Good. I wanted to ask you a little bit more about what you saw. About my husband. And maybe about the runaway girl, too."

"Kerry Mullins," Althea said quietly.

"Right," Callie said. She sat on the edge of the bed. "That's . . . It's a pretty terrible situation. That poor mother."

"Yeah."

When she didn't elaborate, Callie said, "Did you know them? The family?"

"No."

"The police seem to think she ran away."

"You said you wanted to come see me?"

"Yes, I . . . Right."

Shit. She felt so scattered this morning. It wasn't like she'd never been up early before. Back before writing paid the bills, she'd gotten up some mornings at 4 a.m. to write. And that had been sometime *after* having a young son and a puppy, both of whom had awakened at the crack of dawn for years.

She took a steadying breath. "I would really like to come see you, if that's at all possible. Just, you know, sit down, maybe get some lunch. I'm very interested in what you have to say."

"Why?"

"Why?" The question caught Callie off guard. It felt like a test. More like a test, anyway, than a true question. Because wouldn't it be obvious? Althea had claimed Abel's crash wasn't an accident. Who *wouldn't* want to know more?

"Because if something happened to my husband," Callie told her, "I want to know. I want to know what you think. What you . . . know."

"What do *you* think happened?"

This also threw her a bit. "Well, I'm not sure. That's what I'm hoping you'll tell me."

"But you have some ideas."

"No, not really."

Lies.

She fell silent and listened to Cooper's silence, feeling suddenly guilty, or at least wrong. She had ideas, for sure. Loose and scattered, mostly feelings, but they were there. From that first moment in the unmarked police car with Footman, staring out at the crash site, to the snowmobiles gathered last night, she'd sensed something was wrong. Something no one was seeing. Or perhaps willing to see.

Callie was tentative. "Listen, Althea, I don't want to presume anything. I don't know you. But you just . . . you called me up and told me some very interesting things. And it seems like you have more to say, or *want* to say."

"I didn't tell you about Kerry Mullins."

She hustled to recover: "No, you didn't. But you had to figure I would call the police. Not because I was upset at you, but because I wanted to ask them if they knew anything about . . . what you said."

"You checked me out."

"Well, yeah. How could I not? Someone calls up and says they know things? About your spouse, maybe the cause of his condition? And they say that they just know these things?" She let the implication hang. "I'm a regular person. That makes me suspicious."

Althea made no remark.

"And I wanted to know if there was a green vehicle that anyone saw. I wanted to ask the police if there were *any* signs of . . . you know . . . foul play."

"And what did they say?"

It felt slightly rhetorical, like she was expecting Callie to say the police were dismissive. And had Footman been dismissive? Well, insofar as her source was a woman with possible mental health problems . . .

Just be honest and straight with her. It'll be for the best.

The admonition had the mental ring of her own voice, but the tone of her father's.

You get more traction by accelerating *into a curve . . .*

"They said not to trust you. Okay? That's what they said."

"And that's when they told you about Kerry Mullins. That I had tried to help."

"Exactly. But because they never found her . . ." Callie trailed off, waiting. She could hear the younger woman breathing again.

Then Althea said, "If the Mullins family had money, maybe it would matter. But they're poor."

"Yeah, that could be."

"And Kerry used drugs," Althea said. "She went with a lot of guys. That's what they said. So they figured she was just a slut who ran away. And they forgot about her."

The language was harsh. This was more than an armchair opinion; it sounded like Althea had some personal experience that colored it. Perhaps being raised in the foster care system had created a mistrust of the system in general.

"You could be right," Callie said. Then, seizing the moment: "So, what do you say? Think we can get together? I'll meet on any terms — you tell me. It would be doing me a huge favor. I already appreciate you reaching out. I know it's asking a lot. But, please."

"You still want to meet? Why?"

"I just think . . . I want to talk to you. And it's better in person. And I've got nothing else to do." She offered a chuckle, which sounded a bit kookier than she would've liked.

"I can't right now."

The chuckle tapered off. Callie held a breath, thinking it through. "Is there a better time? You tell me. I'm flexible. I spend my days either rattling around alone in the house or driving to see my husband. So . . ."

"Maybe."

A noise broke the background quiet on Althea's end. It sounded like a car had arrived — an engine was idling in proximity.

"Maybe?"

She's in danger. The thought just flashed through Callie's mind, without warning. But there was no reason to think that.

A moment passed. "Yes."

"Great. You name the time and place."

"I'll call you." Althea sounded like she was once again in a hurry to end the call.

Callie felt a shiver. "Althea, are you okay?"

"Yes."

"Do you need . . . Is there anything I can do for you?" It was impulsive, yes; here she was offering aid when this woman had initially called saying *she* could help. But it felt right. That was twice now Althea seemed worried or pressured by someone or something in her midst.

In the background, the engine shut off. Callie thought she heard — just barely — the crunch of footsteps approaching, as if over gravel.

"No."

Before Callie could say another word, Althea said, "I'll be in touch," and hung up.

CHAPTER FOURTEEN

Callie's head filled with the things she might have said.

Do you feel safe? Signal to me if you're in trouble . . .

Twice now, Althea had seemed like she couldn't talk in the presence of someone else. It could all be some sort of game, another trick to lure her in, or she could be in danger.

Althea had reacted strongly to what she felt was dismissive mistreatment of Kerry Mullins. Like she knew about such things firsthand. What if she'd been abused?

What if she still was?

On the other hand, her odd behavior might be part of the mental illness Footman had implied. Althea Cooper could be calling people up at random, pretending to see things — maybe she wasn't prepared when someone called back. Someone who followed up.

Like Callie Sanderson.

"Oh, good for you," she said to herself sarcastically. "Showing up the disturbed woman raised in foster care. What a badass you are."

She got dressed in her outdoor gear, adding snow pants to the wardrobe. A good ten inches had accumulated over the weekend. The Chevy could handle it, but snow in the driveway often melted and refroze with fluctuating late-winter temperatures. Better to get rid of it while she could.

She stepped outside and immediately noticed a car in the road. A sedan, sidled up against the shoulder snowbank, about twenty yards east from the mouth of Callie's driveway. It looked like the car she'd seen on Friday following her to the ferry. It had seemed green then; it looked gray now, in the brighter daylight.

Giving it the side-eye, she went to the shed and picked out the shovel she wanted to use. She shoveled for about ten minutes, starting with the path to the driveway, continually glancing up at the parked car.

At one point, she stopped shoveling altogether. Blatantly staring at the car now, she thought about approaching it. But maybe that wasn't safe. There was a rifle inside the house, a gun Abel used for hunting. Did it make any sense to go get it?

This person could be just sitting there, looking at their phone. A responsible driver, having a chat without endangering others.

Or, they could have something to do with Abel's crash. Maybe they'd started with him, and they wanted her next.

Oh, please. It's not a horror movie.

It could be Althea. Or maybe someone she knows.

Or, like you already thought: it's just some random person.

She continued scraping away the snow. After five more minutes, it was eating at her. She started walking toward the end of the driveway. If anything, just to get a look at the driver.

Before she made it halfway there, the car pulled out. It got up to speed fast, racing by her. Just one person in it, Callie observed, a man behind the wheel. She watched until he was out of sight.

* * *

Abel had an office in the home, really just a corner of the partially finished basement. When they'd first moved here,

CHAPTER FIFTEEN

Footman wasn't answering his phone. Callie hesitated to leave a message. What was she going to say? Hi. Me again. Just can't seem to take your advice about leaving well enough alone, so I'm interrogating possible mental health patients and digging through my husband's accounting . . .

Best to just stick to the facts.

When prompted by the beep, she said, "Hi, Mr Footman. It's Callie Sanderson. I just found out that my husband was working for someone out there in Lake Clear. Well, not working for, per se, but he built some furniture for them. Nathan Marsh. Dr Nathan Marsh." She paused, momentarily derailed when she considered this message from Footman's perspective. *So what? So now we know why Abel was out there . . . It doesn't change anything.*

She thought it did. "Marsh didn't say a word about it when I spoke to him," she said.

Shit. She'd just let the cat out of the bag . . .

"When I was, ah . . . when I was out there. I stopped at some of the houses near the accident, and, ah . . ."

She closed her eyes and pinched the bridge of her nose. No, this wasn't going well at all. Too many dissenting thoughts in her brain. She must sound ditzy, foolish. Maybe even obnoxious. Knocking on people's doors?

". . . and Marsh acted like he never knew my husband. Which is strange, if Abel sold him a hutch. Also . . ."

She second-guessed again, wondering if she should say the next bit, then plunged forward. "I think Althea Cooper could be in danger. Each time I've spoken with her, she's become anxious at the end. She acted like she suddenly couldn't talk. It could be either she's in danger, or she didn't want to say anything in front of someone else, because they—"

A beeping cut Callie off.

She sat there a moment, looked at the phone, and then hit the red circle to end the call. "Crap," she said. She dropped the phone on the couch beside her and put her head in her hands.

This was ridiculous. Everything had made so much sense; the discovery that Abel had conducted business with Marsh felt like a breakthrough. But then, putting it all together, leaving that message, hearing it through Footman's ears . . .

You sound like a lunatic.

Well, maybe not quite that strong. But saying it all out loud did seem to rob the ideas of their power. Yet her husband had *transacted business* with Marsh! And the man had acted like he only knew Abel from the news. What had he said? *My son pointed it out to me.*

Not only had they done business, but Marsh's son owned a green SUV. And even Footman admitted there could have been damage to the rear bumper of Abel's old Toyota.

You put it all together, you had something. Clearly. So why did it fall apart over the phone? Why had she been flooded with doubt, feeling stupid about calling before she'd gotten out ten words?

Because it wasn't enough. She knew how the police worked, how the law worked. People often thought cops could do whatever they wanted — and they did have a pretty broad range of authority to get things done — but that ended once you started thinking like a prosecutor, about courtrooms and legal defenses. Civilians had rights. Cops needed probable cause. They had to prove their case to judges and juries.

She regretted the message to Footman, but only partly. Only because she'd grown self-conscious and stumbled. But it was good to keep him involved. Good he knew where her mind was at, what she was finding, even if he — for now — dismissed it.

And maybe he wouldn't. Maybe he'd look into it. And he'd said they would talk on Monday morning, so she needed to respect that he had a personal life, too.

In the meantime, she'd gather all the information she could, to make her case to Footman as strong as it could be. So far she'd seen evidence that Abel had made custom furniture for Marsh, but for all she knew there was more. Abel also did general contracting. Remodeling, renovations, additions.

Whereas the caretaking documents were labeled by name, and the custom furniture invoices by project, Callie knew the construction jobs were organized by location, so she opened the contracting folder on his computer and searched for *Upper Saranac*. Abel had them arranged alphabetically, so locating the U section was easy. Well, it would've been, if there was anything there, which there wasn't.

Maybe S, then, for Saranac.

Scrolling up to the S section, she stopped.

Shelter Falls. The name of the small town where Kerry Mullins was from. Where she'd disappeared from.

Callie had been afraid for her husband up until now, afraid that he might not recover, or that if he did, he'd have deficits. She'd worried for her son, and the impact this was having on him. But this anxiety gripping her now, this was new.

You don't know anything yet.
Abel does jobs all over the region.
It's just a coincidence.

Oh? And how many coincidences would that make lately?

Callie held her breath and double-clicked. The file opened and she scrolled to the bottom. And there it was.

The summer before, Abel had built a deck for Louise Mullins. Not a huge project, just a small deck, judging by the dimensions. But that was irrelevant.

The fact that Abel was connected to this woman as well as to Marsh — that could be huge.

Abel was meticulous and kept hard copies of everything, using the same system. The dark brown file tower on the far left contained the construction records, again alphabetized by location, and she finger-walked her way back to the S, her heart filling with hope — maybe the computer file was just a forgery, something a hacker had planted — and then deflating when she came across the tab for *Shelter Falls*.

There it was again.

Whatever it meant, Callie's gut told her it wasn't good. Abel was caught up in something. Althea Cooper knew about it — maybe she was pretending to have psychic insights because she couldn't be direct — and it involved Abel getting run off the road.

Callie backed away from his basement office, her mind galloping ahead with next moves. Visit Mullins? Return to the home of Nathan Marsh and confront him? Maybe even record it with her phone? She was jangly with nerves and adrenaline. So much so that when she heard the noise outside, she froze. Like a cat reacting to a threat.

An engine. Someone was here, pulling up to the house by way of the freshly shoveled drive.

CHAPTER SIXTEEN

ALTHEA

I wish I didn't know what I know.

And that is a fact.

Think about me whatever you will, but know that.

I wish I didn't know these things. I didn't ask for them. They just come to me, and then I'm stuck. Do I do something about it? Do I say something? If I do, you might judge me. Judge my life, my family, everything. You might feel sorry for me, or laugh at me. You might even hate me. But none of that matters.

What matters is the girls. The ones he takes.

Their families, the ones that get left behind.

Abel Sanderson is someone I can't help. Not anymore. I can see him; I can *feel* what happened to him. But I can't save him.

I can only think about *them*. The girls. And her — Callie, the wife he left behind.

So, judge me if you have to. I can take it. Roll your eyes, cross your arms, shake your head. What could I possibly know? How could I know it?

I wish I couldn't! I wish I didn't!

But the fact remains: when I close my eyes, I can see him. I *become* him, in his head, his memories a part of my own.

I can see the girl, the one who dresses in those cut-off jeans and skimpy tank tops. It's summer, I get it. And she ought to be free to dress how she wants to dress, look how she wants to look.

But there are no men to protect her. That much is clear.

I worry that someone will take advantage of her. The way she walks across the yard in those bare feet. The chickens run along beside her. She's coming to me with a cool drink. This deck is a simple project, easy, but it's hot out. It's August and it's hot. The air conditioning rattles in the window of the single-wide trailer where her mother lives. Her mother, basically a shut-in.

Leaving this poor young thing all alone. Purring around the property like a cat in heat.

Waiting.

Just waiting for someone to come along.

CHAPTER SEVENTEEN

Mac?

The spell broke and Callie left the basement, hurried up the stairs. She found her boots by the front door and yanked them on, then plunged into her parka at the same time she tried to get a glimpse of who had arrived. The angle of the house made it impossible to see the whole driveway; she spied the back end of a car.

Not Cormac's little hybrid Chevy Volt. This was bigger. Official looking, like an unmarked police car.

She opened the door, feeling her heart thumping in her chest. The man coming up the walk was tall, dressed in a long coat and leather gloves, his breath puffing. He smiled at her, but it lacked good humor.

"Mr Footman," she said from the small porch.

He stopped a few feet from her. "How are you, Mrs Sanderson?"

"I'm good . . . I just called you."

"I know."

He waited, and she realized she ought to invite him in. She held the door and said, "Please."

"Thank you." He took the two steps up to the small porch and moved inside, his musky aftershave wafting to her as he passed.

"Can I take your coat?"

"Sure, yes." He pulled out of it, and she hung it from a hook just inside the door. After removing her own parka, she invited him to sit. "Coffee or tea?"

"No, thank you." They sat adjacent to one another in the adjoining living room, him in the easy chair, her on the couch.

"Water? Anything?"

"I'm fine, thank you." He put his palms together between his knees and leaned forward slightly.

They both started to speak at once. She was about to ask if he'd listened to her message, and he was going to say whatever he was going to say. He smiled at the cross-talk, then said, "Please. You first."

"No, I'm sorry. You're obviously here for a reason."

"Maybe you were going to ask if I listened to your message? I did. But I was planning to stop by anyway. I know we said we'd talk tomorrow morning, but I understand how difficult this is for you. And I feel bad about keeping you in the dark about certain things."

Callie felt her stomach knot. Her heart had just started to settle, but it picked up again. The feeling of things not being right, just generally being off — gaps in information, vague suspicions, misalignment — it was all suddenly going to be justified. She didn't know if she was ready.

"Okay," she managed.

Footman took a breath and studied the floor a moment. Then his eyes came up, direct and blue. "I listened to your message, yes. I don't know about Nathan Marsh. But I know about someone else — Louise Mullins. Your husband worked for her at one point not quite two years ago."

"Yes. I just found that out." A trill of hope cut through the dread. Maybe this was going in the right direction. Maybe Footman had some answers.

"Okay," he said. "You saw some paperwork, or . . . ?"

"An invoice, yes. On his computer and in his files."

"All right, well, I'm going to need to look at those. Okay? In fact, I'm going to need access to all of your husband's devices."

The dread trickled into the back of her brain. "Why? What's . . . ?"

"Mrs Sanderson, I first became aware of your husband six months ago. Long before the crash."

She was too stunned to speak a moment. "What? Why?"

"Louise Mullins had already provided me information about Abel. That they'd conducted business. She showed me her copy of the agreement. The invoice."

"Why? Why were you talking about Abel to her?" Callie's lips tingled, as if going numb. She scratched an itch at the base of her skull.

"Her daughter disappeared. Kerry Mullins."

"I know." She scratched some more, became aware of it, and removed her hand.

"It was my job to get information on all the people in Kerry's life, in case anything bad had happened. So, as part of the routine, your husband's name came up as a general contractor."

Minimal relief. Maybe it was just procedure.

Footman said, "He'd done work on their house. He'd finished the job, actually, just days prior to her disappearance."

"A deck, I know. But what does it matter?" Callie's whole body felt twingey now, like she might need to get up and run. Her intuition was racing ahead, fearing the worst. She'd been so stunned by Footman's appearance she hadn't realized he was carrying a small black valise. He unzipped it now and pulled out a file.

Before opening it, he looked at Callie again. "I didn't pay too much attention to your husband at first. You know what I mean; I didn't worry about him. I talked with him, but it was very brief, by phone. I asked him if he'd seen anything noteworthy while he was working on the deck. He'd said that each day, Louise mostly stayed inside — she's a bit of a shut-in — and Kerry was coming and going from her job at the grocery store."

"Okay." Callie struggled to remember Abel ever mentioning the call from Footman. He hadn't. Not any of it. She might've known one of his projects was building a deck. And she could remember hearing about the missing Mullins girl. But it all felt very much at a distance.

"Anyway, he was cooperative. And as someone with no police record — I mean, nothing of consequence — someone who was a family man with a solid employment record, I pretty much forgot about him. But then that changed."

Callie's chin wobbled, her lip quivered. The backs of her eyes started to sting. *You don't know anything yet. You don't know anything yet . . .*

Footman opened the file. He slid out a picture and placed it on the coffee table between them. Callie looked at the young woman there. A vaguely familiar face.

"This is Naomi Bannon," Footman said. "Sixteen years old, from Glass Lake."

Callie knew Glass Lake, a small hamlet south of Hawkins by forty minutes.

"Miss Bannon was reported missing by her family a little less than two months ago," Footman said. "Seven weeks, to be exact. One week before your husband's accident."

Callie studied the picture. Her nerves continued to chatter, her eyes threatened to spill, but curiosity won out. "I think I remember hearing about that. They thought she got lost hiking? Or skiing?"

Footman was watching Callie closely. "Cross-country skiing, yes. Your husband never mentioned any of this to you?"

She met his gaze, unflinching. "Never. Not that person, anyway. I can say for sure. We might've talked about the Mullins girl, but it would've been brief."

"Does that strike you as odd?"

"That he didn't mention it?" She shrugged. She hoped she was doing a good job of covering the terror she felt. "Like you said, you spoke with him, it was brief; he told you what he could. He might've thought to tell me, and then it slipped his mind. I don't know." She thought back, trying to see through the fog of memory. "Last summer I was working on a book. It's a project that got . . . derailed by things. But when I'm in a book, I can be oblivious to the outside world. For months."

"Was it your Josie Mariner series?"

"It was."

He smiled. "My sister reads those. She's a big fan."

"Thank you. That's nice."

The smile faded. "So, okay. Maybe the Mullins thing didn't come up. Understandable." He waved a hand. "But here's the reason why I'm here. Abel has shown up connected to Naomi Bannon as well. In fact, we only just made the connection."

An icy chill twisted through Callie. She searched Footman's eyes. "But I just *went* through his files. I didn't see anything. Bannon? No. I didn't see anything. How do you know?"

Footman only looked at her. He wasn't going to reveal it.

"I don't understand. This is crazy."

"Mrs Sanderson, your husband is connected to both victims. The odds are pretty bad that it's a coincidence. And so I just wanted to come and tell you in person: Abel is a person of interest in the cases of two missing girls."

CHAPTER EIGHTEEN

Hearing these words from Footman, a feeling came over Callie unlike anything since she'd first been contacted by the police about Abel's accident. After the initial shock, the initial visit to the hospital and overnight stay, those first few days had been black with despair. She'd come home, mostly to shower and change, and to hope to get a few hours' sleep, and the house had been profoundly empty. Cold; the woodstove had gone out and the thermostat was set low, to fifty-five, for the oil heat. She'd seen traces of her breath as she'd sat down on the bed, as she'd looked at his empty side. After the rush of everything, the business of those first forty-eight hours, everything had slowed to a crawl.

Now, that feeling of claustrophobia — that sense of being an animal caught in a trap, with fate looming near — was back.

Footman must've sensed she needed some time to process, because he stayed silent.

Abel was a person of interest in two missing person cases? Did she need a lawyer? Was this public information?

"Why now?" she finally managed.

Footman lifted his eyebrows, as if he wasn't fully sure of her meaning.

"You said Naomi Bannon disappeared seven weeks ago. What came up that linked her to my husband?"

Footman wore a poker face. His eyes seemed kind but his lips were pursed, his hands folded neatly together. "Again, I can't discuss that. I'm sorry."

"It must be something that just happened. That's why you're telling me today . . ." She searched her recent memory. What had changed? Nothing. At least, not on her end. Her life had routine: visits to Abel, calls to Cormac, sad, lonely meals in front of the TV or over the sink when the hollowness in her stomach became unbearable.

But somewhere out in the world, something had happened.

When Footman got to his feet, she did the same. He finally said, "It may help to remember that a person of interest is not necessarily going to develop into a suspect."

"My husband's in a coma. There's not much information he could have for you."

"Well, true, at the moment. But he could wake up. We hope he wakes up — right? And his records might tell us something, too."

"You're going to take his phone? His laptop?"

Footman started for the door. "I'm afraid that might be needed, yes."

"Have you prepared the warrant?"

He stopped inside the door, his hand on the knob. "I'm actually working on it, Mrs Sanderson." He squared his shoulders, directly opposite her. He was taller by almost a foot, and looked down into her eyes. "I'll be setting forth the basis for the search warrant. I'm confident the judge will sign it. It will cover all devices and platforms supporting the digital life of your husband." He continued to regard her, not unkindly, but with that professional distance. "I could've just asked your consent . . ."

"But you want to cover yourself. In case this turns into something."

She watched his Adam's apple bob up and down as he swallowed. "Yes, Mrs Sanderson."

* * *

Ten minutes after he'd left, Callie was still reeling from Footman's revelation.

True, he'd said *person of interest*, a term substantially different from *suspect*. He wanted Abel's phone and laptop ostensibly to locate any information he might have pertinent to the case.

But it could also be true that the police just didn't have anything solid yet, and they were fishing. The fact that the girls were missing would making things difficult. You couldn't get DNA samples from a crime scene that didn't exist or check for trace evidence under the fingernails of a missing victim.

No, Footman didn't have enough evidence for Abel to be a suspect. But he could. He was about to start going through Abel's life with a fine-toothed comb. She shouldn't stand in his way, of course, but her defenses were up.

She knew Abel didn't have anything to do with two missing teenaged girls. He couldn't. It just wasn't him.

How had this become her life?

She googled *Naomi Bannon missing* on her phone.

Links to news articles appeared. There seemed far fewer of them than for Mullins. Maybe because it was more recent? Seven weeks ago was roughly the first week of January. *Family Gathered for Holidays Struck by Tragedy*, one headline read. The article focused on seventeen-year-old Naomi Bannon going cross-country skiing alone in the woods and not returning.

"She was an outdoor enthusiast," one family member said.

Callie tried to absorb all the names. Lots of Bannons and McNamaras. Someone named Amelia Denson, a friend. A search that went on for more than two weeks yielded nothing except her skis and poles. "It's like she just vanished into thin air," said Teresa Bannon, Naomi's mother. "Just vaporized and left her skis behind."

Callie read until she felt she'd gotten all of the information she was going to get. Naomi Bannon was from a big family. She was well-loved. Callie got the sense that some of these people surrounding her weren't the most upstanding of citizens — a little too backwoodsy to be fully trusted — but maybe that was her being judgmental.

How did Abel know them?

Maybe it was pure coincidence. Him being in the wrong place at the wrong time. He'd helped Louise Mullins finish her deck, so maybe he was planning some job for the Bannon people.

He often visited before taking a job. A free consultation and estimate. She hadn't seen anything on the Bannons in her earlier search of his records, but that could be because he simply hadn't gotten to writing it down yet. He'd wound up in the lake instead.

There would be some record of the initial contact, though. A phone call or a text.

Callie went downstairs to get Abel's phone. The act of it prompted a scary question: why had Footman essentially warned her he was getting a search warrant? He could've just waited until he had it.

Maybe he wants to see what you do.

Now *that* was paranoia. What could he possibly expect her to do? Try and scrub her husband's records because she was complicit in some kind of crime? Obviously he didn't think that, or he wouldn't risk it. He knew about her father being retired law enforcement; maybe it was professional courtesy.

Regardless, she was going to look at her husband's iPhone. No doubt about it.

It had been recovered from the crash intact. Abel generally carried it in the upper pocket of his parka, where he had fast access to it. It was that habit which had spared the phone from the icy water. It was still in that accustomed location now.

She fished it out, getting a slight whiff of the sawdust-and-oil smell of Abel's jacket. Scents that had worked their way into the down feathers and stayed there, even though the parka had gone into the water with him. She couldn't even remember the day she'd taken it home. From the hospital, maybe? Or had the police given it to her?

The phone battery was dead; it hadn't been charged for weeks. She plugged it in and waited a few seconds for it to boot up. It was an iPhone SE, the rubbery case scratched and flecked with paint.

Abel's lock screen wallpaper was a shot of their creek, the pristine water purling over medium-sized rocks, dappled with sunlight. She swiped the screen and was prompted for either his fingerprint or a password.

"Shit," she said to her imaginary version of him.

She'd been able to retrieve the bank account password from his small notebook, but not for his phone.

She set it in her lap and sat looking at it.

"You have to do it, babe."

The only way to access it would be Abel's own thumb.

CHAPTER NINETEEN

Her phone rang on the drive to the hospital. With it plugged into the Chevy, she was able to talk hands-free. "Hi, Mac."

"Hey, Mom. Sorry it took me so long to call back. Everything okay?"

"Yeah, everything's good."

Cormac paused. "You driving?"

"I am."

"Coming back from seeing Dad?"

"I'm just going to see him, actually."

After another moment: "Isn't it kind of late for that?"

She glanced at the dashboard clock. Going on seven. The coma ward at the hospital had visiting hours, but not for spouses — she had access to his room whenever she wanted. "I was busy this morning. No big deal."

"You sound kind of funny . . . You sure you're all right?" He added, "You eating enough?"

"I'm fine, honey. Remember, I'm the parent, you're the child. How are *you*?"

"I'm good. Yeah . . ." A bit reluctantly, it seemed, he told her about his weekend. She listened, always happy to hear his voice, always interested. And if it didn't completely eclipse the thoughts about Abel and the missing girls, it turned the sound down on them, just a little.

". . . but it sparked the usual debate, you know?" Cormac was relating a discussion he'd had on social media. "It's like, how do you prevent the politicization of the media when it's so profitable? How do you stay competitive and objective when what people want — I mean, basically, we're consumers — is our preferred truth? You gotta pay the bills, but you gotta be objective, too."

"Right."

Growing up, Cormac had spent time with friends as much online as he had in person. Maybe even more so. Hours in his room, laptop balanced on his knees, earbuds nearly hidden in his ears as he yakked with invisible people.

Abel and Callie had regularly checked in with him: *Who are you talking to? You're not giving out any personal information, are you? Is your homework all done? Are you still able to walk and perform basic physical tasks?*

Cormac, to his credit, had mostly balanced his academic responsibilities with his zeal for entertainment. He hadn't finished top of his class, more middle of the pack, but he'd been a happy kid. At some point, Callie and Abel had decided that was what was most important.

Now at college, he still spent a good deal of time on the computer. He was explaining about some troll on Discord (Callie was dimly proud of herself for knowing what those words meant), when she realized she hadn't said anything for a while.

"Mom, you there?"

"Yeah. Sorry."

"You gonna tell me why you're seeing Dad so late?"

She thought about it. In fact, it almost came out in a rush: *I'm going to verify why Detective Footman thinks your father is a suspect in two missing person cases. Well, person of interest, but it's really the same thing; I could see that in Footman's eyes. And then I'm going to see what else I can find, because obviously I think your father is innocent.*

But there was no way she could lay all of that on her son. It would only worry him and disrupt his life. He'd want to come home. He'd already threatened to quit school once, insisting he need to be there for her, help with the house, to work. She needed to maintain boundaries. "Everything is all right, honey. There's something, but I can talk to you about it later."

"Did Dad's condition change? Did they say something?"

"No. Dad's condition is the same. I mean, he's doing real well, everything looks good, and we're hopeful. Nothing to worry about."

Cormac seemed to accept it but added, "I really think you need to be writing. It's good for you. When you're not writing, it's like . . ."

It's like you're a boat without a port to sail for. That was how Abel once described it. There had been other colorful analogies in the past, too. All loving and understanding. Her husband's creativity was expressed in his woodworking. He was an exacting person, with a head for math and science, while she was much more abstract and seat-of-the-pants. *I'm the soil and you're the flower,* he'd once told her. *It's my job to ground you. But when you're not writing . . . it's like you're seeking anything else to occupy your time. And I mean* anything . . .

She didn't wholly accept that assessment. No, she wasn't some boozy novelist who couldn't so much as brush her teeth if she wasn't writing. She was a wife, a mother, a homemaker. It was true that when she was deep in a rough draft, the laundry was less likely to get done, and some dinners were cold from the fridge. And it was also true when she wasn't working, she could get stuck on some random hobby or idea. *New drapes for the windows! Repainting the house trim! Learning to cook Asian food — hey everyone, it's pineapple fried rice!*

But, over the years, Abel had learned to adapt. And for Cormac, well, things had always been like that.

"I know," she said about the writing. "I've been thinking about it."

"And you need to eat."

"Mac . . ."

A silence developed between them. The Chevy barreled down the interstate, traffic thickening as she neared the Albany area.

"All right," Cormac said. "Listen — if you need anything, I'm just two hours away. I'm happy to come back any time."

"Thank you. I know."

"We can even talk story ideas. Remember we used to do that?"

"I do." She felt a smile. "Sounds good."

"All right. I love you."

"I love you too."

She ended the call and her smile dropped away.

CHAPTER TWENTY

In Abel's hospital room, she pulled his phone out of her pocket and woke it up. "Okay," she said, glancing at the door to the room to confirm it was closed, "I need you to do me a favor."

His only answer was the breathing machine, pumping its air through the tube in his mouth. His green eyes remained closed.

"I need your John Hancock on this," she said, and gently grasped his right hand. The tension of the ligaments kept the fingers slightly furled. She straightened his thumb, then pressed it against the home button. The phone shook her off. It prompted her for the password.

She tried again, twisting her body around, getting his thumb to make solid contact. This time, it worked. The phone opened. She was in.

The first thing she did was navigate to his settings. She'd thought about this on the drive over; these damn phones closed you out after something like ten seconds of inactivity. Then you had to do the thumbprint all over again. She sought to disable it but was prompted for a password.

"Dammit."

All right then, she'd have to be nimble and quick.

"Let's start with your contacts." She kept talking as she operated the phone. Partly because she always talked to him, but also because she felt guilty for invading his privacy.

"First, let's see if you have anyone in here named Louise Mullins . . . Okay. Here we go. Bingo. Hi there, Ms Mullins. All right, let's look at your call list . . . Good, last call to Mrs Mullins was August. Before that, looks like she called you once, and you called her a total of three times. No voice messages. Any texts?" She opened the text app and scrolled down, looking for Mullins.

She reached the bottom without finding any. "Makes sense," she said. "You tend to talk to your customers, not text them, don't you? Okay . . ."

It occurred to her, while she was in his contacts, to look under "F." She found a Federline, a Freemante, and a Foxx Lumber, but no Footman.

She knew the detective's number by heart, though, and she spent a minute combing through the call log around the same time.

And there it was. Two calls, not one, from Footman. One from Footman to Abel that looked like a message, then Abel's return call.

She found the message and listened.

"Mr Sanderson, this is Investigator Michael Footman with the New York State Police. I just have a couple of questions for you, sir, regarding a job you recently completed. You're not being sued or anything like that." Footman even chuckled, then left his number, even though it was already logged by his having called.

That was it. Short and sweet. Abel called back twenty minutes later. The call duration was twenty-four minutes. That seemed about right. Footman would've been thorough, plus the initial small talk.

No other calls appeared.

Maybe it was simply that Abel forgot to mention it? Or, more likely, that Callie had been too deep in her work to talk?

"Okay. Now let's see about Bannon . . ."

She searched the Bs with no luck. Moving on to the call log, focusing on December, there were several numbers she didn't recognize without a voice message to help. She jotted them down, resolving to call them all and put a name to them at some point.

For now, the voicemails, starting with those left since the crash. Several had been received, most of them soon after the accident, before people learned what had happened.

Listening to the messages made Callie the most uncomfortable yet. Like she had leveled up somehow.

And she worried about what she might hear.

"*Hello, I've been trying to reach you about your car's extended warranty,*" said the obvious robo-voice. It was a welcome relief. There were three more just like it from the past two weeks.

The next most recent call reminded him he was due for a dental cleaning. At least it was a real person who called, though she sounded new, like she was going down a list and unaware of Abel's situation.

The day before that there was a call from his brother.

Callie braced herself. Garr Sanderson lived in Telluride, Colorado. He hadn't been to visit Abel since the accident. Callie had called him, knowing that Garr tended to stay off the grid and wasn't on any sort of social networks. He was a backcountry guide for rich tourists seeking snowshoeing and alpine skiing adventures in that region.

Despite being similar in their careers, the brothers weren't close and hadn't seen one another since their mother's funeral several years prior. Garr had expressed genuine care and concern for Abel's situation but hadn't indicated he would make the trip.

His call was a bit scratchy and muffled, like he'd been having some trouble with his phone or maybe had used a landline — Callie didn't recognize the number. "*Hey Abe, it's me. I'm not sure how you're doing, but . . . I didn't want to bother Callie. I'm sure she's got plenty to deal with. I just didn't know if maybe there was a chance something happened, if you were awake or whatever, but I thought I'd check in . . . All right. You know, heal up, man. Come back. I'm sure your wife misses you. And your son. You gotta come back for them. All right?*" He sniffed, but it was hard to say if it was from emotion or maybe cold weather. Then he hung up.

Callie felt touched by it at first, but it left her feeling empty, a little bitter. Abel and Garr had lost their parents relatively young; Abel orphaned at thirty, with the elder Garr being thirty-two. Their father had lived a hard life. Hypertension and atherosclerosis were the reasons given for his relatively early death, but Callie knew alcohol was a factor. Their mother was more cut and dried — breast cancer had gone into her lymph system and gotten her early.

Then there was Leila, an older sister who'd died decades before, when the brothers were just boys. The details of her death — like the emotional distance between the brothers — remained unclear to Callie, even after all these years. As much as she'd tried to coax it out of her husband, he'd managed to avoid clarifying. And to somehow be charming in the process.

She felt a small chill, as if her husband's ease in side-stepping a difficult conversation was, now, a potential sign of something worse.

The next two voicemails were work-related, and she listened to these carefully. One was an update on a back order of lumber. Another was a request for an estimate. Didn't anyone read the paper? *Abel Sanderson is in a coma, people! Vegetables can't remodel your bathroom.*

And that was it for messages received post-crash.

She moved backward to a time when her husband was still conscious and ambulatory. The first voicemail had been left the day Abel went into the lake. It came from a property owner, Janice Reyes, with a question about pipe insulation for the winter.

The next had been recorded the day immediately before the crash. It began with silence. Callie put a finger against her free ear to muffle the machines in the room.

Finally, the caller — a woman — said, "*Hi, Mr Sanderson. I won't be here for the delivery, but if you can just get it up to the porch, that would be tremendous. I look forward to it being in the home. If you have any questions in the meantime, or you need to change plans, just give me a call. Thank you.*" She hung up.

Callie considered it. The caller had sounded educated. Or maybe sophisticated was the word. The number began with a 315 area code, same as Althea Cooper's. Callie skipped back through the log and didn't have to go far before she found it again — a call had been placed from Abel to the number the day before.

Continuing back, several weeks before the crash now, the number showed up again as an incoming call. This one had a message, too.

Callie listened, realizing her mouth felt dry, her palms sweaty.

"*Hello, Mr Sanderson. A friend referred me to you, and so I'm making an inquiry about your availability. My name is Cynthia Marsh.*"

CHAPTER TWENTY-ONE

The fine hairs spiked on Callie's arms. Her spine stiffened. This was further confirmation that Abel had worked for the Marshes. Callie leaned forward, as if it would help her to better hear the message. She listened as Cynthia Marsh described a project she was hoping Abel would consider: a new hutch for their kitchen and dining area. The way she described it, the order was a way for Abel to prove his mettle. Marsh hinted at a bigger remodeling job in the offing — replacing all the cabinetry in the kitchen, new countertops, maybe more.

She reiterated that he'd come highly recommended, then said, "*If any of that sounds possible to you, if you'd like further details, please give me a call. I hope you do. All right . . .*"

Callie sat on the edge of the bed, her heart pounding. This was significant. This gave Abel a reason to have been out in Lake Clear that day, a reason to have been at the Marshes' house — he'd been delivering furniture. Maybe even doing an estimate for the rest of the work.

More, it solidified her feelings about Nathan Marsh. She wasn't just being paranoid — he'd lied to her. When she'd shown up at his house two nights ago, he'd acted like she was a complete stranger.

"That your husband had a reason to be out there? We'd assumed it." He cleared his throat. "Mrs Sanderson, at this time, I'm really strongly advising you to leave the forensic investigation to us, okay?"

She closed her eyes briefly, feeling frustrated. "Mr Footman — I feel like you're not hearing me. Dr Marsh made no indication that Abel was working for them. But his name is on the invoice. That's not even the phone message. That's on his computer."

"Yes. I understand that." Footman's own patience was beginning to wear thin. *Good.*

"Dr Marsh is acting like he doesn't know anything. What if he's involved? I mean, when I was out there—"

"Yes, you saw a green car. Because a stranger called you up and told you about it. We talked about this, Mrs Sanderson."

"No, I went *out there* because there were things about the accident — you admitted this, too, sir — suggesting someone hit him. You've even said there were scratches on the rear bumper."

Footman cleared his throat. "We always thought there was a reason your husband was out in Lake Clear, ma'am. So now you've found it — he was seeing about a job. But that doesn't change the facts. Okay? I'm going to urge you to let this go. You haven't deleted any of the messages in his phone, have you?"

"Of course not."

"Well, even if you did, we can still get everything from it if we need. Apple products aren't impenetrable, no matter what people might like to think."

"I said I haven't deleted anything."

He sighed. "Mrs Sanderson, it's late. I'm at home. I care about your well-being, and my humble advice to you is to go home yourself, get some rest. Tomorrow is a new day."

She tried to stay poised. Footman was a decent man, she felt that to be true. He was doing his best. But there had also been mistakes. And she felt like, on top of being obtuse, he was now, quietly, condescending to her. But confronting him wouldn't help. Even if he'd told her about Abel to see what she'd do, he could be decent and strategic at the same time. But he wasn't going to budge on the Marsh thing. That was clear.

"Mrs Sanderson?"

"I'm still here."

"I want us to talk in the morning. Okay? When you've had a chance to relax."

"Sure," she said.

He hesitated. "You're all right?"

"I'm all right, yes."

"Good. And in the meantime, I would advise you to leave the Marshes alone. Okay?"

"Good night," she said, and abruptly hung up.

She stood there a moment, unmoving. It took her a moment to realize how deeply the cold was sinking into her bones. She turned for the side exit and grabbed the handle and pulled, but the door didn't open. Shit. It had locked when it closed.

She jogged for the main entrance, feeling adrenalized, feeling more awake — more alive — than she'd felt since this whole thing had begun.

Leave the Marshes alone?

We'll see about that.

CHAPTER TWENTY-TWO

MONDAY, FEBRUARY 27

She slowed as she came to the private drive. The last time she'd been here, the daylight had been fading. But it was familiar in the morning light. The wooden black bear held the mailbox on its head, and the mailbox still read, *The Marshes.*

She sipped her coffee and stared down the twisty road. Then she let off the brake and turned in.

The green Pathfinder was not there. But Marsh's brand-new RAM 1500 was.

When he came to the door, Nathan Marsh seemed curious, maybe a little worried, but not displeased. "Mrs Sanderson. Nice to see you again. What can I do for you?"

"I'm sorry to just show up. I know I'm trespassing . . . again."

"Of course not." He shook his head. "We're not strangers."

He was handsome in an urbane way. Callie had always preferred a more rugged look. Not that looks mattered most, but she was partial to a beard and a flannel shirt.

He smiled and stepped back, inviting her. "Would you like to come in?"

For a moment, she hesitated.

"Thank you."

* * *

The home was beautiful, true to the "great camp" décor of the region. The floors were hardwood; the ceiling post and beam. A clerestory room featured several sets of bookshelves towering seven or eight feet high. Behind them, an open staircase rose to a balcony that fed several upstairs rooms.

The hutch was in the kitchen. Abel's work was distinct, but mostly it was the newness of the piece that drew attention. The fresh coat of polyurethane gave it a sheen. And while the rest of the kitchen was farm-style, with old brass fixtures on the cabinet doors and ornate crown molding against the ceiling, the hutch was understated and modern.

Seeing it filled her with a mix of feelings — vindication, sadness, traces of fear.

She dragged her gaze from the furniture and followed Marsh's lead into the open dining room. Several large floor-to-ceiling windows formed the far corner. The windows overlooked a deck, and beyond it, woods that had been select-cut for the view of the frozen lake, the mountain range beyond.

She sat at the antique dining room table — the same vintage as the kitchen fixtures, if she had to guess — with the hutch still in view. "Coffee? Tea? Anything I can get you?" Marsh was smiling, seeming oblivious that her attention was so captured. And why.

"Well, Dr Marsh," she cleared her throat and tried to get her nerves under control. "I'm not sure how to say this. When I was out here two days ago, I mentioned my husband. His accident."

He looked concerned. "Yes. Of course."

"You said you'd heard of it. That your son — Eric? — had pointed you to an article in the newspaper."

"That's right." Marsh tilted his slightly, like he was intrigued where this was going.

She pointed past him at the hutch in the kitchen. "I'm pretty sure that my husband built that."

Marsh kept his gaze on her a moment, his brow slightly wrinkled. Then he turned and followed the direction of her finger. "That?"

"Yes."

It appeared sturdy, well-built. Two drawers at the bottom. A two-doored cabinet in the middle. On top, an open space where a couple of elegant plates had been propped up on display, along with some candles, fancy salt and pepper shakers, and an ancient-looking tea kettle.

Marsh kept looking. "Your husband built it — you're sure?"

"Yes. Well, I'm ninety-nine percent sure."

Marsh turned back, his eyes lively with thought and speculation.

Callie said, "I found an invoice." She'd printed it out and brought it; now she pulled it from her back pocket and handed it to him. Marsh took it and studied it.

"I'm sorry," he said after a few seconds. When he raised his eyes to her, there was something new in them, unexpected. Suspicion. "I'd never heard of your husband before Eric pointed out the article. And you're handing me an invoice with my name on it. But there's no signature, no other identifying information."

Callie was momentarily speechless. She hadn't exactly prepared for a flat denial, nor any implied accusation. She'd expected some excuse from Marsh, and if it made sense, good. If it was bullshit, she'd planned to make a hasty retreat and call Footman again.

But he was doubling down. He even managed to look upset. If it was an act, he was gifted.

"I also have a message from your wife recorded on my husband's phone," she said.

Marsh's demeanor changed instantly. His forehead seemed to lift and clear; his shoulders dropped.

She continued, "I don't have the phone. But there were a couple of calls between them. It sounded like, after the furniture, they were considering doing more work together. Your wife alluded to a remodeling. The kitchen, I would guess."

After a while, Marsh began to nod. He looked chagrined. "Okay. I think I understand what's happened here."

"Tell me."

"It's quite possible this is something that I wasn't aware of." He shook his head, as if with regret. "I think this is something that my wife did on her own."

Callie felt herself relax a bit — but tentatively. Were their lives that separate?

Marsh turned to look at the hutch again. He did some more nodding. "Okay. It makes sense now. I knew she ordered the furniture, but I assumed it was from a company, not a local craftsman." He turned back and checked the invoice again. "I don't always look at all my credit card charges."

"Your name wouldn't necessarily be on there because you paid. It could be the address. Is the house in your name?"

Marsh looked at her, a bit blankly. His mind seemed to have drifted elsewhere. "Um, yes. For now."

For now?

"Maybe I could speak with her? With Cynthia? Is she around?"

His attention jerked back to Callie — he'd been staring into the space in front of him. "No, she's not here."

"Okay . . ."

The ideas sprang up too fast to catch them all. Callie tried to sort through them: Marsh's wife not mentioning to him hiring a contractor was one thing — in fact, the more she considered it, the more it seemed reasonable, like something that probably happened a lot. But the problem: once Abel had suffered the accident, wouldn't they have discussed it? Marsh's son had pointed it out, and Marsh had then read about it in the paper. Did Cynthia Marsh not know? Did he not think to discuss it with her? And where was she now, and why was he so vague about it?

Marsh seemed apologetic again, but there was a darkness at the back of his gaze. Like they were getting into sensitive territory.

For the first time, Callie started to worry about being in this house. Who knew where she was?

No one.

CHAPTER TWENTY-THREE

ALTHEA

I can't tell you how I know what I know. For that, I'd have to kill you.

Isn't that what they say?

I'm sorry. I have to make light of it. I have to try and marshal some control over the situation. Because when these thoughts come, these alternative memories, they just force their way into my life.

I don't want to know about the young women, the man who stalks them; the man who brings them out to such a remote place where he can do what he wants.

I've seen enough in my own life. My brother and I had a hard time going from house to house. He always looked out for me, always protected me. I was a weird kid — even back then, I had things in my head that didn't belong there. None of the adults would listen, so I stopped telling them.

The worst times were when Casey and I got separated. He wasn't there to take care of me, and I had to learn to fend for myself. Which is fine — every woman should be able to defend herself. But it wasn't always easy. Some of those other kids at the homes were even more messed up than I was.

That's the thing — it's not always the foster parents. Sometimes it's the other *kids*.

Anyway, I had enough to deal with. Biological parents who were too young and selfish to raise their own offspring. I know having twins probably made it hard. But still. They left us in state care, and that meant a lot of growing up fast, a lot of knocks along the way.

The last thing I ever needed or wanted was someone else's memories crowding my own. Someone else's nightmares blending with mine.

They sneak up on me. In the shower, going for a walk, sometimes when I'm driving, I'll just—

Is someone following me?

I look in the rear-view mirror. I can see my own green eyes, my bearded face. The road behind me is wintry and white.

See? It happens just like that. Suddenly I'm someone else. Somewhere else, at another point in—

I've just come from a big house, a strange house that looks too square, too cubic for the forest around it.

The man who owns it, I know he's a doctor. Just like I know there's a green car parked in the driveway.

There are bears everywhere: small statues inside the lavish home, a framed painting of a mother and her cub. Outside, two sentinels atop the steps.

Am I fleeing from this house? Yes. I'm desperate to get away from here. There's something I now know, something that I can't un-*know. Though I wish I could.*

And I'm hurting. My head is pounding, blood running from my ears . . .

Is he back there on the road?

He is. Oh God, he is. The light of revelation is nearly blinding. The light of his headlights, bearing down on me.

And then I'm swerving, I'm losing control, I'm sliding toward the lake and I can't stop.

I can't stop until the truck comes to a rest, and the frigid water pours in.

CHAPTER TWENTY-FOUR

"My wife and I are separated," Marsh said at last.

It felt like a release of pressure. The air seemed to lighten some, the sunlight to reach a little closer. "I see," Callie said.

"We're not really speaking right now. We're just communicating through the lawyers."

"I'm sorry to hear that."

"I'm not."

It was ambiguous; Marsh was hard to read. Did he mean it as dry humor? Was he being plain? Any relief she felt was suddenly darkened by fresh doubt.

He studied her. "You thought I might've lied to you? About your husband?"

She didn't know what to say. The urge to leave grew stronger. "I've had a lot happen in the past couple of days," she managed. It came out sounding sorry for herself, and she regretted it. But no matter — it was time to go. Cynthia Marsh had attempted to hire Abel. She hadn't told her estranged spouse, even after Abel's accident, probably because she didn't know about it. Not something Callie wanted to get in the middle of.

And anyway, it was like Footman said — all this did was establish a reason why Abel had been out here. Green cars and anything else were coincidences and hokum peddled by a troubled woman.

At least, maybe it was better that way.

Callie started to excuse herself when Marsh leaned closer, putting his hand up, as if in apology. "Of course," he said. "You've had an incredible ordeal. I can't imagine a loved one of mine in that situation. I don't know what I would do. You're handling it remarkably well, I can tell."

"Thank you." It was the polite thing to say.

"In fact, it makes me think — life is short. I wish my wife and I weren't having the troubles we're having. Sometimes you just look at things and you wonder — is this worth the stress? People hold on to things."

Maybe it was Marsh's vulnerability; Callie settled back into the seat. And she had other questions to ask, as long as she was here.

"I'm sorry you're going through that," she said first. "When was your wife here last?"

He looked up, thinking. "Ah, that's a good question. She was up here for the holidays. We both were, but at different times. I took Christmas; she had New Year's." His eyes found her. "When was it that she contacted your husband?"

"The first time was mid-November. Abel had the accident on January thirteenth — I think he was delivering the hutch that day."

Marsh nodded. "That makes sense. Well, like I said, I thought the hutch was ordered from Wayfair or something. And I certainly didn't have any idea she was thinking of — what did you say? Kitchen remodeling?"

"She mentions a few things in the message. Redoing the cabinets was one of them."

"Okay. Well, she went back home on January tenth. Days before the accident. So she might never have known."

It made some sense, Callie thought, but how about in the weeks that followed? If they'd made some arrangement for future work, hadn't Cynthia wondered what happened to the carpenter she'd hired?

Unless they hadn't come to an agreement. Abel might've decided to pass on the job . . .

Callie noticed Marsh watching her, as if sensing her work it all out. He pursed his lips and shrugged. "I wish I could be more help. I didn't come back until this month. Second weekend in February. Been here since."

Callie would've liked for Marsh to contact his wife, find out a few more details, but he'd made it clear they weren't speaking.

She stood up, sensing the time had come after all.

Marsh rose next. He looked sheepish a moment, like he wished their acquaintance could be in better circumstances. Then he extended his arm, toward the door. She started for it.

Halfway there, she picked up the sound of an engine. Instinctively, she glanced at Marsh to see how he was reacting.

He smiled vaguely. "Oh," he said. "That sounds like Eric. Looks like you'll get to meet my son this time."

CHAPTER TWENTY-FIVE

Eric Marsh was tall — taller than his father, anyway, who was about six feet to begin with. When he first came into the room, his eyes — a bright, penetrating blue — riveted to her. It wasn't until after his father made some hand gestures, sign language, that Eric smiled. He took a step toward her and made a sign of his own.

Marsh translated. "He says hello." Marsh then glanced at her, a flash of apology across his features. "Do you sign?"

She shook her head. "No, sorry. I've always really been impressed by signing. It's really something, to know all that."

She was babbling. Why was she nervous? Eric Marsh watched her with a detached bemusement. Maybe he read lips, too. She noted the plastic bags he was holding. Hadn't his father shown up with a couple of bags when she'd been here before? Not that it meant anything. When people went out, they came back with things. Callie caught glimpses of cleaning products, duct tape.

Eric made a nod toward the kitchen, and his father stepped out of the way. Marsh made signs as he spoke: "Yeah, son. Go put that stuff away."

Eric smiled politely as he moved past. He was handsome, she supposed, clean-shaven, his hair shaped into a fashionable pompadour. He wore a solid blue work shirt beneath a brown L.L. Bean winter jacket. His jeans looked well-worn, and his Sorel galoshes tracked melting snow behind him as he ventured into the next room. The picture of northern chic. As he passed, she caught traces of fresh air, with some slight chemical odor — like bleach — beneath.

Callie noticed the other boots, lined up neatly by the front entrance — three men's pairs that rested in a rubberized tray to catch the snow and dirt. Hanging above these, several men's jackets, parkas and sweatshirts. Even a full-length snowsuit, mostly buried by the rest. But no women's clothes that she could see.

"Well," she said. "I appreciate you tolerating me when I keep showing up. And it was nice to meet your son. I should—"

"We're going to try to share the house," Marsh said.

"I'm sorry?"

"My wife and I. My soon-to-be ex-wife and I. I just . . . I thought maybe a minute ago, when we were talking about it, it must've seemed odd. Usually people getting a divorce divvy up the spoils. But we both really love this place. We didn't want to fight over it. So we're treating it sort of like a child. One person gets it this month, the other person gets it the following month, or holiday — that kind of thing."

Callie was nodding along politely. Why wasn't there a woman's jacket among the hanging clothes? Was Cynthia Marsh taking everything she owned each time she left?

"I hope it works out for you," Callie said. "It really is a nice home, very pretty here." She used a tone to convey she was ready to leave.

But Marsh was still talking about the impending divorce: "Maybe this place is just too much for one person. We have the house, eight hundred feet of lakefront; the whole thing is almost two hundred acres. We own the land all the way back to the road."

They were still in the hallway, the area that served as the foyer to the entrance. Eric was out of sight in the kitchen. Putting things away, it sounded like.

"Well, thank you again. And, ah . . ."

"Before you go, it's just been something I keep wondering — and maybe it's none of my business — but how did you know to come out here?"

She faced him, finding it difficult to meet his gaze. Call it being a cop's daughter, but his question struck her as telling. The guilty always wanted to know how close the authorities were, or where they might've gone wrong.

Guilty of what? It's an innocent question.

"I was just trying all the houses in the vicinity."

"Oh. I see . . ."

Like he didn't believe her.

"I knew Abel had been to this area."

"Because of the crash."

"Right. Exactly. But I didn't know why. We don't have any friends or family out here."

Marsh nodded and broke eye contact.

She took a breath and held it. Time to go.

Marsh looked up at the kitchen entrance, where Eric was standing, signing something. Marsh signed back, saying, "Sure, that's fine. Whatever you need to do."

Sensing Eric was leaving, Callie summoned a smile. "Nice to meet you."

He made a gesture.

"He says nice to meet you, too."

Eric gave his father one last glance before continuing down the hallway. The door at the end opened to a stairway. His footfalls faded as he descended.

Callie moved to the door, and Marsh followed. He spoke before she got there. "So you were just . . . stopping at houses? There's a lot of places out here, no? A lot of long driveways."

She reached the door. Being on the edge of leaving, perhaps, gave her a boost of confidence. "I was actually looking for a vehicle."

What are you doing?

She had to stop being scared. Especially if she wanted to get to the bottom of things. Abel had been here because he

121

was considering a job for Marsh's wife — that was now established. Who Althea Cooper was and how she knew about a green car remained unclear. Unless she believed in ESP or clairvoyance. Which she didn't. Not really.

Marsh's eyes had widened. "A vehicle?"

She nodded. "Something green." She felt sheepish, but bold, too — if she wanted the fullest picture of what happened to her husband, it made sense to lay all her cards on the table.

Marsh processed it. "Like Eric's?"

"Yes."

Different emotions seemed to mix in his eyes. "Why? Why were you looking for my son's vehicle?"

"Because of what a woman told me."

"Who?"

"Her name is Althea Cooper."

CHAPTER TWENTY-SIX

"Althea Cooper?" Marsh didn't seem to have heard the name before. Unless he was hiding it extremely well.

"She called me up out of the clear blue," Callie went on. "She said that she sees things. And that she saw a green SUV."

"Is this someone you know?"

"No."

"And she . . . saw a green SUV? I don't understand. Has she been here?"

Now it was Callie's turn to protect the truth. Another cop move: let the suspect lead. See what he knows, what he admits. "I don't know if she's been here. I don't think so. But she gets feelings, images. Like she's a psychic."

"I've never heard of her."

Callie cleared her throat. "I thought maybe it was possible she was a patient."

The fact that Marsh denied knowing Cooper had gotten Callie's heart going. He was a doctor specializing in the brain; Cooper was someone with a possible mental disorder, living in the same region. Someone who knew his house, the color of his son's car.

Callie was feeling nervous again, the front door pulling on her like a weight. She opened it, letting the cooler air swirl in. "I've taken up enough of your time. Maybe Ms Cooper is someone your wife knows. You could ask her lawyer, maybe. All right. Have a good—"

"You know what?" Marsh pulled his phone out again and wiggled it. "I'll call her right now. This is obviously very important. We can put our business aside."

"Oh . . ."

He seemed to want to keep her in the house.

"It's the right thing to do. Come on back in, and I'll give her a try."

Shit. Now you really *need to get going . . .*

Her truck sat in the snowy driveway at the bottom of the steps. She looked at it the way a parched woman looks at a fresh glass of water.

But if she really felt Marsh and his son were dangerous, she never would have come alone. She would've asked Footman, at least.

Then again, Footman wouldn't have come. This had been the only way to find things out.

And it still was.

Marsh waited in the hallway, his hand open as if to take hers.

"I really don't want to put you out," she said.

He frowned and shook his head. "Let's clear this up. See what she says."

Callie breathed. In the end, avoiding social awkwardness was such a powerful force. She told herself everything was going to be all right. And she pulled the door closed.

CHAPTER TWENTY-SEVEN

Feeling heavy, Callie walked back through Marsh's kitchen, following him as he beckoned, and then sat back at the table where she'd been before.

He poked at his phone a moment. "You sure I can't get you a drink?"

"I'm still good. Thank you."

A thump came from somewhere downstairs. Marsh glanced up, then at Callie, then back to his phone. His thumbs were busy. "Think I'll text her. No one answers the phone anymore, anyway."

She smiled in a way that felt plastic on her face. The urge to flee was almost overwhelming. What kept her? This terrible human tendency to avoid social discomfort?

No. It was because less than two months ago, she'd had a good life. The best life, really. The greatest and luckiest life anyone could've ever asked for. She'd been a modestly successful novelist with a son at college, a loving husband who divided his time between carpentry and caretaking. They'd had some hardships — Abel losing his mother, and before that, their family losing Breezy — but for the most part, they'd lived happily. The biggest grievances were usually the lack of dine-out options in their small town. Sometimes

Abel seemed a bit distant; sometimes she was the one feeling estranged. But they'd always found each other again. Always came back together.

Now he was wasting away in a vegetative state. He hadn't spoken to her, much less opened his eyes, in forty-four days. Their son was barely hanging on — Cormac was resilient, but this was a huge burden on him, a terrible and inescapable hardship. It would only get worse if she ran out of money, if there was no mechanism to keep Abel safe. And it was only a matter of time before word spread that her husband was a person of interest in two missing person investigations. Which could easily, let's face it, turn into homicide or human trafficking cases.

It felt like the truth — finding it — was all she had. Her only play.

"Okay," Marsh said, though he was still typing with his thumbs. A moment later, he finished, yet kept his attention on the screen as if reviewing what he'd written. "Let's see if she—"

Another loud thump emanated from somewhere below, powerful enough to vibrate the table, the chair she was sitting in.

Marsh got a worried look, there for just a second, as he stared off toward the hallway. Then he seemed dismissive. "That's just Eric."

A third thump felt like it rattled her spine. It took all her courage to stay seated.

Now Marsh looked thoughtful. "Maybe he needs my help with something. Let me just go check . . ." He walked out of the room and she heard the door in the hallway open, the one that led to the stairs going down.

For a moment, there was music. And a woman's voice? Singing. But why? Eric was deaf.

The more Callie listened, the singing sounded like moaning. It was as if her senses recognized it, her *body* recognized it, before her brain could take full measure.

She stood up, as if shocked. This was the final straw.

Get out. Get out right now.

She could go the way Marsh had gone, through the door from the dining area to the hall, but she chose to walk through to the open kitchen and out the door on that end instead. Both led to the hallway, but this one was closer to the front door. To the way out.

She stepped out of the kitchen just as Marsh stepped back out of the stairwell, pulling the door behind him.

They locked eyes down the length of the hallway. Marsh seemed confused at her position but raised his phone. "She wrote back already," he said about his wife.

Callie swallowed over a lump in her throat. When she spoke, her lips felt numb. "Does she know her? Does she know Althea Cooper?"

Marsh didn't answer immediately. Callie realized she'd been backing up when she bumped into the pile of coats and boots inside the door. She turned to look. Her movements had displaced some of the outerwear. The full snowsuit was revealed. It was black, with yellow stripes across the sleeves and legs.

A flash of memory — two nights ago, snowmobilers at the crash site, one of them dressed exactly like this.

It was like a bomb going off in her brain, scattering her thoughts to the corners of her mind. Nothing made sense.

A kind of cold fear spread through her, radiating from the stomach out.

Get out get out get out . . .

She grasped the doorknob beside the coats. For a terrifying moment, it wouldn't turn.

Marsh started walking her way. "She doesn't know any Althea," he said. "And actually, I have a confession to make . . ."

The doorknob turned at last. Relief flooded her in a wave. Callie yanked the door open. She was mumbling something. "I'm sorry. I really have to go." It didn't matter what. It only mattered that she left.

Marsh's eyes drilled into her. His head cocked at that inquisitive angle, like she was some vaguely interesting MRI scan on a lightbox.

Abel must've found something, she thought.

He was out here delivering furniture the husband didn't know about and he saw something he wasn't supposed to.

"So sorry," Callie stammered. "Just forgot I had to do something, thank you . . ."

Meaningless words. All that mattered was to pull the door shut on this man. To close it on his face, his eyes. To get free. To run now, to scramble down the snowy steps and not fall — *be careful!* — to not fall and break something.

She did, she scrambled, taking the steps fast one by one, imagining her husband — *seeing* her husband in her mind's eye — as he'd done something probably very much like this just less than two months ago. As he'd discovered something terrible and fled, fled to get a signal, to call police.

But he hadn't made it.

As she reached the bottom of the stairs and ran toward the truck, she wondered — was the same thing going to happen to her? Was Eric going to come up from downstairs now and chase *her*? Run *her* off the road with his green SUV?

She flung open the door to the Chevy. She stepped on the runner and hauled herself up — or tried — her foot slipped and she bashed her knee against the door frame and cried out. A moment later, she risked a look back at the house.

Marsh was in the doorway, staring down at her. He had his phone in his hand, holding it the same way as he'd done in the hallway, his other hand on the door. He stared at her, his face blank and inscrutable.

Callie climbed into the cab and pulled the door shut.

The keys, the keys.

Through the windshield, she saw Marsh retreat inside.

Where were the keys?

She checked her coat pockets until she found them tucked away, pulled them out, almost dropped them, got the right one, stabbed it into the ignition, and rotated the key chuck. The Chevy's engine roared to life.

The front door opened again. Marsh reappeared. He'd put on boots and a jacket. He started down the steps.

"No no no no," someone said. Callie realized it was her. She dropped the shifter into reverse. She let off the brake and got going just a bit before she had to suddenly stop.

"Oh God," she said. "Oh God."

The green Pathfinder was behind her. Eric's vehicle. He'd boxed her in.

She was trapped.

CHAPTER TWENTY-EIGHT

Marsh came toward the car. His lips were moving. Callie didn't stop to hear what he was saying. Part of her felt irrational, but more of her felt terrified — an alarm had been tripped, and it was time to run away as fast as possible.

As she shimmied back and forth to get the Chevy turned around, she bumped into the Pathfinder. Something cracked. Marsh stopped in his tracks, holding up his hands, as if in a sign of peace. *Whoa, whoa — take it easy!* Callie kept making the micro-movements with the Chevy, back a little, forward a little, until she was finally turned around. Then she roared off down the bumpy, twisty drive.

She didn't look back.

* * *

"Calm down," Footman said. "Let's take it one step at a time."

"I think Abel saw something. Or maybe he even heard something. While I was there, there was this awful thumping. And a voice, like moaning . . ."

Callie hated how this looked, how it sounded — she was like one of those hysterical main characters in a psychological thriller. Always jumping to conclusions and flying off the handle. She'd left Marsh's place at high speed, jouncing over the terrain, the Chevy thundering, only stopping to call Footman once she was several miles away and had cell service. The state police headquarters in Ray Brook were on her way home, and Footman was in his office.

She stood in front of his desk, too keyed up to sit. Another investigator had joined them, standing beside Footman's desk. She wore a navy-blue pantsuit, dirty-blonde hair pulled back in a tight braid. Footman had introduced her as Investigator Stephanie Sacony.

"Can you be sure it was a woman's voice?" she asked.

"Yes. It was a woman's voice."

Sacony looked thoughtful. "But, I mean, a woman physically in the house? Not someone on TV, maybe, or . . . ?"

"It could have been, yes. But he can't hear. So if there was music or a TV on, I can only think he was trying to cover up some other noise."

"Like what?" Sacony asked. "You think he was doing something to someone while you were there?"

"I know how this sounds. But it was the whole thing. The thumping, the stuff in his bags. I think I saw duct tape in one. And then I saw the snowsuit hanging there . . ."

"The snowmobile suit," Footman said, glancing at the notebook on his desk. "The one you say resembles what you saw a man wearing at the site of your husband's accident."

"Not resembled. The same. I mean, it's possible there are two identical suits. But not likely. It would be a huge coincidence. And you're always . . . Police don't believe in coincidences."

The investigators glanced at each other. Footman asked, "What's your theory on why they were at the crash site?"

"I don't know. Because I was there. Because I'd come out to the house. They went over to look at it. To see what I might have done there. I don't know."

He scratched his neck.

Callie hurried on. "I just . . . I'm sorry. I don't in any way mean to tell you your jobs. But do you think you might check this out? I know I'm not doing the best job of explaining here. I was pretty scared. But this is just . . . There's too many things to ignore."

"Absolutely," Footman said finally, after another quick glance at Sacony. "We're going to look into it right away."

"We just need to have all our facts straight," Sacony said. "Can you tell us again — why did you visit the Marsh home for the second time?"

Even though she already had, Callie explained how finding the voicemail from Cynthia Marsh got her thinking Nathan Marsh hadn't been forthcoming. "Which I told you about," she reminded Footman. *Even though you weren't very compelled.*

Sacony said, "So you went to see Marsh yourself? Thinking he might've lied to you, and it could have something to do with foul play in your husband's case, you went out there alone?"

"Mr Footman had just told me my husband was a suspect in two missing person cases. I can't just . . . sit there."

"And what is it that you do, again?"

Callie sighed. Some part of her always dreaded this question. "I'm an author."

"An author?" Sacony lit up for the first time. "Is your stuff around here in the bookstores or . . . ?"

"No, it's not. It's mostly e-books."

"E-books . . ."

"Amazon Kindle? Tablets? You know, electronic books?"

"I understand," Sacony said.

Footman turned his head to look at her. "Not a lot of bookstores left these days, really."

Sacony explained, "I just thought, maybe, local bookstores. Things like that. There's the one in Lake Placid."

Callie cleared her throat. The cops returned their attention to her. "Listen," Sacony said, after a moment, "we are going to take this very seriously. I'm going to try and reach Cynthia Marsh, for one thing. And we'll get to the bottom of her relationship to your husband."

"Thank you."

Sacony started out of the room, then stopped when Footman said, "We are still going to need your husband's phone and laptop, Mrs Sanderson. Someone will be at your house this morning."

"I understand."

He nodded, as if that settled it. Sacony resumed walking to the door, opened it. "It was nice to meet you, Mrs Sanderson."

"You too."

Footman rose from the desk after Sacony pulled the door shut behind her. "Officer Sacony is a good investigator. Been with BCI for fourteen years. Just transferred in, and I'm glad."

Callie gave a half-interested nod. The morning's events were fading, doubt filling up in their wake. Had she really heard a woman moan? Why was she so afraid of Marsh and his son? Did she have some kind of bias or prejudice because Eric was deaf? Just because he couldn't hear — maybe he still liked the vibration of music.

And the snowsuit . . . Exactly why *did* she think Marsh and his son would've raced on their snow machines to visit the crash site so soon after she'd left that first night? She didn't have an answer to that. The doubt then spread to all other areas.

Footman was watching her with concern. "Are you all right?"

"Yes. Sorry." She got moving toward the door, then stopped. "Can you tell me how Abel is connected to the Bannon family?"

Footman looked grim. "I can't."

"You really think my husband had something to do with two missing girls?"

He didn't answer, only looked at her with detectable pity in his eyes.

"Why aren't you asking me any questions?"

"I will be, in time. And we might need to speak to your son, too."

She felt nauseated. "I don't understand."

"Think of it this way: this is a process of elimination. I want to eliminate your husband from the list of suspects."

She could have written the line herself.

"Are there a lot of suspects?"

"I . . . can't really answer that, either. What I can say is we can connect your husband to both missing girls. They went to different schools, they didn't travel in any of the same social circles; they're not even friends on social media. So being connected is significant."

"He built a small deck for Louise Mullins. That's it. And he has some relationship to the Bannons that you won't tell me about. So it seems pretty tenuous to me." She spoke to Footman in a familiar tone because it felt like they'd been through a lot together already. Like he was a distant family member, even.

But he wasn't. He was a police officer, and she was pushing her luck. The room tensed.

"I'm sorry," she said.

He waved a hand. "This is a tough situation. Let me take a look at your husband's phone and laptop. And Investigator Sacony is looking into the Marshes. Okay? In the meantime, try to take it easy."

* * *

There was no taking it easy. Not for the rest of the drive home. Not when she inspected the Chevy and found she'd cracked the rear taillight backing away from the Marsh place. And not when a van showed up with a group of three crime scene technicians. She let them in and showed them to the basement where they spent the next hour in Abel's office, eventually leaving with several of his belongings in bags marked *Evidence*.

No. Easy was not how she took it.

CHAPTER TWENTY-NINE

Footman wanted to speak to Cormac, so Callie had to head him off at the pass, to warn Cormac ahead of time. Footman's phrase, "person of interest," really was a euphemism for "suspect." Callie didn't want Cormac finding out via a phone call from a stranger. She had to tell him.

And maybe she could feel out what had been going on between him and Abel. If the talk they'd sought was over anything serious, or just typical father–son stuff.

Of course, he didn't answer. She glanced at the clock in the kitchen — it was half past two. She'd had Cormac's schedule memorized but temporarily forgotten it. Was he in class at this hour on a Monday?

"Mac, hi. It's Mom. I know . . . obviously. You've got me in your caller ID. But you've got to start somewhere when you're leaving a message . . ."

She was trying to keep it light, but she probably sounded humorless anyway. "Listen, bud. I have something I need to talk to you about. Dad's okay, but there's something that's going on with the police. They think that he might have information relating to a certain case . . . but they obviously can't talk to him. So they're talking to us. They took his . . . ah . . . they took his phone and laptop . . ."

She could feel herself unravelling and quickly wrapped it up. "Anyway, just call me. You might hear from Michael Footman — he's the state police investigator — but call me first, if you can, all right? I love you."

She hung up, trembling. Not bad, though. She'd prepared him without alarming him. And even if Footman got to him first, she didn't think the investigator was looking to upset her son.

She hoped.

* * *

She took her usual walk around the property, down the switchback trail toward the water, along the river, past the huge boulders and caves. Her knee ached a little from bashing it against the truck. The subtle throb was a reminder of how crazy her life had become. She wanted to forget that a little bit, if just for a moment.

It had been a while since the last snowfall. Animal tracks crisscrossed her path — rabbit, fox, deer. She stopped when she saw what she thought were human footprints.

Nope, no forgetting.

Well, it wasn't entirely unheard of for people to walk through here. Abel had posted a few No Trespassing signs when they'd first bought the place, but occasionally kids from Hawkins wandered down by the river. One summer, Abel had found the makings of crystal meth in a backpack stashed among the big rocks and notified the state police. A "one-pot bag," it was called, meaning it had enough precursor ingredients to prepare the drug for a single user. There were even signs the trespasser had spent a night or two in a cave formed by two of the larger boulders while making his drug.

But that had been a couple of years ago. Callie didn't recall seeing tracks down here for a long time.

They seemed to meander along the rocks, then come back to the river. She followed them, lost them, and picked them up again on the eastern edge of the property. Where the land sloped up to the road.

And she thought of the man in the gray car from the day before, parked right at that spot.

Had he been down here? Why?

* * *

When her phone rang, she'd been dozing on the couch. She'd gotten four hours of sleep the night before, maybe less. The walk had made her extra tired, her knee even stiffer.

It was just after 4 p.m., and it was Footman.

"Mrs Sanderson? Did I wake you?"

"No, no," she lied. "What is it? Everything okay?"

"I've been thinking about the whole thing with Marsh going through a divorce." He let the statement hang a bit.

"Okay . . ."

"Not knowing his wife's plans. And it occurred to me: maybe your husband inadvertently got in the middle of that."

Callie sat up on the couch, sore knee forgotten. "I thought of that. If maybe Cynthia Marsh never told her husband she had plans to renovate."

'Right," Footman said. "And that's why she never mentions Abel to him, even after the accident. She hid it because it could give Marsh ammo in the divorce. They have this deal to share the place, but probably any remodels or updates have to be approved by both parties. She does an end run around that for some reason — maybe just to mess with her soon-to-be ex — but then the carpenter she hires drops into a coma. Plans foiled."

Callie picked it up, feeling alert now: "Maybe she was unaware Abel had written an invoice for Nathan Marsh."

"My thoughts exactly. Eventually, she would've directed Abel to bill her instead."

"But in the meantime, I found the estimate and let the cat out of the bag. Now Nathan Marsh potentially feels he has the upper hand. He could leverage this in the divorce."

"Exactly," Footman said again. "We're on the same page." He added, "And we're back in reasonable territory."

But none of it exonerates my husband from suspicion about two missing girls, Callie thought.

"Have you been able to talk to Cynthia Marsh about this?" Callie asked. "Maybe get her side of the story and see if it fits with what we're saying?"

"Unfortunately, Investigator Sacony hasn't been able to reach her yet. But it's just been a few hours."

"Usually when someone calls from the state police, you call right back."

"True," he admitted.

The notion of Cynthia Marsh being unresponsive got Callie's mind spinning again. *Maybe because the poor woman is locked in their garage.* She reeled herself back in. "Are you going to talk to my son today?"

"Yes."

"What are you going to tell him?"

"I just have some general questions. I'm sure he's a smart young man — he's going to want to know why I'm calling. I'll be courteous, mindful that this has been difficult."

"Thank you." She almost blurted: *You don't think my husband actually did anything. You just have no other suspects, no other decent theories about what happened to these young women.* But she kept that thought to herself, too.

"One last thing," Footman said.

She waited.

"You floated the question the other day, 'Why up here?' Meaning why was Althea involving herself with events happening four hours away. Well, it occurred to me — Marsh is from Syracuse. That's where his practice is."

"He's a neurosurgeon."

"Correct. Now, the other thing is, Althea Cooper has an interesting medical history. Part of it involves neurological issues. That's all I can say."

"I asked Marsh if she was a patient. He said no."

Footman was quiet a moment. "Well . . . I don't know. But if they're connected, it might explain some things. Depending on their relationship, it could give her motive to implicate him in something. Just to mess with him."

"Yeah," Callie said, her mind wandering ahead again. She talked with Footman for another couple of minutes. Ending the call, she considered how both Footman and Marsh were professionals bound by confidentiality. Maybe they couldn't say things directly about what they knew.

But Althea Cooper could.

CHAPTER THIRTY

Althea Cooper's automated voicemail fielded the call. Callie didn't leave a message. This time, she'd wait.

In the meantime, the cupboards were bare. The fridge contained a few condiments and a leftover pizza from time immemorial. She threw it out, along with some other moldy leftovers, and headed into town.

Hawkins was quaint without pretension. One main road — Church Street, rather than Main — bisected the downtown area. A grocery store, a hardware store, two small bank branches, two churches — Episcopal at one end, Roman Catholic the other. Not much different from Lake Clear.

Callie's father had been raised Roman Catholic, and she had memories of being in a church on Christmas Eve. Her father's delighted eyes contrasted with her mother's set mouth and rigid posture. Wendy Baker-Pavlis didn't like church. Gregory Pavlis liked it just fine.

How a religious cop and an atheist college professor had ever hooked up — let alone stayed married for forty-three years — was beyond Callie's comprehension. Though she did suspect that her own arrival in the world had had something to do with it.

She lingered over the produce aisle, not really seeing anything, distracted by her conversation with Footman and her own churning hunger. When had she last eaten? Had she even had breakfast? She went to the deli counter and ordered some sliced cheddar. Maybe a grilled cheese sandwich would hit the spot.

When she felt like she was being watched, Callie turned. No one was there. At least, no one who appeared to be watching. An older woman considered the leanest package of bacon, and a man pulling an oxygen tank on a small cart — the tube went under his clothes and up to his nostrils — was eyeballing a plastic box of donuts. But the feeling had been intense — her skin felt rough with gooseflesh.

Outside with her cheese and bread and a few other items, she scanned the parking lot. No one there. Across the street, though, halfway to the gas station on the corner of Church and Park streets, a figure stood beneath an oak tree. He faced this way. He seemed to be watching.

Callie loaded her car, keeping one eye on the man. Was he smoking a cigarette while he waited for a companion to pump gas? It didn't seem so; both of his hands were in his pockets. He wore a ball cap that obscured his face. She thought he was big, though. Tall. Like Eric Marsh had been tall.

Finished loading, she rolled the empty cart to the kiosk, where other carts were stashed willy-nilly. She tried not to stare as she walked back to her vehicle. But when her phone buzzed in her pocket, it made her gasp out loud.

Callie dug for it. She was familiar with the incoming number by this point. And maybe because her nerves were up, she didn't waste any time with pleasantries.

"Are you a patient of Dr Marsh?"

Althea had a ready answer. "No."

Interesting. The innocent answer would have been: *Who?* The "no" suggested she knew him. Maybe at least knew *of* him.

"Is that the truth? Or are you hiding the fact that you knew this doctor in the woods, the one you halfway implicated on the phone, because you're worried what I'll think?"

"And what would you think?"

"I wouldn't believe you. I would suspect something." Callie stood at the driver's side door. She opened it and climbed into the cab of the Chevy. When she looked back at the tree by the gas station, the man was gone.

"All I can say is, I've seen him before. Well, I've been close to him."

"Close to him?"

"Near him." Althea paused. "He's weird, isn't he?"

"I don't think he's weird," Callie lied. "Did you know he has a vacation home in the Adirondacks?"

"Is this really what you want to talk to me about?"

"You were right. There are statues of bears. One at the head of the driveway, two at the top of the stairs."

A pause. "You're angry with me."

"That's a tactic. What you're doing right there. That's distraction."

"I wish you weren't angry."

"I'm angry with a lot of things," Callie said. *Scared, too. Maybe even seeing things.* She took a cleansing breath. "Why are you being vague? Why should I believe you that you didn't know the house you described belonged to your . . . a doctor? Can't you see how that's tough to swallow?"

Althea was silent, just breathing.

Callie said, "I'm gonna level with you, Althea. I think—"

"You think I have mental problems."

"Do you? Do you have neurological issues, maybe? The police won't tell me exactly, but they've alluded to it." She was as delicate as possible. "If you have a condition that inclines you to magical thinking, it wouldn't be your fault."

"What if there's no difference?"

Callie pondered it, and Althea resumed, "What if what we think of as mental health problems are really signs of something else? That the only way we could understand them was to think of them as problems?"

Again, Callie chose her words carefully, mindful of the precarious nature of mental health. "I'm not an expert. I've done some research and talked to therapists. But none of that qualifies me to make any kind of assessment about you. Other than just my own personal feeling. Maybe you're right — there could be all sorts of things we don't understand about psychology, about how the mind works — but I have no idea. All I know is that you started something. You know something. And, to me, my experience tells me it's probably because of some physical, logical connection. Not because of some extra sense."

"It doesn't seem extra to me," Althea said. Her voice was almost too quiet to hear. "It feels more like a deformity. Like I'm a freak."

Callie took a moment to consider whether Althea was fishing for sympathy. Maybe. But that didn't necessarily disqualify what she was saying. Here was someone who didn't seem to be scamming anybody — not in any way that made sense. She wasn't asking for money. She didn't seek attention. Callie had to make a decision. Try to get to the truth through reason, or maybe to go along.

"Okay," she said. "So you've . . . been *near* Dr Marsh — how many times?"

"Once."

"When?"

"A couple of months ago. Before Christmas."

"Have you ever met his wife?"

"No."

"How about his son?"

"No."

"His daughter?" Callie felt a pang of regret. She didn't like to mess with people, and Cooper was especially vulnerable. But it was just a small test — Marsh never said he had a daughter. Eric was an only child, like Cormac.

"No. I never met his daughter."

143

"Okay. Let me ask you, though — do you think that's significant? That you met this man, and he happens to be the one who owns the house where there was a green SUV, bears everywhere — the things you told me were in your vision?"

Althea didn't answer right away. Then: "I think it is. Yeah."

An unexpected answer. Callie waited for more.

"I think I have to get close to the person. I mean I have to be near them. And then something . . . transfers to me. It's been that way since I was a kid."

"Okay. So you were physically near Marsh more than two months ago, but you just called me the other day. With these things that you know. These alternative memories."

"Because they're like any other memory. Well, first they have to transfer from the other person, I guess. I don't even realize it. But then maybe something triggers it. Like, I suddenly thought about a man in his truck. Trying to get away. Trying to get away from this house, and from another man."

Callie ignored the chill it gave her. "So, you see Marsh before Christmas, it creates this alternative memory of my husband that doesn't really get activated until just recently. And then you called me."

"Right."

It was a hell of a stretch. Convenient, really — a way to fill certain holes. But she fell silent, considering the difference it might've made if Althea Cooper had called her weeks ago instead of just the other day. Not much of any?

Something else moved to the top of her thoughts: "You said to me — when you first called me — you said you thought he was a doctor. The man whose house my husband was at. You said he was at a house nearby. He was talking to someone."

Althea agreed tentatively: "Yes . . ."

"And didn't make the connection to Marsh?"

"I know multiple doctors, so I didn't assume. I told you, I'm not his patient. I just met him the one time."

Callie sighed. They were going in circles. "First of all — Marsh wasn't there when my husband was. Do you know

144

who was?" She let the question linger until it felt like a bad attempt at a "gotcha" moment. The kind of thing people try on psychics: *Okay, so what am I thinking now?* Callie answered her own question. "It was his wife, Cynthia. My husband didn't have any direct dealings with Dr Marsh. It was her he talked to. They exchanged a few messages, and he was meeting with her to see about doing a kitchen remodeling job."

"Oh. Well, he could be lying."

"True . . ." Callie waited a moment, thinking. This line of conversation wasn't really bearing fruit. Something else occurred to her: "What about Kerry Mullins, Althea? If you think Dr Marsh might've been the . . . touchpoint for my husband, then do you have any idea what the touchpoint was with Mullins?"

"Yes," Althea answered quickly. "I do. That was what I saw first. A girl. Two girls, actually. At a cabin. And then Kerry Mullins was missing — I saw it on the news — that was the trigger, so I called the police. But it was the same situation. I didn't call right away. I had to see if the memory persisted. Sometimes they're false."

My God, Callie thought. *The complicated life of a clairvoyant.*

She reined in the sarcasm and instead weighed up what to say next: *Because the police are thinking my husband is a suspect in Kerry's disappearance. That and another girl's . . .*

"Maybe you should," Althea said.

"I'm sorry?"

"Well, it's only because you went out there — you met Doctor Marsh, and then you talked to me about him — that's how I know he was the connection."

Callie tried to follow the logic.

Althea said, "Maybe you should talk to Kerry Mullins's family, and then you can tell me what you find. That way, I might know why I saw what I did."

Callie was quiet a moment, considering it. How much of this was manipulation? Before she could respond, Althea said, "I just think you need to ask questions. Maybe even of people you wouldn't think to ask."

"What does that mean? Who?"

"I don't know."

The conversation seemed to have run its course. They talked for a few more minutes, but the young woman merely repeated things she'd said. At times, she sounded unconvinced herself. As if she doubted the things she was saying, too.

* * *

Driving home with the groceries, Callie talked to Abel.

"Maybe the Marshes hurt her. Or she thinks they did . . . And she tries to get back at them by coming up with this story."

It was far-fetched. Hard to believe.

"Or she's just completely crazy," Abel said.

It spooked her, for a second, how much it had sounded like he was in the truck with her. But he wasn't. He was just another voice in her head.

One thing that seemed clear: Louise Mullins was the next person to talk to. Either she or Kerry had a connection to Althea Cooper, or Cooper just saw something in the newspaper and intervened. That was what Footman thought. Maybe he was right. Callie would find out.

She didn't get too far, though. As she approached her house, she spotted a vehicle parked in the driveway.

CHAPTER THIRTY-ONE

Garr Sanderson climbed out of the dark blue Jeep. He was taller than Abel by several inches. They looked alike in certain ways — their smiles, mostly, and in some ways through the eyes — but otherwise you might not know they were brothers.

He gave Callie a quick, stiff hug. Garr was not affectionate — at least, not to her. The one time he'd put his arms around her was at her wedding to Abel. He'd said, "Welcome to the family," and given her the briefest of hugs. They'd never spent much time together, either. It was only the big events — weddings and funerals — when she saw him.

"What are you doing here?" She stepped back from their quick embrace.

"Well . . ." He glanced at the house, the property. "It's a bit of a story. How are you? You okay? Everything okay?"

"That's a bit of a story, too." A sense of etiquette finally broke through the shock of his arrival. "Would you like to come in?"

"Sure, yeah." He gave the Jeep another look, as if deciding whether he needed something. The gray sweatshirt he wore said *Sanderson Guide Services*, with flecks of white paint dotting the right sleeve.

When he seemed ready, she led him up the snowy walk-way to the front door.

* * *

Inside, she made tea. Garr sat at the dining room table. The dining room was open to the kitchen, like it was at the Marsh place. It was on the tip of her tongue to tell him everything, but she wanted to hear from him first. Why he was here.

"So, how's Abe?"

"He's . . . you know. He's okay."

"Yeah? Any change?"

She thought of her husband withering away, day by day. Literally and metaphorically shriveling into the bed that had become his place of indefinite rest. She was surprised at the rise of bitterness she felt, there one moment and gone the next, leaving a slick of guilt in its wake.

Garr was watching her — she realized she hadn't answered his question, and that her hesitation itself was a response.

"No change, really," she said. "They're still optimistic . . ."

He nodded. "Good," he said, and sipped his tea.

It was normal to feel resentment, she told herself. In one of the online forums she frequented, a spouse of someone permanently disabled had noted how the survivor's guilt could be terrible, but you didn't have to be a perfect person.

Loss created resentment. That was natural. Resentment toward the world, toward God, toward the doctors and nurses who seemed ineffectual at doing anything other than dabbing at his bedsores and shrugging their shoulders.

"So . . ." Callie said.

Garr kept nodding, as if responding to an unspoken question. "Yeah. So, I bought some property out here."

"You did?"

He seemed to glance around the house, eyes briefly alighting on her, moving on again. "I did. Well, my girl-friend and I did."

"Oh." There was such little communication between Abel and Garr, it was interesting how he now spoke of things as if Callie would have any clue. "That's nice."

"Her name is Lynn. I actually guided for her out in Telly. Her and her family." He meant Telluride, where he worked as a backcountry guide. Callie remembered the message he'd left on Abel's phone: *I just didn't know if maybe there was a chance something happened, if you were awake or whatever, but I thought I'd check in.*

"That was a little over a year ago," Garr said about meeting Lynn. "We met and hit it off. And we just kept talking. She found out I'd grown up back here in the Adirondacks. She said she'd always wanted to get a place here, something she could rent out and then stay in when she wanted to get away, things like that."

"Nice. And so — she did?"

"Yeah, she closed on it a couple of months ago. Everything went through. Did Abel ever say anything about it?"

"About you — or your girlfriend — buying property?"

"Yeah. That, and Lynn wanting to build on it. Like a tiny-house Airbnb type of thing. I gave her Abel's information. This is before his accident, obviously. But he never mentioned?"

Callie stepped away from the kitchen counter and moved a little closer to Abel's brother. "I'm sorry, Garr, things have been a little crazy around here. A lot of stuff has happened. But I don't think he mentioned it, no." Callie thought back to the records she'd been reviewing: had there been someone named Lynn on any of the invoices? Maybe one of the numbers Callie didn't recognize, or a voicemail she'd skipped over?

"Did she actually hire him?"

Garr shook his head. "It ended up not working out. I was just curious if he said anything."

She stared a moment. Not only had Garr never been affectionate toward her, this was probably the most they'd spoken in twenty years.

"Honestly, Garr, we never talk about you. I had no idea you had a girlfriend or property or anything."

Callie knew that the emotional distance between him and Abel probably went back to their childhood. But the few times she'd pressed Abel for details, she could tell it was too painful for him, and so she'd relented. Garr wasn't going to be any more forthcoming, that was for sure. Not even with his brother in a coma.

He said, "Well, I didn't want to bother you."

"It's not bothering me."

He made a small nod, as if he accepted her admonition. "I'm your sister-in-law. We're family."

They fell silent, and she could feel herself hoping for an apology from Garr. Something about the distance he'd been keeping despite the situation. And how when he'd finally shown up, it was unannounced.

But she got the sense Garr wasn't practiced in saying sorry. He'd never married, for one, and marriage was where men cut their teeth on emotional maturity. Maybe Lynn would be the one. But for now, if Callie wanted an apology, she was out of luck.

She shifted subjects. Sort of. "When did you get here?"

"This morning. Flew in and rented a car. Lynn is on her way. She lives in Connecticut — she's driving up. I got here a little ahead of her. Wanted to come by."

And what? Callie thought. Was he checking on her, or here to help? She realized she was being a bit hard on him, but it had been a minute, and things were a bit of a mess.

"I'm glad you came," she said.

"So how's, um, Cormac? He's in college?"

"Yes. His second year."

Garr shook his head. "Damn. I remember when that kid was just a wee little guy."

Callie thought Garr had maybe seen Cormac half a dozen times since he was born. She wasn't even sure if Cormac knew where Garr lived or what he did for a living.

You're awfully judgmental, she thought about herself. *Given the state of your own family.*

It was true, she knowingly kept an emotional distance from her parents. But they talked to Cormac on the phone. They sent him gifts. They'd sent money to pay for his graduation party when he'd finished high school. Maybe they weren't a big part of his everyday life, but they weren't *estranged*. Not the way Cormac was from his uncle Garr.

Grandparents have more of a role to play. Uncles don't have to be part of a kid's life. It's not the same.

Whatever. She agreed with Garr that Cormac had grown up fast. She said that Mac was doing well — and he was, despite recent events.

"He seems like a tough kid," Garr said.

Callie thought of Mac as anything but tough. Maybe he could be rough around the edges, but, like his father, the inside was made of mush. Love and emotion. Again, she came close to letting it all spill out. To telling Garr everything: that some part of her had always doubted Abel had just skidded off the road, and then she'd gotten a strange call. The call had set off a chain reaction, and somewhere in the midst of things, the police were telling her they thought Abel had information about two missing teenaged girls.

What would it mean to Garr? His eyes would widen and he'd listen intently, saying *holy shit* at certain moments, but what would he do? What *could* he do? Nothing.

She was about to move on, start giving indications she had things to do, places to be, and he'd get the hint and leave. But something Althea said recurred to her.

I just think you need to ask questions. Maybe even of people you wouldn't think to ask.

Okay, then.

"So, you're meeting Lynn tomorrow?"

"Yeah. She's going to leave bright and early, she said."

"Cool." Callie gave it a beat. "So where's this property located?"

"Not far, actually. It's just south of here by an hour. You know North Creek? That area?"

"I do. It's nice down there."

"It is. And people are buying up things like crazy. She really got in at just the right time — the market has gone through the roof just in the past couple of months."

Callie nodded, like she knew, though it was something she scarcely paid attention to. Mostly she was thinking about the location of North Creek. That neck of the woods and what was around there. She tried remembering the villages.

Garr stood. He'd finished his tea. His body language and expression suggested he was about to make his exit.

"All right, well, listen. I don't wanna . . . you know. You have things to do, I'm sure."

"I'm happy for you to be here," she said. She was itching to take out her phone and have a look at Google Maps. Why did she think North Creek mattered?

At the same time, she tried to ask her next question delicately: "Do you think you're going to be able to visit him?"

"Oh yeah, absolutely. That's the whole thing. That's why I'm here."

"Okay." Callie felt a little stunned. "Well, that's great."

He scratched his head and frowned a bit. "Is there anything I have to do? They probably just need to see my ID, right? Or is there like a list, or . . ."

She smiled though her mind was racing. "You're fine. You're his family." She took out her phone to check the time. Just past 2 p.m. "You don't have too much time left, though. Visiting hours are over at five."

"Even for you?"

No, they weren't. And something in his eyes was so earnest, so suddenly boyish, her heart swelled. "I could call," she said. "If you think you'll be late. Call and say you came in from out of town . . ."

"That would be amazing. Thanks."

He started toward the door, continuing to look around as he walked. "Place looks great."

"Thank you." She followed him, phone in her grip.

"So this Lynn, huh? You guys serious?"

He gave her a look that made her suddenly feel she'd gotten too personal. But he said, "Yeah. Could be."

Garr held the door open and gazed outside. "She loves it up here. Always did. It's funny how, you know, we met out there in Telly, but we were right near each other when we were growing up."

Callie was just inside the house, behind him. "What do you mean? Didn't you say she was from Connecticut?"

"Originally, yeah. She was born there, went to school there. But her family, on her mom's side, come from up here. That North Creek, Pottersville area."

Pottersville. That was it. And the lake in Pottersville . . . Callie's throat went dry. "Glass Lake?"

"Yeah, yeah. Exactly. Her mom's family had a house on Glass for years." Still holding the door open, cold air rushing in, he narrowed his eyes at her. "Why? You know them or something?"

"Is their last name Bannon?"

She knew what he was going to answer before he said it. Like she, too, had developed some kind of sixth sense.

"Lynn's last name is McNamara," he said.

"Okay . . ." Callie exhaled.

"But her aunt is Teresa Bannon." Garr blinked. "Why?"

CHAPTER THIRTY-TWO

After she caught Garr up on everything so far, she had to stop him from driving out to the Marshes. Physically. He was big, the type her father would've said was "built like a brick shithouse," but she put her hand on his chest and he stayed.

They'd come back inside and stood in the living room. "The police are already going out there to talk with them," she said. "I was at the police station this morning. Late morning, right after I was out there."

Garr finally relented. He backed away some, shaking his head, as if boggling at the connection. "Naomi is Lynn's cousin. When she went missing, we were in Telluride. Lynn flew back for a week and helped with the search. They were dragging the frozen lakes and rivers, everyone was looking for cabins in the woods . . . God. This psychic person called the police about it?"

Callie talked him through what she knew about the Kerry Mullins case. Garr wasn't retaining much, though. He still seemed too angry. And her gut told her he wasn't going to ease up until she threw him a bone of some kind.

Maybe Louise Mullins. She'd planned to visit Mullins; Garr could join her.

"Yes." He nodded vigorously. "Yeah, that's a good idea."

"But after we visit Abel. You need to see your brother."

Garr took a deep breath, considered it, and nodded. She was right. But he insisted they take his rental car. She conceded. "We'll talk about Naomi on the way."

* * *

"All I know," Garr said, driving, "is that Lynn called Abel up and then he went down there to the property. After that, I don't know exactly. I assumed he was considering the job. Like I said, we don't talk much. It was really her business, and I go on and off the grid. I did some guiding in there, taking people into the backcountry. This one family, this guy was a tech entrepreneur, and he brought his wife, plus this woman he was working with, and I swear they were—"

"Why didn't Lynn hire him?" Callie asked, bring Garr back on track.

"I mean, it was the disappearance. Lynn told me she was coming back because her cousin was missing. I figured the kid, Naomi, you know . . . she'd run away with some guy, or maybe she'd had a bit too much fun partying in the woods and they'd find her all frozen up somewhere. I mean, she had her skis, I guess. So maybe she went skiing with some guy."

"Did Abel ever meet with Lynn, about the project?"

"I don't think so. But he did go down there."

"He did?"

"I remember she said he went down and looked around at the property, the spot where she wanted to build. There's this great view — you can just see the lake through the trees."

They were coming into Essex, a quaint little town on the edge of Lake Champlain. The ferry to Vermont was there.

Now you know, Callie thought. *Abel's connected to two missing girls, just like Footman said. Now you know how.* And perhaps even more importantly, it meant that twice, despite his being connected to someone *who went missing*, he'd never said anything to her about it. Nothing at all.

A kind of dread formed in the pit of her stomach. A cold emptiness. Like hunger pangs.

Don't get ahead of yourself.

It was becoming like a mantra.

But how could she not entertain the idea? Why had her loving husband never said anything? When something shocking happened, you spoke to your loved ones about it, if you had *any* sort of connection at all. *Oh, so-and-so disappeared? I just saw them last week! Oh, so-and-so went missing? She's related to this person I almost worked for!*

Not to mention: *Did I tell you my brother's girlfriend called me about possibly building a tiny house for her?*

Instead, zilch. Yes, it had been a busy summer; yes, Mac had been graduating, and Callie had dived deep into a writing project right after that. But still.

"How exactly is Lynn related to Naomi again? I mean, you said cousins, but how?"

Garr clucked his tongue, like it eluded him. "I think, ah . . . Well, Lynn's mom is named Lauren, and her sister is Teresa. That's Naomi's mom."

"Maybe we can talk to Lynn?"

At first she thought he was going to say no, the way he cut his eyes to her. But, "Yeah," he said. "We can do that." He paused. "Now?"

"Please. That would be great."

He seemed to suspect something, but they got Lynn on speakerphone. The reception wasn't good this close to Lake Champlain, but they were able to make introductions. "It's nice to meet you," Callie said.

"You too." Lynn's voice was on the sultry side. She sounded good-looking. "Though I'm so sorry about your husband."

"Thank you. So, how well did you get to know him?"

"I mean, I'm sorry to say — well."

"Did you say, 'not that well'? The phone's cutting out."

"Yeah. Not that well. We just had the — calls. He — once, but I wasn't here."

"You weren't there? When he did a site visit?"

"Right. — was."

"Who was? Sorry?"

Garr had reached the ferry dock and was pulling up to the pillbox to pay the fare. "Hang on a sec." He rolled down his window and smiled at the attendant. While they transacted, Callie's gaze drifted to the other cars boarding ahead of them, just six vehicles. The ferry was close, coming from Vermont, cutting silently through the water about a hundred yards out.

Garr took his change and ticket, thanked the attendant, and sent the window back up. "Sorry."

"No problem," Callie said. "Lynn, you still there?"

"Yeah."

"Who did you say met with Abel?"

"I asked my uncle to do it. Todd Bannon."

"Okay." Callie wrote it down in her phone. "That's Teresa's husband?"

"Yes."

"Would you mind if I called him? Just to ask him a couple of questions?"

After a moment, as though growing suspicious, Lynn relayed his number. "Can I ask? I mean, is everything . . . ?"

Callie didn't know quite how to handle this part. She'd been focused on asking Lynn about her interactions with Abel but hadn't figured out how to tell her he was a person of interest in her own cousin's disappearance.

The lined made three soft chimes and went dead. Call dropped. Callie was saved.

"I'll see if I can get her back," Garr said once he parked. He tried twice, but it went to voicemail each time. That sultry voice: *Hi, this is Lynn McNamara . . .*

The cars from Vermont disembarked. Garr and Callie awaited their turn to drive aboard.

Callie said, "What are the thoughts about the girl? About Naomi. Is there still hope, or . . . ?"

He considered it. "Well, it's been, what, more than six months? Her parents are still looking all the time. They hired a private investigator."

"Really?"

"Yeah. I mean, they don't have much money. I think this investigator is pretty low-rent. Not doing too much." He took a full breath and let it out slow. "But the other people in the family, like Lynn said, a lot of them have let it go. Or want to. But it's a tough spot to be in. A dilemma. Do you let go and grieve? Or do you hold out hope?"

"I get that," Callie said.

He faced her, and seemed to understand how perfectly that description of things encapsulated her own situation.

It was time. Garr put the car in gear and rolled up to the ferry worker taking tickets. After he handed his over, they pulled aboard.

CHAPTER THIRTY-THREE

Garr stood at the bed, looking at his brother like he couldn't quite understand what he was seeing. He seemed squeamish and kept a distance, not touching Abel. As if it might be catching.

No, she corrected herself. *To touch him would make it too real.*

"So how does it work?" Garr asked, after several minutes of silence.

"How does what work?"

He looked around at all the machines, the lights, the suspension harness for lifting Abel up to bathe him. "Insurance covers everything?"

"We don't have insurance."

He looked at her, and his eyes widened. "You're paying for it all?"

"I am." She kept her voice quiet, as if Abel could hear them.

"How much longer can you keep that up? Sorry, probably not my business."

"As long as I need to."

The words felt heavy with a kind of negative charge. Neither of them spoke for a few seconds. The machines beeped and hissed and the hospital corridor occasionally murmured or softly rumbled as something passed on wheels.

Callie said, "I'm going to give you some privacy, all right?"

Garr looked like it was a mixed blessing. "Okay, sure."

She slipped out. She went downstairs and out the side door. This time she found a rock, wiped off the snow, and wedged it so the door wouldn't close. She keyed the number Lynn had given her — she'd already put it into her phone — and called Todd Bannon.

"Hello?" He had a rough, husky voice.

She had some trouble deciding exactly how to explain who she was and how she had gotten his information. "Hi, Mr Bannon. My name is Callie Sanderson."

In the end, she decided to wait and see how he reacted.

"Sanderson?"

"Yes, sir."

"What do you want?"

His choice of words, tone of voice — they told her a lot. The police had talked to him about Abel.

"I'm Abel Sanderson's wife."

"I figured that."

"You don't have any reason to talk to me — I would understand if you don't want to — but hoping you will."

"How did you get my number?"

"From Lynn McNamara. Her boyfriend is my husband's brother, Garr."

"Oh. Yeah. Lynn."

Callie was about to continue but decided to wait. Bannon sounded like he might say more. "Ma'am, your husband seemed fine to me. A normal guy. But my daughter is missing. So, it's complicated."

"I understand that. I do. Could you just tell me how you met my husband?"

Bannon cleared his throat. "He came down here to look at the property Lynn bought."

"Right . . ."

160

"The day he came, I was over there. Lynn had asked me to handle meeting the potential builder, so I swung by. I had Naomi with me. He met her."

Callie was grateful to have the connection clarified at last. But she felt heavy with it; it was more confirmation that Abel had been keeping things from her. To have been considering work for his brother's new girlfriend and have met with members of her extended family — and not to have mentioned it?

"Okay, I see, thank you," she said to Bannon.

"All right. Is that all you wanted to know?"

"Garr said you'd hired a private investigator. Has he or she been able to help?"

"He's done a few things . . . Ma'am, see, there it is again. I'm not saying I think your husband did anything. Or that you did. But, like, what if? And now I'm talking to you? And you're asking me these questions?"

"I'm sorry. I really am." She realized she hadn't thought this through very well. She'd been worried about what Lynn might think, and Lynn was only the girl's cousin. This was Naomi's father. He knew Abel was a person of interest to the police.

"I only have one other question, and I'll leave you be. Can you just tell me who your private investigator is?"

"And why would I do that?"

She took a quick breath. "Because I'm in a similar situation. Your daughter is missing, and my husband is in a coma. And I have a son, and neither of us has any answers. In my heart, I don't believe my husband had anything to do with your daughter. I think there might be some other people involved. But I don't know. I don't know anything for sure. Just that I've seen a man outside my house. And footprints at the back of my property. Even someone watching me outside the grocery store. And I'm just trying to figure out if it's someone — like the private investigator you hired — or if I'm losing my mind."

It had all come out in a stream-of-consciousness rush. Having no idea how Bannon would react, she held her breath.

161

"His name is Tim Watkins," Bannon said. "He's tall, dark-haired. He drives a gray Ford Taurus. Kind of an older model."

"Thank you," she managed.

"But I'm not saying any more. Whatever he's found, or whatever he knows, I'm just not going to say."

"I understand."

"If he's looking at you, looking around your area, then he's doing his job."

"Yes. Right. I understand that. I—"

Bannon hung up.

* * *

Back upstairs, she found Garr had moved a chair beside the bed and sat staring at his brother.

Callie entered quietly and sat in the chair in the corner.

After a few more seconds, Garr spoke. "You ever heard of a guy named Martin Pistorius?"

"I have."

"He was in a coma for, like, twelve years. But he was aware of everything the whole time." He stared at Abel. "Maybe he is, too."

"I've thought about it. But I don't think so. And I've been here with him a lot."

Garr looked at her, again striking in his boyishness. This big man, rugged, with such a childlike visage at times. "But you read to him, you said."

"I don't think he's trapped like Pistorius was. I just think . . . we don't know. Maybe sounds and familiar things work on a subliminal level." She stood from the chair and went to him. Daring herself a little, she took Garr's hand. "I mean, you can talk to him. Even if he doesn't hear you exactly . . . maybe there's something. A feeling."

Garr surprised her by wiping away tears. He looked at Abel, who lay beneath the red-checked fleece blanket. Unmoving. Eyes closed.

She thought Garr might do it, might say something, but his lips stayed pursed. He looked into a corner, and his hand left hers.

"That's okay. I think, ah . . ."

"Anyway, Pistorius had locked-in syndrome, what they call a pseudo-coma. And it wasn't twelve years. He was vegetative for three or four, then he started to regain consciousness. In three more years, he was fully conscious and communicating with his eyes."

"You know a lot about it."

"I read everything I could find when Abel was officially diagnosed. I wanted to know what the rules were, for one thing. If there was any time limit, how it all worked. Because I knew *nothing* about it, at first." She added, "And Pistorius lives a healthy, happy life now. You can't ever give up."

"Yeah." Garr looked out the window, where night was coming on. "Lynn asked me if he had a DNR. And I didn't know."

It felt like someone had squeezed her heart.

Garr faced her when she didn't speak. "Does he?"

"I'm not sure."

She told him about how it worked. Patients asked their primary care doctors for a DNR. And the doctor kept it in confidence. "If he did, I wouldn't know until something happens, I guess. If his condition changed for the worse. If he had no brain activity. They'd give it a little time, but . . ."

Garr stayed on her a moment with those wide eyes, then turned back to Abel. "This shit is scary."

"Yes," she said, suddenly stung with tears herself. "It is."

Very gingerly, very softly, Garr reached out and touched Abel's forehead with his fingertips. The wound had healed, but there was a scar.

"That's from hitting his head," Callie explained. "When the truck struck the tree."

For a long time, Garr didn't say anything. "What if they found out that it happened before the accident?"

She felt another tightening of the chest. She'd actually never thought about it before. In the midst of everything else, she'd accepted that part of the accident involved Abel hitting his head. "They said he probably hit it on the driver's side glass," she told Garr. "When the truck hit the tree, he hit the glass."

But now she wondered. After everything she'd seen and felt at the Marsh home, it could be possible.

"Did you ever see pictures?" Garr asked.

She thought back. The past six weeks were a mix of clear and hazy. Especially the days immediately following the crash. She remembered Footman, his classy demeanor. And her, sitting in his office, arms limp at her sides, staring at pictures as he'd talked about the vehicle . . .

"I'm sure I looked at everything, but I really don't remember. One thing I do remember — they had other pictures. From before the crash. Maybe from Facebook? Or maybe I gave them to him. They were pictures of us, ah, camping last summer. And we had the truck, which was just an old beater, with the back bumper already kind of falling off. So they said, you know, it was inconclusive. If there'd been a collision."

"But did you ever see a picture of the driver's side window?" Garr was facing her now, and his spine had seemed to stiffen. "Was there a crack? Was it smashed? Was there blood?"

"I don't know," she said at last.

They both looked back at Abel and the scar above his left eye.

CHAPTER THIRTY-FOUR

Things you never think about: Putting your affairs in order. Deciding who takes the kids if both of you die.

Or you do think about it, but kick it down the road. *Another day. We're young yet.*

Callie was surprised, though, in retrospect, that Abel hadn't. He was fastidious, an organized and mindful person. She could excuse herself; she was too unconventional for insurance and wills. Some people fought their way through another career before writing. They were a lawyer, a doctor, a cop, or a therapist. The most she'd ever done was wait tables. Never held a nine-to-five job, never worked in an office. Thinking about life in terms of pensions and retirement had never been her style.

She realized now it was fear. She didn't want to think about life winding down. Didn't want think about death. Maybe some people knew how to compartmentalize that; she didn't.

Turning down a short dirt driveway, she faced a double-wide trailer on the edge of a forest. Gray against dark green. A mangy, short-haired mutt with floppy ears came running her way, kicking up puffs of snow as it barked. It jumped up on the vehicle, nails clicking loudly and scratching the metal. Callie winced as its teeth and flailing tongue flashed beside the window.

"Whoa," she said, her heart going.

It would've been nice to have Garr still with her, but they'd parted ways after leaving the hospital. Lynn's family was expecting him. He couldn't spend the whole day driving around with Callie. And this way, he could get more information from the Bannons, too, and report back. So after she'd gotten a hold of Louise Mullins on the phone and convinced her to meet, she'd gone off to do so by herself.

The dog ran alongside the Chevy, barking, as she made their way to the end of the drive and stopped a few yards from the other parked vehicle. Callie wasn't sure of the make and model, but it was one of those cars shaped like a toaster. Honda Element, maybe.

Various junk littered the property. To her left, what might've once been a garage had almost entirely caved in. There was enough room for bales of hay and a small tractor, along with various garden-type tools sticking out of the snowdrifts. To her right was the deck Abel had built. Small but sturdy, it connected the trailer to an aboveground pool, the snow denting the middle of the tarp that covered it.

More buildings. A chicken coop, a small barn, a bunkhouse. The property seemed to stretch back a ways; Callie thought she glimpsed a couple of goats and at least one donkey in the distance.

The dog continued to bark and jump at the truck.

She was about to get out slow, act natural, when the front door opened. A large woman in a purple muumuu stepped out, smoking a cigarette. She pulled the cigarette from her lips, and, with her other fingers, made a whistle. The dog flinched, as if shocked, then trotted over to her, its shoulders rounded, head down as if ashamed. The woman scolded the dog, gave it a whack on its hindquarters, and sent it inside.

Callie was already out of the truck, calling over, "It's okay. He was just saying hello."

"*She*," the woman corrected. "Trixie knows better than to jump on people's cars. Who're you?"

"We spoke on the phone. Callie Sanderson."

Louise Mullins stood looking. She had to be three hundred pounds. She took a long drag on her cigarette, blew the smoke into the cold air. "The one that got called by the psychic."

"That's right."

"All right, then," she said. "Come on in, I guess."

* * *

Inside, Mullins took a seat in a ratty burgundy-colored recliner. She dragged on her cigarette and squinted through the smoke. "You sure you're not a reporter? Or a cop?"

"No. I'm just a concerned wife. I know my husband worked out here, and that you and I have both gotten calls from the same person, Althea Cooper. She said she had information on my husband's car crash. I'm just trying to figure out what's going on."

"What exactly did she say she knew?"

"Just . . . where he'd been. What he'd been doing."

"That he'd been here?"

"No, not that part. I found that out going through his records."

"So he's been keeping stuff from ya."

"I'm still figuring that out."

Mullins smoked and scratched her leg, threaded with blue veins. "I think you're not telling me something."

Callie decided to level with her. "Althea Cooper told me my husband was chased. By someone in a green vehicle."

Mullins looked puzzled by the possible significance.

"The house that Abel was visiting — their son, he has a greenish car. A Nissan Pathfinder."

"So there you go." Mullins tapped the long ash of her long cigarette into a nearby beer can — Keystone Ice.

"Well, ma'am, I mean . . . Yes, there is some concern there."

167

"Why don't you tell the cops?"

"I did." Callie settled in. "Can we talk about you for a minute?"

Mullins gave Callie a shrewd look. A bluish haze of smoke filled the air between them. "Uh-huh."

"What was Althea's phone call to you like?"

"I don't know. . . I didn't expect it. I'd never heard of her. I thought maybe she was pranking me at first. But then she seemed a little nervous. Like she was scared."

"Did you ask her how she knew what she did?"

"No. I just listened."

When the woman didn't elaborate, Callie tried a new tack: "Did she have any relationship to you? Or maybe your daughter?"

Mullins shook her head. "I'd never heard of her before. Never met her. Kerry didn't know her, either."

"You're sure?"

"Uh-huh."

"How can you . . . ?" Callie trailed off. Mullins looked like she didn't want to be pressed on it. So Callie took out her phone. She had taken a screenshot of Naomi Bannon from her Instagram page. She stood and crossed the room, parting the cloud of smoke, and held it for Mullins to see. "How about her?"

Mullins looked briefly. "I don't know her. Police showed me the picture of her, too. And I've seen her on the news. But I never knew her."

Callie retreated to the chair, pocketing her phone. "And you're sure Kerry didn't."

"Right."

Seated again, Callie took a breath. "How about Dr Nathan Marsh? Does that name mean anything to you?"

"Can't say it does."

"Okay. So, this woman you've never met calls you up. She doesn't know you, she doesn't know Kerry. But she says she has an idea where Kerry might be. And afterwards, you called the police and told them. Why believe her?"

Mullins just stared a moment. "Because I was willing to try anything. I thought if I saw words in my alphabet soup, I'd follow the signs. Kerry had been gone for days. And no one was paying attention. Well, they were, but . . . they didn't seem to care all that much. They had bigger fish to fry. She was a runaway, they said. She'd done it before. I said this time was different. They had a look around, they talked to Stan, talked to my parents, talked to her friends, but nobody knew nothin'. So they basically gave up. And then I got this call. This woman said she knew things. When I asked her how, she told me something about a . . ."

When Mullins seemed at a loss, Callie said, "An alternative memory."

"That's it. Things that just popped into her head. I used to see people like that on TV. The psychic hotline. Remember those?"

Callie did, vaguely. Maybe Mullins meant "900 numbers," from back in the eighties and nineties. You called and got billed by the minute. At any rate, she was finally unlocked and holding forth, which was what Callie wanted.

"I remember," Callie said.

Mullins nodded. They shared something now — a piece of time, of culture. She sucked on her cigarette, and her lips released with a subtle "pop" as she exhaled. She dropped the butt in the Keystone Ice can, where it hissed. "So, I listened to her. Heard what she had to say."

"Did she say anything else? Other than about the cabin?"

"Well, it wasn't what she said, it was what I asked her. I asked her if Kerry's boyfriend was involved. And she said she didn't think Kerry *had* a boyfriend."

It reminded Callie of her own test of Althea. "And does she?"

"No. Last boy she dated was Moses Lynch. And that was months and months ago. He hadn't come around here since the summer, maybe. No, Kerry didn't want nothing to do with boys. She was getting her life together."

Mullins grew distracted, searching her purse. She came up with her pack of cigarettes and shook one out. The bluish haze from the last one had yet to disperse. It had been a while since Callie had been anywhere with someone smoking indoors. Her father had, for years, until her mother made him quit.

"So I listened to her," Mullins said. "Most of these crackpots, they ask a lot of questions. And those questions make them seem like they got something. You know? They'll ask . . . 'Hmmm, I'm getting someone in your life that starts with an L. Anyone start with an L? And you go — 'Moses Lynch! My God! This person is psychic!'" Mullins laughed, and the laughter turned into a coughing fit.

Callie felt herself grinning. "So she didn't seem tricky."

"No. She didn't come across as phony to me. She seemed, like I said, kinda scared."

"I felt the same way about her."

Mullins looked thoughtful. "The one question she asked me, actually — she said, is your place by the woods? I said yes. She asked if there was a river, I said no."

"And she asked about a cabin?"

"Not especially. I told her about the bunkhouse, where Kerry sometimes hangs out with her friends. She said that might have something to do with it. But Kerry was out in the woods, she thought. I thought maybe a hunting camp." Mullins paused a moment. "I know I could've been a better mother."

Callie didn't know what to say. "I, um . . ."

"I know that when she was little, some of the men who came around . . ." The woman stared into space. In the other room, the dog started to howl. A sad, plaintive sound. Mullins hopped tracks again. "Kerry was taking care of the animals. Now I got Stan doing it, and he doesn't know about adding grit to the chicken scratch."

Callie let all of it settle. One thought stuck out: Althea had never specifically said *cabin*.

Mullins lit her cigarette and continued to gaze at nothing.

"Ms Mullins?"

"Mmm?"

"Do you remember talking to Detective Footman?"

"Yeah, yeah, I do. I remember his funny name."

"And Footman took it pretty seriously. You told him that someone had called you?"

"I did. But I didn't say too much. About her being psychic and this and that. It might put him off. Maybe he'd focus on her instead, figuring she was up to something."

Callie had thought along similar lines. But it seemed like such a risky strategy for Cooper. If she was involved, how did pretending to "just know things" shield her? Or make her credible? It did neither. Footman had gotten the background on her and found mental health concerns. She'd have been better off just calling anonymously.

But she'd given a name. She'd been shaky and uncertain, and yet held to the claim that she knew what she did for reasons she couldn't, or wouldn't, explain.

It crossed Callie's mind at that moment — what if Cooper was a victim?

How? In what way?

She didn't know.

"So I just told him, you got to check the woods, check all the camps and cabins. This woman seems to know she's out there."

"But the search found nothing."

"They had dogs out there. They had people covering miles and miles. They checked every nook and cranny, turned over every rock. Looked at every cabin they knew about, every abandoned camper. And nothing turned up. Nothing."

The women were quiet a moment.

Finally, Mullins said, "You're not the first one who's been here asking me all this."

"Well, the police, right?"

"Another one. A man, younger than you, I think. A private investigator."

"Tim Watkins?"

"His name might've been Watkins, yeah. He asked me most of these same questions. Plus a couple extra. I might have his card around here somewhere . . ."

"What did he ask?"

"He asked me about your husband working on my deck. Who he hired, who he had with him to help, things like that. We talked about Kerry, and how she was looking at colleges. Driving herself, mostly, to go visit them. She was gonna get out of here. Make something of herself."

Callie had many questions, but one rose above. "Do you remember what Watkins was driving?"

Mullins blew smoke and nodded. "I can see everything from my window. Just like I seen you pull up. And I know my cars, too. He was in a Ford Taurus. Probably an '04 or '05. It was gray."

CHAPTER THIRTY-FIVE

Back in the truck, Callie called Garr. "Tim Watkins, the PI the Bannons hired, has been making the rounds."

"Really?"

"He's been to see Mullins. She thought he left a card, but she couldn't find it. He's been to my house, too. I think he might've even been following me."

"When was he there talking to Mullins?"

"She said just recently. Since Abel's accident."

"Well, they only hired him recently, I think. Just after Christmas. Did he say anything interesting, or . . . ?"

"He just asked questions. All the questions I asked," Callie said. "Except one I didn't. He asked Mullins if Abel had anyone with him when he'd worked on the deck."

"And?"

"She never saw him do the work. I guess she was staying with her sister. But Kerry was here. She was here alone."

"Shit. All right, well, I'll see if Lynn knows anything about Watkins, or what he's found. She can ask Todd — he's got the contact info for this guy."

"I talked to Todd already," Callie said. "He wasn't too happy about my call."

"Ah. Well . . . we'll be discreet."

It was getting dark. It was only a little after five, but in the North Country, in February, the daylight ran out quick, just a fading orange in the west. She merged onto Interstate 87, headed south toward home.

She continued to talk using the hands-free system. "Mullins said something interesting. About how DEC searched all the cabins they knew about. What if there were places they didn't? Hunting camps, wilderness cabins, private property. Stuff not on a map?"

"Well, property owners would give over that information freely to DEC, right?" he asked. "To search teams?"

"You'd think so. I'm not sure exactly how it works. But I think it would be really interesting to know if anyone refused a search."

"Oh, I doubt that. Especially if they . . . you know, if they had something to hide. Refusing to let DEC and police onto your property to look for a missing teenaged girl would be a glaring red flag."

"No, that's a good point. You're right."

"Still be interesting, though," Garr conceded. "What if someone just didn't answer the phone, you know? They were out of town, something like that. Never returned DEC's call. Didn't refuse, per se, but didn't give permission, either . . ."

They considered it in silence.

* * *

Footman called once Callie was back home. "Mrs Sanderson. I went out to the Marsh residence this afternoon."

"Okay . . ."

"I spoke to Dr Marsh. And to his son. They were kind enough to invite me in and let me have a look around."

She waited.

"Everything seemed in order to me, nothing concerning. I said that you'd come to us this morning. That you had concerns. There was really no other way to explain my presence there."

"I understand. Did you—"

"I asked Dr Marsh if anyone was staying with them. He said there was no one. He invited me to look around."

"And you did? Was there anything?"

"Mrs Sanderson, no. Now, I want you to know, Dr Marsh was very considerate of your situation. He understands your need for answers. So he's not going to make an issue out of you running into his son's car."

Footman let the statement hang there, like a lead weight.

Damn. She shut her eyes. She'd been hoping it was only the Chevy that was damaged. "I was rushing."

"Yes. He said that. And you hit the front of his son's Pathfinder."

She opened her eyes. Damage to the front of the Pathfinder? That could be the truth, but it set off distant alarms for her. Marsh could be claiming damage from Callie's Chevy in order to conceal the evidence of rear-ending Abel's truck two months earlier . . .

"He wishes he could be of more help."

"I bet he does," she mumbled.

"I'm sorry? Can you say that again?"

"Nothing. I'm . . . What about his wife? Officer Sacony was going to try to reach her. Has she?"

Footman didn't respond right away. His end of the line was very quiet. "No. I don't believe that she has."

"That's a little odd, isn't it?" Callie regretted the words instantly. Every time she spoke to Footman now, she felt embarrassed. An irritating, even gullible woman with too much time on her hands. Maybe at first, she just seemed like someone who was spending too much time looking for answers. By now, though, she surely seemed driven to extremes over her guilty conscience. Trying to cover the tracks of her troubled husband.

"It's only been a day," Footman said. "We'll keep trying to reach Mrs Marsh. In the meantime—"

"Wait, just . . . I'm sorry. So you spoke to them and . . . were you able to search the property?"

"Mrs Sanderson . . ."

"I'm just wondering."

"I looked through the house."

"I know, but I mean — they have two hundred acres."

"There's not enough probable cause to search their property."

"What about during the Kerry Mullins search? Was the Marsh place included?"

"It's fifty miles away. No, it was not included. Mrs Sanderson, please listen to me." His voice was getting an edge. "I understand this is difficult. We've all been very understanding. But—"

Callie broke: "This isn't about me or my husband's coma," she said sharply. "Two young women are missing. I'll do whatever it takes. I don't care if my husband is implicated, I want those girls to be found. But if my husband did find something, and that's why he was run off the road — or maybe even hurt first — then, to me, it seems like a very good place to be looking."

Footman was silent.

Callie added, "And, if you don't mind, I'd like to see the pictures of the crash again. Of the vehicle."

Footman sighed. "So, this is the next thing . . . Now you think he was hurt first?"

"I'd just like to see them."

"Fine. Come to the barracks."

"I will."

"Listen to me, okay? Kerry Mullins could very well have run away. We've been talking with her boyfriend—"

"Moses."

"Yes, Moses Lynch."

"They're broken up."

Footman paused. "We've been talking with him, and he's revealed some more about Kerry's plans. About how she planned to get away from her mother, and Stanley Gruber, her mother's sometime boyfriend. She didn't want to be there anymore. She's had . . . trouble over the years with her mother's friends. Male friends. We're working with the FBI at this point, Mrs Sanderson. So it's possible, *very* possible that your husband knowing Mullins was just a coincidence. It's also possible he'd witnessed an altercation between Kerry Mullins and Stan. And we wanted to talk to him about that. But, obviously we can't. So . . ."

Callie started to speak, but Footman cut her off. "Althea Cooper talking about Kerry Mullins being out somewhere in the woods was a wild goose chase. We searched. No signs. Now you're being led on a wild goose chase. So save your energy. Leave the investigation to us, and take care of yourself and your husband and son in the meantime. Okay?"

She almost let loose with a *Don't-you-tell-me-how-to-take-care-of-my-family* tirade. But Footman had been good to her. He was just doing his job.

She thanked him instead and ended the call.

The Chevy cut through the twilight. Almost home now.

She knew Footman was right. That leaving this to him was the right thing. Where had this pursuit gotten her?

Time to give up the ghost. Let the professionals handle it.

She cruised along for a moment, then decided. *Just after this one last thing.*

And ten minutes later, over the phone, Althea agreed.

"Okay. I'll meet you."

CHAPTER THIRTY-SIX

TUESDAY, FEBRUARY 28

Red's Market was located in Speculator, in the middle of the Adirondack Park, with a deli and a gift shop. Althea's brother Casey was part owner.

Speculator was in Hamilton County, which had probably the lowest population density in the state — not much around but primeval forest and ponds, everything now under a coating of ice, a thick cream of snow. As Callie pulled off the road and into the parking lot, she felt anxious. She was about to meet the woman who'd started this whole thing, Callie's erratic pursuit of the truth. The woman who, for the past several days, had become like a voice in her head. Urging her to go further, ask more questions — to look a little more closely. It all had the feeling of meeting someone in person for the first time after a long period of online flirtation.

An electric chime startled her as she entered the store. Past the shelves of local maple syrup, coffee mugs bearing the store logo, and handmade soaps was a small dining area. A countertop with stools against the wall, and three sets of table and chairs. Althea Cooper, sitting at the middle table, looked up from her phone. She smiled. "Hi."

"Hi," Callie said, moving closer.

The young woman stood and offered her hand. Callie shook it — a smooth grip, not too dry or clammy. She was naturally blonde, it seemed, with red-brown eyes the color of cognac. Freckles dotted the bridge of her small nose, and her complexion was otherwise unblemished. Healthy-looking, with creamy skin and a natural flush to her cheeks.

She was just about as nice and normal as could be, Callie thought. And it hit her: the moment she'd heard "mental health" from Footman, she'd imagined a person with limited functions. A fragile wallflower in oversized glasses and fingerless gloves.

If anything, Callie thought, *I'm the one who looks like shit.*

"It's nice to finally meet you," she said.

"You too." The smile on Althea's face seemed genuine.

Neither of them made a move to sit down. Callie had been in the car for two hours drinking coffee and needed the bathroom. Althea seemed to be waiting for Callie's cue for what came next. Callie noticed they were about the same height. And that Althea wore snug-fitting blue jeans. Callie would have to see them from behind to determine if they were designer, but the woman knew how to size a pair of jeans, that was the point. A Henley top covered by a blue-checked flannel shirt and an emerald parka over it. On the table, a winter hat and gloves.

"Do you want anything?" Althea asked. "I got a coffee while I waited. Are you hungry?" She seemed to assess Callie's gaunt figure.

Callie checked the deli, where a woman in a hair net chatted up the young male cashier.

"No, thank you. Is there a bathroom here, though?"

"Yeah, totally. I'll show you."

Callie followed her out of the dining area and deeper into the store.

* * *

After the bathroom, Callie returned to the seating area. For a moment, she panicked: Althea was not there. But then Callie saw her outside, exhaling a cottony boll of vapor into the cold air.

Ah. Not so perfect after all.

Callie pushed out the door, and Althea turned toward the noise. "Sorry, just sneaking a smoke. Coming right now."

"No problem." Callie glanced around the near-empty parking lot. The wind came through with an icy chill. Althea was turtled into her parka but didn't seem too bothered. She blew out the last drag of vapor, and Callie held the door for her.

Back inside, they drank coffee at the table. An awkward moment passed with neither of them speaking or knowing where to rest their gaze.

"How are you?" Callie asked.

"I'm good."

"Your brother is part owner here, you said?"

She nodded. "He is. For a couple of years now. Him and another guy he's known for a long time."

Callie couldn't help but wonder about it, how a man who was the same age as his sister — twenty-eight — was able to afford a business. Unless he'd made some money at an early age, there were probably big loans involved.

"Is he here?"

Althea nodded. "Yeah, he is. He's dealing with an HVAC issue and meeting with one of the managers about inventory, which is what he usually does mid-week."

HVAC — she meant the heating system, presumably. "Is everything all right?" Callie asked.

"Yeah. It got so cold last week that some pipes almost froze, I guess. They're fixing it. It'll be okay, he said."

You don't sound like the woman on the phone. Callie swallowed the words. But it was true — not only did Althea look different than expected, she had more confidence, poise. Sitting here across from her, you'd never suspect she had any sort of concerns, neurological or otherwise.

Or, like you thought before, it's all just an act.

180

"Does your brother know we're meeting? Does he know I'm here?"

Althea didn't answer right away. The longer she looked back at Callie without speaking, the more Callie wondered if she'd offended her: *I'm a fully functioning adult, lady, and he's my brother, not my nursemaid or my conservator. I can come and go as I damn well please.*

"Yes," she said finally. "He knows. I drove up with him. I mean, he drove; I don't have a car. I figured it would be easier for us to meet halfway than for you to have to come all the way down."

"That's nice," Callie said. But for the first time since arriving, she sensed deception. Nothing major, just something Althea wasn't saying yet.

"The first time you called me and wanted to meet, I felt bad," Althea said.

"It sounded like it was hard for you to talk."

"I mean, yeah, but . . ." She was contemplative. "I don't think I've ever met someone I've, um . . . intervened with."

"I'm glad you decided to."

Althea smiled and looked down; it was the kind of innocent blush of being flattered. Like she wasn't accustomed to too many compliments.

Callie found herself looking around the place, the sights and sounds taking on new significance. She'd been here at least once, years ago, but it had been renovated since. She noticed a couple of teenaged boys. Aside from them, a young family — the father was currently trying to pry his daughter away from a small toy section. Stepping from the bathroom, a gray-haired woman in a flannel shirt.

All kinds of people came through here, it seemed, which made sense. The route connected the northern and southern sections of the Adirondacks, and it was one of the only ways to go if one was traveling to or from Syracuse. Or anywhere in Central New York, really.

"I actually thought about something else, too," Althea said. "And maybe it's a little selfish."

Here we go . . .

But when it seemed she might not go on, Callie prompted her. "What?"

"I don't ever visit the people I . . . see." Althea took a deep breath. "Or the *places* I see." Her eyes came up, bright and direct. "I was wondering if you would take me up there."

Callie blinked, unsure what to say. And she didn't even know which place Althea meant, exactly.

"Up to . . . ?"

Althea glanced around. Her gaze hit something in the upper corner. Callie saw a camera there. She slowly returned her attention to Althea as the young woman whispered, "To Dr Marsh's house, I think."

It was almost too low to hear. Callie leaned in, just to be sure. "You want to go to Marsh's house?"

Althea met her gaze and nodded.

Callie sat back. She took a sip of her coffee, hoping it might've spontaneously turned to bourbon. After wiping at her mouth, she leaned closer again. "Honey, I just, ah . . ." She wasn't sure what to say, but what she was thinking was clear: the police, Footman, the Marshes. She'd just about exhausted the patience of all three.

"I don't want to bother anyone," Althea said. "I just want to see." There was pleading in her soft, whispering voice. A dance of light in her eyes. "I want to see if it's like I pictured."

Callie remained reluctant. "I've been to that house. Twice. The police have been there . . ."

"Not the house. The property. And what might be *on* the property."

Both women fell silent. When the chime rang over the door, a big man entered — a trucker type with a beard and a big baseball cap high on his head. He was tall enough to be seen above the shelf separating the eating area from the entrance. His footfalls vibrated the floor.

The property.

What might be on *the property . . .*

Althea was still looking at her. "I just want to see," she repeated.

"Thanks." Althea lowered the window, then took a drag. The vapor she exhaled smelled like strawberry candies Callie remembered from some vague time in her youth. Left in a bag in the sun, turned to hot goo.

Does Casey know you're a clairvoyant? Or that you tell people you are? It was on the tip of her tongue to ask. But now it felt rude, too intrusive.

Callie slowed as she reached the second car trailing the plow. This was really not good. If it was just the plow, she might be bold enough to pass. *Maybe* she'd pass it with one trailing car, if there was a long enough straightaway. But a plow plus two cars? She was relegated to hoping one of them would take the initiative.

"*Callie*," Althea mused about her name. "Is that short for something?"

"Calista."

"Oh, that's nice."

"My grandmother was named Calista. So it's an heirloom." Callie omitted that the name meant *beautiful*. That always felt awkward. Althea was the one with the looks, anyway. "I'm pretty sure 'Althea' is Greek, too. Did you know that?"

"I think so, yeah. Are your parents from Greece?"

"No," Callie said. "My great-grandparents were. On my dad's side. But *my* parents were from White Plains. You know where that is?"

"I think it's Westchester County?"

"Exactly. My father was a policeman there. My mother taught at Purchase College. I was born down there, but when my father got into investigations, they wanted him upstate. So, we moved. I was almost ten."

"Wow. That's cool."

Cool, Callie thought. Not quite the word she'd use to describe those years. Her father was happy, but she and her mother were made miserable by the move. She'd had to leave all her friends, and her mother hated her new job — so much that she quit only a year later.

But Althea didn't know any of this. Callie wondered how much the young woman even knew about her own origins. And then Althea said, "I don't think my birth parents were Greek. Their last name was Tausinger."

Callie remembered that fact from an earlier phone call with Footman.

"And Casey isn't a Greek name," Althea said. "But he says they were Deadheads. And that's where we got our names."

It took Callie a moment to realize the meaning. She was talking about the Grateful Dead.

"They followed the band around. I guess that's something people did."

"Go on tour, yeah."

Althea paused, holding the vape stick to her lips. "They had us on tour, actually. We were born the last year of it. The same time the main guy died?"

"Jerry Garcia."

"Right. Exactly. Jerry Garcia." She bit her nail, examined it. "So they named me Althea. Because that was their favorite song. And that Casey Jones song, that's where he got his."

Althea went on vaping, staring into space. The more time Callie spent with Althea, the more the young woman revealed her humanness. Which was usually how it went with people. "That's pretty interesting," Callie said.

If memory served, Casey Jones was a real-life locomotive engineer who was killed in a train crash. An odd choice for a baby name perhaps, but then, the world of the Grateful Dead didn't necessarily have to make a lot of sense.

Althea faced her. "Did you get into all of that? Were you a fan?"

"No, not really. That whole thing kind of passed me by. I didn't really get into following bands. I mean, I liked music and everything, but I never went to concerts. And when I did listen to music, it was weird stuff." She laughed and sounded self-conscious.

Althea smiled, but it didn't touch her eyes. She seemed to have drifted away. The confident young woman from the market had been replaced by a more reminiscent, broody one.

Did you know your birth parents? When did you go into foster care? What happened? Did you stay together, always, you and Casey?

Callie just drove. The questions would keep for now. One of the cars between her and the plow had turned off a mile or two back. They were coming up on a straightaway. Now was the time to make her move . . .

Althea toyed with the vape stick, holding it like it was a flute. Then she suddenly yanked it away from her mouth and pointed. "Watch out!"

Callie had just drifted into the oncoming lane and was about to pass. The car coming at them was white, no headlights, blending in. Callie hadn't seen it right away. She dropped back, her heart pounding, and eased fully back into her lane as the car — it was a truck, actually, similar to hers — passed in a rush of snow and wind.

"Sorry about that," Callie said. "Thought maybe I had it."

They drove in silence. Callie glanced at Althea; she didn't seem shaken up or anything, just lost in thought again. After ten seconds or so of not talking: "Casey thinks I try to get attention," Althea said.

Okay. Here we go.

"What do you mean?"

Althea gave her a quick sideways look. "About knowing things. Remembering things that aren't my memories."

"He thinks you're just . . . ?"

"He thinks I'm just being dramatic. That I see something in the paper or hear about it on TV, and then I forget it for a while, until something makes me remember. And then it seems like it's my memory." She gave Callie another furtive look. It seemed to embarrass her to talk about it. She was on guard, as if waiting to be ridiculed.

"And that bothers you. That he feels that way."

"Well, yeah. You know, at least he doesn't think I'm just making stuff up. But he does think it's . . . that my head isn't right."

"And what do you think about your head? Have you had any medical problems?"

Callie was thinking about Marsh, a neurosurgeon. Maybe Althea Cooper was suffering some condition after all. Nerve damage. A traumatic brain injury. It could be anything.

Althea dodged the question. "It's just something that happens. I can't really explain it better than that."

"Sure. I understand." She added, "It's got to be really tough. Having something going on with you that you can't explain. And that people are sort of geared not to understand."

Althea looked at Callie carefully, as if deciding whether to trust her.

Callie wasn't paying lip service. She didn't believe in psychic powers, per se, but *something* was going on with this person, and she'd get further by being kind and open-minded.

Plus, she could relate. "I think it's hard for people to understand what I'm going through with my husband. They see him as alive, and there's every chance he'll recover. But they don't know what it's like to be waiting. With no end in sight. No clock, no timer."

"You're all alone in it," Althea said.

"Yes."

This time, the quiet was more comfortable. The car in front was kicking back lots of salt and snow. Callie spritzed the windshield and ran the wipers, dropping back a little. She decided to share something. It could seal the bond that was tentatively forming. But mainly, it might comfort the woman beside her.

"My father told me a story once."

Althea raised her eyebrows.

"It was a cop story. From toward the end of his career in investigations, about a case."

Althea turned her shoulders toward Callie, vape forgotten.

"A woman had disappeared. They had a press conference and a hotline. Another woman called in, a clairvoyant, said she knew where the missing person was."

Callie glanced at Althea. She still seemed riveted, but maybe a touch unsure.

Callie said, "This woman, she took the police right to the missing person. Dead behind some building, buried in the trash. There she was, right where she said she would be. And of course, they arrested her."

Callie paused, giving Althea a chance to say something. She didn't.

"But after they arrested her, they couldn't find any connection between her and the victim. They took DNA samples, everything. In the end, all the evidence they collected pointed to the victim's domestic partner. He was a man who'd been in trouble before, for assault. There was even a record of a domestic dispute between him and her. The victim."

"But still no connection to the clairvoyant?"

"Still no connection." Callie took a breath, keeping her eyes on the plow, as it finally turned on its right blinker, like it was going to pull off and let the trailing vehicles pass. "And the clairvoyant had no connection to the man, either. But all the evidence was enough to convict him. He went away to prison. Boom. And he's still there." She added, "Unless he's dead."

Althea exhaled like she'd been made nervous to hear it. "And what happened to her?"

Callie chose her words carefully. "My father would say that, to this day, he didn't know how she knew. Didn't know if it was something he missed, or some magic he couldn't understand. That's how he put it. 'Some magic.'"

"It's not magic," Althea said. But Callie could sense the woman regaining some equilibrium. A growing trust. That made her feel good; she wanted Althea to feel comfortable. *Whatever Casey thinks about you, maybe he just doesn't understand.*

Althea dipped her head and seemed to nod to herself. She studied her hands.

The snowplow turned off into a parking area. The car ahead of Callie surged forward. She pressed down on the gas and got up to speed, finally. The momentum was good.

Althea lifted her head, took a breath, and then spoke. "I haven't been completely honest with you."

Callie gave her a quick glance.

"I haven't told you everything. About what I've seen."

Callie felt anxious waiting. "What more is there? What do you need to tell me?"

At last Althea turned to her, and those red-brown eyes seemed to fix on Callie's soul. "I've seen a lot more about your husband."

CHAPTER THIRTY-NINE

"I've seen your husband with a woman who isn't you," Althea said. "I know that sounds terrible, but I wouldn't say anything unless I was sure. And I'm sure." She gave Callie an apologetic look.

"Who?" Callie felt split: The implication of Abel with another woman confirmed her fears about infidelity. Insecurities she decided every spouse or partner harbored at some level. Yet it also raised her skepticism about Althea a notch; it was possible a connection to Marsh explained some of the woman's revelations, or that media coverage of Kerry Mullins led to her "memories" of being in the woods, but claiming to know something this specific about Abel? This intimate? It smacked of a scam.

Of course, that could just be your defense mechanism . . .

"What does she look like?" Callie asked.

"She's tall, brunette. She's very pretty. And young. Maybe my age."

Callie checked the woman beside her. Althea wasn't in some trance, nor was she twinkling about the eyes like she was up to something. If anything, she looked slightly confused. Frowning, she absently rubbed her cheek, as if she had a sore tooth.

"What are they doing when you see them together? Can you be specific?"

"I've seen them at her house, but I don't know where it is."

"Are they . . . together?"

Althea paused. "It seems like it."

"What does that mean?"

"I'm upsetting you. Ugh. This is so uncomfortable."

Oh, you're *uncomfortable?*

Callie and Abel had a strong relationship. He was a good husband. She'd never suspected him of cheating. But there were . . . things. Normal things, she'd always thought. The usual rough spots in a marriage.

He was a supportive spouse, and a predictable one. He rose at the same time every day, ate the same lunch, went to bed with his socks peeled off and dropped beside the bed each night.

It wasn't often that he had a temper, but when he did, it could be scary. He'd never hit her, not even close, but there were a couple times she'd felt fear. Once when he dented a door with his fist. And once — only once — when he flipped over their dining room table.

It was never any one thing that seemed to set him off. He was like Mount St Helens, prone to occasionally erupt in order to release pressure. In a way, it was just another part of his consistency. Once every year or so, you could expect Abel Sanderson to lose his shit.

But in the weeks he'd been unconscious, lying there in the bed, still and silent, she'd wondered. Her life had effectively stopped, and so she lived more in the past and the future, holding out hope, than in the present. How much did anyone really know someone else? The question seemed like a cliché because it got to the heart of life.

There were things Abel didn't know about her. Running away from home when she was a teenager, putting her parents through hell. Sleeping with a man nearly ten years older, her father finding out, hence the running.

If there were things about her, it stood to reason there were things about him. He had a brother he never talked about, and a sister who had died young. He'd never shared the details of her death or his feelings about it. What else didn't she know?

Maybe she was overreacting. Using Althea's visions to shape — and validate — her vague fears.

"This is why . . ." Althea broke off, shaking her head. "This is why it's so hard. I wish there was a thing, you know? Like a stamp of guarantee. But here it is, okay? I haven't seen your husband doing anything specific or incriminating. But these aren't just mental pictures. It's not like a video camera. I get feelings. Of fear. Like when your husband had the crash. Before it, really. I could sense him feeling afraid as he drove."

It grabbed Callie's attention. "Before he went into the water?"

"Like he was hurt. That's why I thought it was more than an accident."

Callie realized she'd planned to visit Footman and look through the crash photos. The trip to pick up Althea had derailed her.

"Why was he hurt?"

"I don't know."

"Where? On his body, I mean."

Callie found it hard to watch the road. She almost lost control when Althea raised her hand to her temple. "Here, I think."

"In the head?"

She nodded. "I mean, it's always hard to know if I'm filling things in because of a feeling. Does that make sense?"

"I don't know."

"I feel like he was hurt in the head."

Callie considered pulling over to vomit. "What about the green SUV? Following him?"

"Maybe following him. Or, in the road. Something in the road. Something he needed to avoid."

A chill. A recall of her own dream. "In the road . . . what? The SUV?"

Althea continued to frown, almost as if she were squinting at the past. Her version of it. "Maybe a car or . . . something else."

"Snowmobile?"

She stared at a point in space as she searched her mind, then she fell back against the seat, her eyes fluttering closed. "I'm sorry. It's like any other memory a person has. Sometimes it changes. Or you're not sure."

Good god. A woman in Abel's life. A possible head wound that preceded his accident. And maybe something in the road that caused him to swerve. A snowmobile? That's what it sounded like. Like Abel had been chased. Not by the green SUV in the driveway, necessarily. As difficult as it had been to recreate the crash, the police had always seemed confident that no other car had been involved. But the area was frequented by snowmobiles. There were tracks crisscrossing every which way.

So Abel found something out. Someone hurt him. And he tried to flee. To get to an area with phone coverage and call for help.

But they ran him down. Maybe road-blocked him. And in his panicked state, he lost control.

Somehow, Althea knew about it all. She was involved, or knew someone who was. And she was possibly crazy, or brain-damaged.

As they bumped down the private drive to the Marshes' house, Callie felt mostly numb. Maybe she should've felt scared. Or exercised better judgment, deciding right now that this whole thing was a terrible idea, and they should leave. But she felt nothing. Like her limits had been already tested, and now there was nothing left.

* * *

The Marsh house appeared quiet and unoccupied, with an empty driveway. No green Pathfinder, no RAM 1500.

Their absence was not comforting.

Callie stopped and put the Chevy in park. She expected Althea to sit a moment, to hesitate — hell, maybe "Miss Cleo" would have herself a vision right then and there — but the young woman just opened the door and jumped out.

Shit.

Callie steeled herself and climbed out next, hopping to the ground. She wasn't too worried about tracks, tire or foot — the snow had been plowed and packed down. But there could be cameras. There could also be someone inside, whether the place seemed abandoned or not.

"Althea . . ."

The young woman moved slowly toward the house. "This is it," she said, sounding incredulous. Like she'd said at the market, she never visited the places that her mind conjured. "This is the house where your husband was." She looked up to the porch where the carved black bears formed the top of the handrails. "More bears," she whispered.

The desire to flee grew in Callie's belly, like heat. It was one thing to be safe in the Chevy, with some woman who could turn out to be delusional in her claims about head wounds and snowmobiles. It was another thing to be here, trespassing again. Especially if there was any truth to it. She reached for Althea.

The young woman moved to the garage and stood on her tiptoes to see in the windows. Then she came back down on her heels and looked away, into the woods surrounding the house.

"Listen, all right. Let's just get back in the truck." Callie closed the distance and took Althea gently by the arm.

Althea just stood there, looking into the forest, breathing. She seemed to focus on something, and Callie followed where she was looking: a path carved through the deeper snow on the ground, winding through the trees.

"Out there," Althea said. Her voice was barely audible.

"Okay . . . Let's just . . ."

Althea's arm came up and her finger unfurled to point. "The cabin is out there."

CHAPTER FORTY

There was no use trying to stop her. Callie wanted to wait, to call Footman, maybe. At least, get *someone* out here. But Althea had already charged ahead, and Callie was hurrying to catch up.

"Hey — wait!"

The path had been made by machine — it had the ridges of a snowmobile track — but was still deep enough in places that the snow went right over the edges of her hiking boots, slowing her down. Althea seemed to stay on the surface and not break through. How long until they crossed over onto someone else's property? Marsh's voice surfaced in her memory: *The whole thing is almost two hundred acres . . . We own the land all the way back to the road.*

She remembered the time Abel had their land surveyed. She'd marveled at how big it was, with places she hadn't explored to this day — and that was just ten acres. Two *hundred*? It could very well be that the cabin Althea pictured was within the Marshes' borders.

The younger woman moved fast, taking big strides. Callie, winded, tried to keep up, plunging through the snow-pack in places. Her mind buzzed with too many things. The idea that Nathan Marsh was involved in wrongdoing had occurred to her many times, but it was always vague. They were thoughts she hadn't wanted to follow through to the end. Women trapped on the premises. Captives chained up in some cabin where they were sexually assaulted by Marsh. Maybe by his son.

No. She'd repeatedly decided she was jumping at shadows. That Nathan Marsh was merely cultured and reserved, in a way that could make him appear deceptive. That the snowsuit was a coincidence, the moan of a woman's voice misconstrued music or TV. She had fears and suspicions, but proof of nothing.

Yet she kept coming back.

It no longer felt like make-believe; the sense of surrealism was gone. The cold against her skin was real. The heavy snow on the trees, the woman walking fast ahead of her, her arms out for balance as she hurried over the terrain — all very real.

Okay. You're here now.

Think.

The snowmobile path looked fresh. Considering the snowfall from just a couple of days ago, the tracks were pristine, the ridges clear. Someone had been here just recently . . .

Her phone buzzed in her pocket and she fished it out. When she saw the name, her breath caught. "Hello? Mac?"

"Mom?"

"Honey, I've been meaning to call you."

"— you?"

Callie stopped and put her finger to her ear. Althea glanced back but kept moving away, deeper into the woods. "Honey, I can't hear you. Can you hear me?"

"— at the — today?"

"Mac, I'm sorry, honey, you're all broken up. If you can hear me, I'm going to call you back, okay? Let me just get back into town."

His reply was so garbled she couldn't make any sense of it. "If you can hear me," she repeated, "I'll call you back soon. Give me an hour or less. I love you."

She waited, heard nothing, and ended the call. Before she put the phone away, she noticed a message. It looked like Garr had called her, and it had gone straight to voicemail. Recently, too. Everything was happening at once.

She hurried along the snowmobile trail after Althea. The land sloped up for a while, and Althea was gone, having crested the rise. Callie trudged onward and upward, arms pumping, thighs burning a little. She had a headful of things to say to Althea when she got to the top of the hill: *We need to turn around. You need help. This is my mistake.*

It all went away when she looked down into the next valley.

The cabin was quaint, though more a hunting camp than a vacation getaway. Small, maybe only three or four hundred square feet. It had been built homestead-style, with a front porch. Nothing came out of the smoke stack, but a cord of wood sat beneath a tarp and six inches of snow beside the porch.

Althea was halfway there. Callie got moving, her heart really picking up now, between the exertion and anticipation, the fear of what they might find.

"Hang on, hang on," she called as she hurried down the slope. Althea was determined, hurrying ahead.

Suddenly, a voice in Callie's head, clear as a bell:
Stop. It's a trap.

She did stop. She watched as Althea reached the cabin. As she took the door in her hand.

A trap for whom? For Althea? For them both?

Abel's voice, nearly. Or maybe her father's:
For YOU.
This has all been to lure you here. Don't you see?

Callie did see. She suddenly imagined someone inside that cabin — maybe Casey Cooper — waiting for her. Those friendly eyes of his glinting with anticipation as she stepped into his lair and gasped.

This is what they do, the two of them. Casey and his sister Althea. Althea is the bait . . .

CHAPTER FORTY-ONE

The sound of the machine filled Callie with panic. This was exactly what she'd been afraid of. Someone was here after all. Maybe Marsh had lied about leaving. Maybe *this* was the trap.

She hurried around the cabin until she found Althea trying to lift the second window. "Come on," Callie said, grabbing the young woman by the arm. "That's enough. We have to go."

Callie led her back to the snowmobile track, then stopped to listen. The machine was definitely getting louder. Headed in this direction, for sure.

Callie and Althea could abandon the trail, but their tracks in the deep snow would be visible. The porch had been shoveled clear and the area around the cabin was tamped down, but if they left the area, they'd give themselves away.

There was, just maybe, one option.

* * *

The outhouse was a tight fit — just enough footing to stand, with the toilet bench taking up the rest of the space. Althea climbed up on it while Callie stood just inside the door. The snowmobile got louder, drowning out the sound of their hard breathing.

Callie peered through the half-moon cut in the door. The angle wasn't perfect, but she could see some of the cabin, mostly the right side; the big stack of firewood. The snowmobile engine reached its loudest yet, then quieted some. It idled for a few seconds, a kind of mechanical gurgling, before shutting off.

Their breathing seemed very loud once again. Callie braced herself against the walls. Althea, behind her, scuffed the toilet bench as she shifted her weight.

Shhhhhhh. Callie didn't even dare say it. And Althea knew, anyway.

It occurred to Callie that this was absurd. They were hiding for no reason. They'd seen nothing, heard nothing. There was no evidence that the Marshes had anything to do with the two missing girls. None. Footman didn't seem to expect anything, Louise Mullins had never even heard of Nathan Marsh.

The only connection to the missing girls was Callie's own husband. They'd each disappeared shortly after meeting him.

But for some reason, the woman stuck in this vaguely shit-stinking outhouse with her had ideas that Abel was wronged. That there *was* something sinister going on here.

Why? What was she basing it on? What knowledge, what evidence?

Althea just *knew*, apparently. Because she had special powers.

She was magic.

Well, if it were all so absurd, then there was no threat from Marsh or his son, was there?

So step out of the door then. Say hello.

Callie didn't, of course. She stayed where she was, keeping still, trying to breathe shallowly. Mushing her face against the wood, she strained to see as much of the cabin as possible. She could just make out part of the snowmobile. Something behind, too: a sled, full of more cordwood, perhaps. She couldn't see the driver — he'd already dismounted.

But then a second later, he stepped into view. The visor was up on his helmet, but the angle was wrong. She couldn't see his face.

He wore the snowsuit, though — black with jagged yellow bands around the sleeves and pant legs. Just like the one she'd seen on the driver the first night she'd been out here.

Just like the one inside the Marsh home, hanging on the wall.

He turned to the sled behind the machine and started flinging pieces of the wood toward the pile.

Althea whispered behind her, "Who is it?"

Eric.

It had to be. Eric Marsh. The figure seemed tall but agile. Young.

Halfway through unloading the pile, though, he stopped. He stood erect, and then slowly looked in Callie's direction.

Had he seen their tracks?

He stood there and took off his gloves. Tossing them aside, he undid the strap below his helmet. With the heels of his palms, he pushed it up over his head, revealing his face.

Callie stopped breathing.

CHAPTER FORTY-TWO

The man in the snowsuit stared straight at the outhouse. Like he knew they were in there.

Not Eric Marsh.

This man wore a thick beard and had longish hair.

Rory Harper. The Good Samaritan who had called the police the night of Abel's accident. The hero who had ventured deep enough into the cold lake to hook a tow rope and pull the vehicle out of the deeper water. It had saved vital minutes. EMTs arriving on scene had been able to get to Abel before the tow truck arrived. It likely had even saved Abel's life.

But Harper had quickly disappeared back into his reclusive life. He hadn't wanted any recognition. He'd given the barest of answers to police about why he'd been so quick to respond. Callie hadn't suspected him of wrongdoing, necessarily, but now she wondered. Had he done something to Abel when Abel found evidence of his crimes? Then tried to cover it up by playing the hero?

She suddenly saw him in her mind, like one of Althea's own alternative memories, checking to see if Abel looked dead. Hauling him out when he thought he was. Not expecting a coma, and the possibility Abel might someday wake and reveal what he knew, Harper had inadvertently devised his own downfall.

He ran a hand through his wild curls and scratched at his giant beard. He continued to stare, while Callie's heart pounded against her breast plate. Did he know? Why was he just standing there? Was he toying with her?

Finally turning away, Harper walked to the snow machine and lifted its seat. From a hidden compartment beneath, he pulled out a bottle of water, then twisted off the cap and started to drink.

Maybe he didn't know after all.

Maybe there was still a chance.

"Who *is it*?" Althea whispered again.

Callie dared to answer. "Rory Harper. Maybe we can . . ."

"Who?"

Callie didn't answer. Could they run? To where?

He'd definitely been staring in this direction, but he could've been lost in thought. For all she knew, he'd been contemplating whether he was going to use the bathroom. Their best option might be to just wait. See what happened.

The truck, though. He could've seen the damned truck in Nathan Marsh's driveway.

Maybe. Assuming he'd come from their house. And why would he? It was more likely he lived nearby.

Really? A rich hermit?

Well, he *was* an enigma. He'd could've been on the Forbes 500 for all she knew.

Callie shifted her stance. It was terribly uncomfortable standing here like this, bent over, peering out the half-moon hole. She reached a hand up to steady herself by gripping the door frame. Her finger bumped against something cold and hard. She felt for it in the dark. There was the faintest jingle of metal.

Keys.

They almost fell from the narrow lip, but she managed to catch them. Two keys, held together with a standard key ring.

Althea whispered, "What? What is that?"

Callie pressed against the wood and peered through the half-moon. Rory Harper finished drinking, screwed the cap back on, and tossed the bottle into the snow beside the snowmobile. Wiping his mouth with the back of his hand, he faced the cabin and stood looking a moment.

Callie's heart beat hard enough to crack a rib.

The keys she had in her hand — they went to the cabin. What else could they be for?

Then Rory Harper turned toward the outhouse and started walking her way.

CHAPTER FORTY-THREE

Crazy. Nuts. These kinds of things just couldn't happen. Some people were private, some were odd, but no one actually kept girls locked in a cabin in the woods. That was just for crime novels and cheap movies.

But, no, it happened. And guys just like Rory Harper were usually behind it.

Callie froze with indecision. If she ran from the outhouse, she'd have a head start on Harper. They'd come how far from the Marsh house? Half a mile? More? It wouldn't be enough to get there before he did.

She could wait, and not do anything until he opened the door, then jump out. Maybe gouge him with the keys. Where? In his face? Take out an eye? Insane.

There was still every chance this was all fear and paranoia. She didn't have it in her to stab someone with a set of keys, not unless her life depended on it — or someone else's — and she still didn't know.

And, for God's sake, this was the man who pulled Abel out of the lake.

The man who probably saved his life.

"What is it?" Althea whispered behind her, growing more anxious and intent. "Callie? What is it? He's coming, isn't he? Those are the keys to the cabin . . ."

Yes. Yes, they were. These were the keys to the cabin . . .

It was enough to unlock a plan in her own mind. At least, a plan to get her through the next few minutes, keep them safe until she could figure things out.

But she didn't move. *Couldn't* move, really; her feet had turned to lead.

"Callie? Callieeee . . ."

As Althea whined, Callie watched Rory Harper approach. He was bigger than she remembered. Maybe the beard added something, but he stood at least six feet tall and was two hundred pounds. There was no question he was headed here.

The keys. Oh, the fucking KEEEEEYS

She had seconds left. A blankness filled her thoughts as her mind went into survival mode.

"Okay. We're gonna go. We're gonna go to the cabin. Follow me to the cabin." Her lips felt numb as she spoke.

"What?" Althea was losing it. "We're gonna what?" She grabbed Callie's shoulders from behind.

No more time.

Callie flung the door open.

It swung out and then ricocheted back, and she caught it against her forearm. Moving to the side, holding the door open like this, she called for Althea to run. At the same time, she stared into Rory Harper's stunned face. He hadn't been expecting two women to burst from the commode. Not at all.

Althea moaned as she ran. She gave Harper a wide berth, putting her in the deep snow beyond the footpath. Callie ran the other direction — just an instinct — he couldn't catch both of them at the same time.

In her peripheral vision, she saw him sort of twist around to watch her as she ran past. He reached out, as if attempting to grab her. Then she and Althea converged on the path. They got to the porch at the same time and Callie squeezed past her, positioned herself in front of the door.

Two keys, one lock. Maybe the second key was for a door within? She tried the first key. It slipped in, and she twisted it. The bolt lock gave way. She turned the knob, and the door cracked open. She entered with Althea on her heels, then slammed the door behind her.

Now, the moment of truth — it needed to be able to lock from the inside. She twisted the bolt lock and even saw the metal slide down into place. That did it. And the windows were double-paned and small to minimize heat loss; even if he smashed through both panes of glass, she'd bash him in the head with a chunk of wood from beside the woodstove before he could shimmy in.

They were safe.

* * *

Callie tossed the keys to Althea. "Try one." She wanted to keep an eye on Harper, see what he was doing while Althea opened the door to the inner room.

Callie edged to the window and risked a peek. No one in view. But she thought she heard him out there — it was cold enough that the snow made a crunching noise underfoot.

Althea approached the door to the inner room. Callie had guessed the cabin was about four hundred square feet. Roughly twenty by twenty. Inside, it seemed a little bigger, but not by much. The inner room was tiny; it couldn't have been more than eight feet wide, maybe six feet deep. Like a prison cell.

Althea tried a key.

Callie, heart steadying, said, "That's the one for the front door. The other one." She turned her attention back to the window and, for a moment, couldn't move again. Everything locked up, including her breathing. Rory Harper was standing right there, on the porch, looking in the window, inches from the glass. He was so close she could see the tiny icicles in his beard. His gaze connected with hers.

Hurry, she thought at Althea, but for no particular reason. Once they opened the door to discover whatever was in the small room, they would still be trapped in here with Harper out there.

She realized he was moving his lips. It didn't seem like he was speaking — she'd be able to hear something through the glass if he were. He was just mouthing words, almost like praying. She stared back, her breathing shallow, pulse working in her neck. A kind of low-grade electric current seemed to buzz through her body, moiling her stomach, buzzing in her brain.

Rory Harper turned and stepped away.

Althea, behind Callie, got the right key in the lock and turned it.

Callie dragged her attention away from Harper and focused on Althea as the younger woman twisted the knob. She glanced at Callie and hesitated. Callie nodded and steeled herself for what she might be about to see. Bodies, maybe. Girls already dead, maybe chopped to pieces.

Or, still alive. Emaciated, drugged, barely clinging to consciousness, having been abused and tortured.

Althea opened the door and Callie stepped forward, holding her breath again. With one hand on her stomach, like she was about to be sick, she peered into the room.

In there, it was the darkest yet. There were no windows, no natural light. Callie moved closer.

"Hello?" Her voice was a trembling whisper. "Anyone here?"

As her eyes adjusted, she realized she was looking at equipment. Nordic skis, snowshoes, some kind of pack basket. A wooden cabinet, padlocked, not unlike Abel's back home. Could be guns in there, other items for hunting, judging from the set of deer antlers sitting on top. Bags and boxes formed a pile in the corner. A smooshed pack of cigarettes — Marlboro Reds — lay on the ground.

It was a storage room, used for all manner of outdoor and hunting gear. The scents of wood and grease hung in the air.

But no bodies. No missing girls. No signs someone had been kept there, either.

Callie backed out of the room. The relief she felt was short-lived, followed by questions and more fear.

What was going on here?

Callie faced Althea, standing in the doorway to the inner room. Among the many clamoring thoughts was one clear appraisal of Althea's beauty. In the unheated cabin, her fur-lined parka hood was up around her head, her blonde hair tufting out. Her eyes shone with emotion — a kind of hurt there, that went deep. As if she'd been almost *hoping* to find girls here. To validate her visions. And maybe more — maybe some catharsis from her own time as a victim, in some way or form.

For the first time, really, Callie saw through the noise of so-called psychic ability, saw beyond her own concerns for Abel — saw through to a young woman who was deeply troubled after all.

Looking at Althea was like looking back in a mirror, really. One that reversed time to her own earlier years. Her own trauma, shame, regret.

You're here because she led you.

"I don't know," Althea whispered. "I don't know . . ."

Callie returned to the window and looked out. Rory Harper was in view, and on his phone. He seemed to be just finishing up. He turned and saw her in the window. His lips moved, and this time, she caught his muffled voice.

He took the phone away from his head, poked it once, and strode to the cabin.

She shrank back a little as he held the phone out to her. As she leaned in to see what was on the screen, Althea moved beside her.

911.

The number he'd just dialed.

Callie felt the sickness return. She looked at Harper, met his eyes again, but then turned away. Not knowing what else to do, she slowly sank to the floor.

CHAPTER FORTY-FOUR

Looking back, they could have left. Callie could have grabbed Althea and hightailed it out of there.

But her parents hadn't raised her to run from authority.

And she wasn't entirely ready to trust Rory Harper just yet.

Mostly, though, she'd spent the time waiting for the police to arrive just sitting there in the middle of the cold cabin. Wondering how she was going to explain this to Cormac when it inevitably came up. Or to Abel, eventually, when he awoke.

Honey, while you were sleeping . . .

Yes. While he was sleeping, she'd gone on a wild goose chase. Based on the vague murmurings of a troubled young woman who thought she might have extra sensory perception. And motivated, really, by pride. And fear. *Because of what people might've thought, honey. About you being a suspected axe murderer.*

Mortified by Abel being a "person of interest," she'd set out to prove that someone else was behind the disappearance of two missing girls. When really, one had probably run away and the other was dead in the woods, killed in an accident. The only reason Abel was interesting to the police was because he had met them both. Kerry Mullins, because of a job he'd done for her mother. Naomi Bannon, because his brother was dating her cousin. And he'd been out here to the Marsh place the night of his accident to see about another job.

That was it.

Then came Althea Cooper. Possibly a patient of Marsh's who — for whatever reason — had decided to stir up some shit. She'd taken a few things she knew about the doctor and his second home in the North Country and started messing with everyone's head. Callie's the most.

* * *

"Epilepsy," Footman said. After the first police arrived by snowmobile, the women had been ferried out to the main road. Callie sat behind a mesh grate separating the front and back of a patrol car until Footman slid into the front seat. "Ms Cooper has a form of epilepsy, according to her brother."

"Epilepsy?"

"That's what Casey said. Seizures are rare, he said, but it's possible there are delusions associated with the disorder. It's a degenerative organic condition — there is an affected area of the brain, and it produces some of these impulses."

Callie waited for more — surely Footman didn't mean that a brain condition had provided Althea the ability to see things.

"She's been to see Marsh," Footman said. "Once. This is something I didn't know. I knew about the condition. I couldn't tell you, but since Casey and I have just spoken, he gave me the okay. She met Marsh once, briefly, and she never went back. She wouldn't talk about it. Casey thinks Marsh just decided not to treat her, and Marsh either doesn't remember or can't say. But there are pictures in his office, he told me. Pictures of the Adirondacks and of his home. Even one with the green SUV in it. These are all things she could've easily seen while in his office, and then claimed to 'just know.'"

It was along the lines of what Callie had already considered. She could see Althea from here, in the back of another state trooper car across the road. The surrounding trees and the sky reflected in the glass, but she could just see Althea's face behind it all, staring forward.

"We're lucky that Marsh is being so understanding. Harper, too. Everybody can see that she's troubled, and they don't blame her. Or you. With your husband having been out here, and then his situation, and everything that happened. Harper won't press charges. He was more worried about the two of you than anything else. He was afraid you were going to hurt yourselves in there."

Callie took her eyes off Althea. "Is it his cabin?"

"Yes. His property abuts on the Marsh property. The cabin is near the border. You'd just gone over the line by a hundred yards or so. Marsh and Harper have an agreement about hunting; Harper hunts in the spring and fall, and sometimes accesses Marsh's land."

"He's wealthy?"

"I don't know exactly. He's a stone mason. And he does work for people all over the region, like your husband. I think he makes a very good living at it, yes."

"What about the snowsuit?"

Footman's eyes found her in the rear-view mirror. He sighed, as if it pained him to answer. "Harper is friendly with the Marshes. He's done work for them. They're neighbors. He says he ripped his own suit a few weeks back and has been borrowing Eric's until he gets into town for another one. He doesn't go into town much, and he doesn't use the internet."

"That night, though — a few nights ago — when I saw two men on snowmobiles . . ."

Footman nodded. "That was Harper and Eric Marsh. Nathan didn't know, but they were out. They ride together."

It explained how someone could be at the crash site so fast after she'd left Nathan Marsh — Eric hadn't been home.

Footman said, "That was how Eric Marsh knew about your husband, too. He knew about the crash right away, because Harper told him about the whole thing. Then Eric told his father, at some point later."

She thought about it. Her mind scanned for any other possible holes in the story. "When I asked Dr Marsh if he said he knew Althea Cooper, he didn't."

"He sees hundreds of patients. She was there for five minutes, one afternoon last fall. Or maybe he was keeping even that confidential, but probably he just didn't recall her name. Mrs Sanderson, listen. Let's move on. Okay? Has your son been in touch?"

"He tried to call me just a little while ago." The thought of Cormac in the midst of all of this brought back that sense of queasy heaviness.

"Well, I talked to him, as I said I would. I'll let him fill you in. He's a good young man, Mrs Sanderson."

And you're fucking him up with all of your ridiculous antics was what Footman didn't say.

"Okay," Callie said. "I appreciate that." Her mind drifted back to recent events. Harper tossing the wood on the pile. Staring at the outhouse, surely thinking about the key. His face in the window as he watched them inside. "Could you do me a favor?"

"I'll try."

"Could you apologize to Mr Harper for me? I'm sorry if we worried or upset him."

"He seems okay. I explained things a bit, and he was very understanding. He's just . . . a private person. Marsh said he's a little socially awkward, not used to people."

She thought about his lips moving soundlessly as he stared into the cabin.

"You should speak to your son," Footman said.

"What do you mean?"

Footman was contemplative. "Let's just say he has his own point of view on things. Everyone does. And right now

217

. . . well, maybe just talk to him, see what he thinks. And we can talk again later."

Cryptic. But she was too exhausted to press him.

Then Footman clapped his hands, making her jump. "All right. I guess the only question left is, what do we want to do with—?"

"I'll take her home," Callie said.

He gave Callie a look that bordered on sympathetic. Like she was the poor soul being taken in by another's madness. "You sure?"

"I brought her up here; I can get her back home. If that's all right. It's the least I can do."

He blew out some more air and touched his neat hair with a gloved hand. "Okay. Sure. And you'll let Casey know. Or have her call him."

"I will."

Callie didn't wait any longer. Being around Footman felt more and more like she was a teenaged girl getting a lecture from her father. Footman got out and opened the door for her. Together, they crossed to the other car.

"Ms Cooper, you're free to go."

"Okay." Althea avoided eye contact with Callie as Footman helped her to her feet.

Footman said, "Ms Cooper, I don't presume to understand everything about you, or what you feel. But I think you need to take a look at this situation." He looked around, gesturing to the multiple police cars, their red and blue lights flashing, like the view made his point for him. "If there's anything else, I would have you call me before you call Mrs Sanderson. Or anyone. Especially someone directly involved, okay?" He pulled a business card from his inner breast pocket and handed it to her.

She took it without a word.

"Okay," Footman said. "You ladies get home safe."

Someone had brought Callie's truck out to the road. She led Althea to it and got in. With the engine started, she waited a moment while it heated up. Footman talked with the state troopers. One of them smiled and then laughed. She wondered where Nathan Marsh was. Maybe she'd never see him again.

Hopefully, this whole thing was over.

"I'm sorry," Althea said. The young woman slumped in her seat and stared out the window.

"It's okay." Callie reached over and put a hand on Althea's shoulder. "It's not your fault."

She put the truck in gear and pulled out. She checked the mirrors as they drove off. The vibration of the road shook the mirrors and the images within, but she could see Footman in his black coat, among the state troopers, his pale face watching her.

CHAPTER FORTY-FIVE

The sun was setting as Callie reached home. She felt exhausted. While she'd meant it when she'd told Footman she would get Althea home, the thought of a four-hour drive right now was untenable. Althea had seemed happy to accept Callie's invitation to stay for the night. It meant delaying a scolding from her brother, probably. When she'd called to tell him, he'd accepted it, but she'd ended the call with haste.

After that, they'd driven most of the way in silence, with Callie unable to tell if Althea was embarrassed, frustrated, or something else. In truth, Callie wasn't even sure about her own emotional state. It had been one of the strangest afternoons on record, and that was saying a lot, considering how strange in general things had been the last couple of months.

And it was about to get even stranger.

As they came within eyeshot of her house, Callie spotted Cormac's car in the driveway.

* * *

"What are you doing here?"

"I tried calling you. I asked where you were."

"I'm sorry. I was out of range."

He sighed. "I just couldn't do it anymore, Mom."

"Couldn't do what?"

"I know you got all this stuff going on. You shouldn't be alone." Cormac looked at her with pure concern. He seemed to know everything by looking at her. The weight she'd lost. The insomnia. And now all of this stress and running around.

Maybe more; she thought about Footman's comments, about Cormac having a point of view.

"The police investigator called me," he said.

"I know. What did he say to you?"

"He asked me about Dad."

"Okay." Callie didn't follow that up right away, looking instead toward the downstairs bathroom. Althea had headed there after quick introductions. The door was closed, and Callie thought she could hear the fan.

"He said he was still investigating the accident," Cormac said. "We'd talked before and he didn't have much to say then. But he had all sorts of questions this time. What's going on?"

Callie gestured for Cormac to follow her into the kitchen. Althea knew everything, but the desire for privacy was instinctual. And maybe she'd need to say things about Althea she wouldn't want the young woman to overhear.

"What did he ask you?" Callie wanted to know.

"Just . . . everything. About how Dad was the last I saw him."

"And what did you say?"

"I said fine. He was normal. I could only really talk about Christmas, though."

Cormac looked like Abel only a little. Mostly he had her genes — her facial features, anyway. His blond hair was short around the ears and shaved to a hard fuzz at the base of his skull. Wavy on top, close to curly. His marble-blue eyes were intent and intelligent.

"Well, yeah," she said. "But you guys talk, too. On the phone."

He shrugged. "We text a little. But Dad's not very chatty. You know that."

"Yeah." She was thinking about Cormac's message on Abel's phone. *I have something I need to talk to you about.* "Is everything okay with you, bud?"

"Like what?"

"Well, Mr Footman thinks we should talk. And, full disclosure — I went through Dad's phone. Before the police took it."

"You did? Why?"

"Just to have a look at everything. Any work stuff I'd missed. See if I could figure out why he'd been in Lake Clear."

"And did you?"

"I did, yeah. He was seeing about a job out there."

Cormac nodded like this made perfect sense. Then he wandered over to the fridge and opened it.

"You want something to drink?"

"Yeah." He put his face in. "I got it, don't worry."

"There's orange juice, I think."

"Okay. Okay." He found it and took it out, undid the cap and gave it a sniff.

"It's fine."

He glanced at her. There was a lot in that look — that he didn't trust everything was okay back home, for one thing. And could she blame him? Honestly, if she'd been asked to name the contents of her refrigerator, or what she might have for dinner, she wouldn't know.

But there was something else. Something about what he and his father had shared that she wasn't yet privy to.

The toilet flushed in the bathroom, at the other end of the house. The water ran. Callie heard the furnace kick on in the basement. They had no hot water heater, just the oil-fed boiler. Abel wanted to get them off it, put solar panels on the roof.

"I know you miss him," she said, nearing her son. "I miss him, too. So much."

Cormac stood at the kitchen island, drinking his juice. When he set down the glass, she hugged him. He smelled of deodorant and fast-food, like he'd been in the car for a while. "I listened to the message you left," she said.

He pulled away. "What message?"

"The one where you said you wanted to talk to him about something."

Cormac seemed to be deciding whether to be mad at her.

She was quick. "I just meant, if there's anything you need to talk about, you can try me, too."

He held her gaze and seemed to soften, nodding. "Yeah, no, it's okay. I remember that. It was just weird. I wanted to talk to Dad about Uncle Garr."

Callie stiffened. There had been so many odd coincidences. "Uncle Garr? Why?"

Cormac started to explain, but a noise caught Callie's attention. She held up a finger to Cormac — *just a minute, we'll get back to this.*

"Hello," Callie said as Althea approached. The woman stopped on the edge of the kitchen, which opened to the dining area.

Callie looked between the two of them. "So. Are you two hungry?"

Althea had been introduced to Cormac as "a friend" who was "just visiting" and that she lived in the Syracuse area. He was no dummy and knew there was more to it.

"I could eat," Cormac said.

"You can always eat." Callie grinned.

"True." He watched Althea.

"Sure," the young woman said.

Cormac kept staring a moment. Callie knew he was intrigued, that he was attracted. Most men probably would be.

Besides her looks, there was just something about her.

CHAPTER FORTY-SIX

Spaghetti always worked in a pinch. There was half a jar of sauce in the fridge, and it was perfectly palatable. Althea offered to help. Callie liked to save a little pasta water and add it back to the pasta after straining it, plus a little olive oil and salt. It was a trick she'd learned from a chef. One of the many chefs in one of the many restaurants over the years. In what felt like another life.

The spaghetti was good, just a touch softer than al dente, and Callie had found some pickled beets and carrots to have on the side. The three of them mostly ate in silence, with moments of small talk. Althea ate slowly, picking at the food. In the silence, Callie's mind was buzzing. Cormac mentioning Garr reminded her that she'd never returned his call. Lynn was supposed to have joined him today. He could have new information.

And, thinking of things overlooked, she still wanted to get fresh eyes on the accident photos. Only that felt more like paranoia now. The ground seemed to be vanishing beneath her feet, a little at a time.

"Althea?"

The woman looked up, her eyes bright with expectation.

"I'm going to tell Cormac what's been happening, okay?"

She swallowed a bite and nodded. She gave no sign of reservation.

Cormac already looked like he knew, too — at least, knew that what wasn't being said could fill a room. That Althea wasn't just some random friend. He'd been waiting patiently.

"Okay." Callie opened up. She told Cormac everything, from Althea's first call, up to the events that afternoon at the Marshes'. Althea watched and listened. She was solemn at times and looked slightly embarrassed at others.

The entire time she spoke, Callie worried it was unfair, that she was burdening her son, using him to clean her own conscience. But he seemed to take it all in stride. And after listening, he dabbed his mouth with a napkin, sat back, and looked at them, and he seemed more adult than she ever remembered in that moment. Among other things, it broke her heart a little.

What he said next, though, surprised her.

"Dad takes care of a couple different properties. Some of them are pretty deep in the woods."

At first, she didn't know how to respond. "What does that mean?"

Cormac was looking at Althea, and then his eyes slowly homed in on Callie. "I'm just saying. She thought these missing girls could be out in the woods somewhere."

Callie could imagine throwing Althea under the proverbial bus. *So fucking what? She's a lunatic making things up about some doctor she didn't like.* But of course that would just be defensive lashing-out, and not really what Callie thought.

Cormac had more to say, anyway: "The police investigator asked me about them."

"About what?"

"About the properties Dad caretakes for."

Callie swallowed. She looked from Cormac to Althea and back. "Well, maybe Footman thinks your father saw something. That he ran across a crime scene, or evidence of a crime."

Cormac was shaking his head. "That wasn't really it. And I mean, if Dad had seen something, he would have told us. Plus, the only links from these girls to Dad is the one deck job he did, and the property in Glass Lake where he was going to help build some cabin or tiny house. None of the properties he caretakes for are connected."

"So what exactly are you saying?"

But Cormac just watched Callie a moment, and it hurt her to see how his eyebrows turned up, the corners of his mouth turned down. Like he felt sorry for her. For them both. "I'm just telling you what Mr Footman asked me, okay? He asked about the properties Dad takes care of. What I knew about them, that kind of thing. And I asked why. I wanted to know. And he said that they were looking for missing girls."

"Okay, but, I don't understand what you're not—"

"They're trying to get at something. It sounded to me like they suspect Dad is involved."

"He's a person of interest, not a suspect. They think he might have information. That's all. He can help them form timelines, maybe speak to the state of mind someone was in. He's a witness, basically."

Cormac just stared at her a moment, tension in the air. She knew her tone had gotten sharp. He said, "There's stuff about Dad that you just don't know about, Mom. I'm sorry, but there is."

Callie's jaw was working, but no sound was coming from her throat. Sadness and anger formed an undigestible mixture. Finally, the words released, bitter on her tongue: "Cormac, this is your father. He's not a kidnapper, or a killer. *None* of it."

"Okay, right." He paused. "But there's a reason why the police are asking these questions. They don't come up with something like this out of thin air."

When no one spoke, Cormac stood. He picked up his plate and offered to take theirs. Callie's thoughts had scattered, leaving her empty. Althea offered her plate and thanked him quietly. Her face had reddened and she seemed to look anywhere but at Callie. Maybe she was regretting deciding to stay.

Welcome to the family, kid.

Cormac brought the dishes to the sink and put them in, ran the water for a second. Every sound was crisp, loud.

Callie suddenly felt gripped by a kind of panic, a mindless fear that renders everything meaningless and scary. She was a child again, left at a funhouse, lost without parents.

The chair legs scraped the floor as she pushed back from the table. She might've mumbled, "Excuse me," might've only thought it. Cormac moved toward her, concern on his face, but she left him, headed for the bathroom, where everything from dinner came back in a stinging rush.

CHAPTER FORTY-SEVEN

Callie retreated to the bedroom upstairs. The voices of Cormac and Althea drifted up from the kitchen. They'd watched her come back from the bathroom, concern on their faces. "I'm all right. Just need a few minutes. Althea, please make yourself at home. Cormac . . . ?" He'd nodded, taking the nonverbal cue: *Be a good host in my absence.*

She also saw it in his eyes: guilt.

She hated that it made her glad. He was her son, her baby. But this was a tough situation. If her life was a true-crime story — and it was rapidly turning out to be that — weren't the children of the accused always his defenders?

It made sense. Your parents were your protectors. Your father was, in a way, your god.

So what was Cormac thinking?

She wandered to Abel's side of the room. After the shock of his crash had worn off, she'd found herself doing things like cleaning and laundry, routine chores that distracted and comforted. Her husband was injured, but his condition wasn't permanent; he'd be home soon. So, she'd done the dishes and shopped for groceries. She'd vacuumed the house and dusted. She'd cleaned his side of the bedroom, picked up his dirty clothes and laundered them.

Only his jacket and a couple of hanging shirts retained his smell — scents of pine and motor oil. The fresh air. Traces of sweat and tobacco. Abel wasn't a cigarette smoker, but he occasionally puffed a small cigarillo. She'd poked fun at him, calling it a hipster thing to do. But Abel wasn't a hipster. He had a sense of style, he kept a fashionable beard, but he was the real deal. A craftsman and an outdoorsman. He didn't just look the part — he lived the life.

She pictured him as he'd recently been. She wasn't sure what moment in particular it was that came to mind, but she saw him climbing down off their Kubota tractor. He'd been wearing dark brown canvas work pants. A Carhartt jacket that had seen better days. His wavy hair curled beneath a blaze orange hunter's beanie. And he'd grinned at her with one of those cigarillos tucked into the corner of his mouth as he'd taken off his leather gloves, set them up on the big tractor tire beside her. When was that? He'd been coming in for dinner, she remembered. She'd been standing in the front doorway. But instead of going directly to the table, he'd lifted her up, carried her into the house, to the living room, where he'd placed her on the couch and started to take off her clothes. Normally they might've had a shower together, but that night, alone in their home, fire crackling in the open fireplace, they'd made love in the open.

She stood now, lingering over the things on his dresser. A stack of mail that had been accumulating — she'd kept it there instead of his corner office. A small wicker basket, full of bric-a-brac, including a random assortment of nails and screws, a small tape measure. His nighttime reading was stacked neatly — he'd been working on three different books. Two nonfiction and one fiction. Actually, one of them was at the hospital, the one she'd been reading to him. *Crow Killer*.

Could he hear her, when she read? Maybe she'd ask Althea. Perhaps a clairvoyant could see into Abel's mind.

Now you're really losing it. Now you're—
"Mom?"

She startled, and her hand bumped the wicker basket, rattling its contents.

Cormac was in the bedroom doorway. "Everything okay?"

She sat on the bed, not answering.

He took a few cautious steps. "You're upset."

Finally, she raised her eyes to him. "I'm just trying to place everything."

He knew what she meant, she guessed. That she was "trying to place" how he could entertain, even for a second, that his father was guilty of anything. That Abel could hurt anyone.

Cormac sat beside her and she faced him. "What did you say to Footman?"

"Nothing. Really. He wanted to know if . . . Basically, he wanted to know if Dad told me. Where the girls were."

Waves of revulsion and anger. Her eyes blurred with tears. "*What?*"

"He seemed to really think Dad knew where they were."

"*Why?* Why would he think that?"

"He wouldn't tell me why."

"What did he ask you? Tell me exactly."

"He wanted to know how often I talked to Dad, what we discussed. I told him everything I could think of. Then he asked if Dad ever got violent . . ."

"Cormac, no . . ." Callie knew where this was heading.

"I mean, it's true, Mom. Dad can get pretty upset . . ."

She was shaking her head, even though she'd had the same thought when Althea mentioned the brunette. "You and Dad had a couple of arguments before you left home. That's it."

"He threw me through the front door, Mom."

"You'd been gone for two days. Off with your buddies. You told him to 'go fuck himself.' And you're just as strong as he is — it's not like he took advantage of you."

"I'm not as strong as he is," Cormac said quietly. He studied the floor in front of him.

230

Callie, anger melting into love for her son, went back to the bed and put her arm around him. Tears stung the backs of her eyes. "Mac . . . it's Dad. I'm not justifying violence. He was too hard on you. He never should have treated you that way, and he knew it. He was sick about it. But just because you and him had it out doesn't mean he *kidnapped* anyone. Or did . . . anything like that. At all."

"Yeah . . ."

"They're wrong. Okay? Whatever they think, there's a reason. But they're wrong."

Cormac was crying now, too, just barely.

"What else did Footman ask?"

"He asked about Uncle Garr and his girlfriend."

"And what did you say?"

"Not much. That Dad and him weren't very close. That I hardly ever saw him except a couple of times when I was younger, and then those couple of times last year."

It was so out of the blue that it took her a second. "What couple of times last year?"

Cormac wiped his eyes and sat up straighter. He gave her a look. "You know, he was here."

"Uncle Garr?"

Cormac nodded. "Yeah. In the Adirondacks. A couple of times. I saw him in town once. And then I saw him out here — he was just leaving when I was coming home."

Now she was reeling. She blinked a few times, trying to catch up. "You saw Garr when you were coming home? What do you mean, exactly?"

"Just after Christmas. You and Dad were gone, I guess you were at Annie's." He was referring to Callie's friend, the rad-tech. Callie and Abel had dinner with Annie and her husband Bill every once in a great while. The last time had been New Year's Day, about a week before Abel's crash. And the day Cormac was supposed to be returning to school from the holiday break.

"We went to Annie's after you left," Callie said, not understanding.

"I know. I forgot my laptop battery. I drove almost an hour away before I realized it and came all the way back. I didn't want to bother you guys. Anyway, Uncle Garr was here."

"Here? At the house?"

Cormac nodded. "He was, like, on his way out."

"Did you talk to him?"

"Briefly, yeah. He seemed kind of weird, in a rush. We sort of passed each other in the driveway. I said you guys had gone to dinner. He said no problem, he'd get in touch with you. That sort of thing."

Callie thought back. She had no memory of Garr getting in touch on New Year's. Not with Abel, either. He would have said.

Then again, there were many things he hadn't said in the months before the crash. Things he should have.

"And you said you saw him in town, too?"

"Yeah, that was back last summer. Just before I headed to school for the first time. I was in town. I don't know what I was doing — bank, maybe. And I saw Uncle Garr coming out of the hardware store. I wasn't even sure it was him at first. But you know how he kind of looks like Dad, and kind of doesn't?"

She nodded.

"The sight of him caught my eye, and I slowed a little."

"Did he see you?"

"I don't think so."

"And you told all of this to Footman?"

"Yeah."

So, Garr had been coming around to the area and she'd had no idea. "I went to see your father with Garr," she said, sort of to Cormac and sort of to herself. She stood from the bed. "I spent hours with him. He didn't say anything about being here. Not at New Year's, not last summer. He made it seem like he was just coming now. For the first time in a long time. Meeting his girlfriend. Maybe meeting her family for the first time."

Callie didn't know why she hadn't thought of it before. She faced Cormac: "Do you still have your Facebook account?"

"I never use it."

"Well, I got rid of mine. Do you have your phone with you?"

He dug his phone out of his pocket. After poking at the screen, he handed it to her. "Why?"

"Lynn," Callie explained. "I'm going to see if she's on here."

"Uncle Garr's girlfriend?"

She nodded. "Lynn McNamara."

CHAPTER FORTY-EIGHT

Callie located Lynn McNamara within seconds. Or at least, someone with that name. The profile picture was from a distance — presumably Lynn on horseback — so she had to go deeper. Luckily, the images were public.

It was her. Callie lingered over the first picture, not knowing quite how to feel. She knew it was the right person for a couple of reasons — there were pictures of Garr, and she had friend connections with various Bannons.

And she was tall. Brunette. Gorgeous and young — only twenty-five. Just like the woman Althea had described.

Cormac was watching as Callie scrolled. "What is it?"

"You were about to tell me something at dinner," Callie said. "You'd called your father to talk about Uncle Garr, you said."

"Yeah."

"Why? About what?"

Cormac just looked at her. The longer he didn't answer, the more uncomfortable she felt. "Mac? What did you want to talk to Dad about?"

Cormac drew a breath. "Dad never told you about him and Garr?"

"Well, yes and no. There's a lot I don't . . . What about them?"

"Uncle Garr was just . . . he was abusive when they were younger."

She was silent. There was nothing to say. Abel had confided in his son, and that was a good thing.

Cormac continued, "It was some pretty bad shit."

The bad language didn't faze Callie. She had too many other thoughts and emotions running.

"He would get drunk, get Dad to wrestle. And Dad wasn't always as big as he is now. Garr would pin him. He'd put Dad in a headlock until he passed out. Things like that. Brothers fight, but Garr was a bully. A couple times, Dad said, Garr almost killed him. Hurt him pretty bad."

Callie's hand had drifted to her mouth.

"He said he didn't like to talk about it. He didn't talk to you about it, really. But he told me. He wanted to teach me about bullying. When Dad got physical with me that time — I know he was upset, like you said. Because he came to me afterward. He was crying and everything. That's when he told me. He apologized a thousand times. He said, you know, victims of bullying can grow up to be bullies themselves. And he didn't want that."

Callie fell into a recent memory. Seeing Garr standing at Abel's bedside. The emotion she'd seen, the remorse — she'd thought it had to do with their estrangement. But it could've been more.

And frankly, over the years, she'd had her suspicions. Sometimes words were unnecessary; the spaces and silences told the stories. The body language — the way Abel would tense up at his brother's mention.

"I knew that Uncle Garr had been trying to make it up to Dad," Cormac said.

"Make it up to him?"

"Giving him projects. The thing down in Glass Lake. The Mullins deck, or whatever."

"The Mullins deck? Louise Mullins?"

"Yeah. Uncle Garr is friends with some guy who takes care of her animals and stuff. I think his name is Stan. They grew up together. Back when Garr lived here. Before, um, Grandma and Grandpa died. Anyway, when I called Dad, it was after seeing Garr at the house. I just wanted to know how it was going. I knew Dad wasn't talking to you about it . . . so I just stepped in, I guess."

She put her arm around him and tucked her head against his shoulder. "I understand."

Cormac was silent a moment. "The detective was really interested in Garr. And what Dad knew about him. And what Dad said about him. We went over that stuff — the bullying, the jobs — we went over that a lot."

"You and Footman."

"Yeah."

She sat with it. She thought, *person of interest*. Someone with information.

Abel had been working with Garr. Garr had gotten him a couple of jobs.

She was about to ask Cormac more when she heard a floorboard creak in the hallway. "Hello?" Callie moved toward the door.

Althea walked past the room, stopping when she saw them.

"In here," Callie said. "Sorry."

Cormac wiped at his face some more, self-conscious that he'd been crying.

Althea studied them a moment. "What are you guys doing?"

No point in secrets or even vagueness, Callie thought. She scrolled through her phone to a picture of Lynn.

Althea paled. "That's her," she said. "That's the woman I saw your husband with."

"That's Lynn McNamara," Callie clarified. "Abel's brother, Garr — that's his girlfriend."

A series of pictures on Lynn's page showed her and some friends cross-country skiing. It was beautiful country, wherever they were — with trails through the woods, frozen lakes, mountain views.

"That's their new property, I think," Cormac said, looking. "It's pretty nice."

"It is," Callie said. "So Garr recommended Dad to help them build this tiny house . . ."

"Yeah. But then the girl — Naomi — went missing."

Callie continued to scroll. She stopped when she came to a building. A ramshackle trailer. The kind meth dealers used.

"Oh God," Althea said.

"What?"

Cormac spoke first. "That's the old trailer on the property. Dad said they were going to either pull it apart and haul it out in pieces, or try to get it out intact."

"It's on the property?" Callie asked Cormac.

At the same time, she watched Althea. Althea was trembling. And Callie's own mind was working, fast. Putting pieces together: Garr was the one who knew Louise Mullins. And he was the one who knew Naomi Bannon. Not only that, but there was a trailer on Lynn's property. Not a cabin, per se, but like Althea said — sometimes she misread her own visions. Filled in a feeling with an image that wasn't quite right, though the gist of it lined up.

Garr had a girlfriend with a place deep in the woods.

He was connected to both missing girls.

Althea blinked several times in rapid succession and looked at Callie and Cormac. Cormac got to his feet. When Althea's knees buckled, he caught her.

"Shit," Cormac said. He had her full weight — she'd passed right out.

* * *

After Callie helped Cormac drag her over to the bed, Althea came to a little. She mumbled, and her eyes fluttered some more and opened, half-lidded.

"What?" Callie asked.

But her words were unintelligible. It was as if she'd blown a circuit. Callie worried she might need medical attention. Was this the epilepsy? Was it a seizure?

"I'll call 911." She pulled out her phone. As she punched in the numbers, her mind was still half on what she'd just realized, Garr and his connection to the missing girls.

No. She had to concentrate now. Beside her, Althea closed her eyes again. Scrunched them up. Her face crumbled into an expression of pain and sadness. She curled up into a fetal position, gripping herself as she softly cried.

Not a seizure, it seemed, but she was hurting. As if what she knew had gotten too heavy to bear.

"Hang on, honey, I'm calling."

The line for emergency services rang.

Callie looked across the bed at her son, who looked back.

At the same time, they heard an engine. Someone was here.

CHAPTER FORTY-NINE

"Nine-one-one, what is your emergency?"

Callie saw Garr from the hallway dormer, walking up the snow-swept walkway toward the house. It looked like the vehicle was still running, someone sitting in the passenger seat, but it was too hard to tell for sure.

"Hello?" the dispatcher asked.

Cormac had followed Callie out into the hallway. When Garr knocked on the front door, she ushered Cormac back into her bedroom.

"Mom, no."

"Get in there. Stay with Althea." She pushed him, then shut the door.

On the phone: "Sorry, I didn't get that. Hello?"

Garr knocked again as Callie moved down the hallway to the next room — Cormac's bedroom. She slipped in and pulled the door shut, staying away from the front-facing windows. "This is Callie Sanderson." She gave her address. "I need police response and an ambulance. I have an intruder and an injured woman." It just came out that way.

Downstairs, Garr knocked a third time. She heard a muffled voice: "Hello? Cal? You here?"

He had to be suspicious. The Chevy was in the driveway in front of him, not to mention Mac's vehicle.

"Ma'am? I can hardly hear you. You said an injured woman? Injured how?"

"Please just send the police and an ambulance." She relayed her address again, loud as she dared, and hung up.

There was one more knock from downstairs, but it sounded weak, like he'd already given up. Staying low, Callie crept to the bedroom window and risked a look outside. Garr was moving back toward the driveway. He slowed and turned and looked up at the house. She jerked out of sight. *Dammit.*

When she poked her head out for another quick look, Garr was no longer there. The car remained. It still appeared as if someone sat in the passenger side, but the driver's side was empty.

The back door.

Had she locked it?

There was a thump from downstairs. The sound the back door made. His voice drifted up. "Callie? Cal? It's me. I'm coming in. Hope that's okay."

She racked her brain. What did he know? He knew she went to see Mullins. He'd acted like he was going to go, but then ducked out. No wonder. But he couldn't have known what Althea had said about Lynn, or the dots Callie how now connected. Although he could easily suspect . . .

She needed to answer him.

"Be right down! Just give me a minute!"

He didn't respond right away. Then, "Oh, okay! I wasn't sure." He said something else, too low for her to hear.

Her phone vibrated, the screen lighting up in the dark. It was Footman. What did he want?

Quietly, she answered. "Hello?"

"Mrs Sanderson. What's going on?" He sounded, for the first time ever, alarmed. "I've just been notified you called nine-one-one."

"It's my brother-in-law," she blurted.

240

"Mrs Sanderson, I can't hear you. Did you say brother-in-law?"

"Yes, Garr. He's here at my house. He might be responsible for the missing girls."

She was ready for Footman to blow her off again. To tell her that this time she'd finally gone too far. To seek therapy immediately. She didn't care if he did or not.

"He's there now?"

"Yes."

"Mrs Sanderson, are you sure?"

"Am I sure what? *He's in the house*," she whispered harshly. "He's been coming around for months, and I didn't know. Working with Abel. And he's dating Lynn McNamara, Naomi's cousin."

Footman was quiet. "Cynthia Marsh said he was at her house."

Callie felt struck. "What?"

"We finally got in touch with her — he's been to her house. With your husband. They delivered the furniture together. Your husband and his brother."

The impact of that hit her. "Garr and Lynn bought property. And there's a trailer on it . . ."

"It was Garr and Lynn who searched that area," Footman said.

"Oh my God . . ." The implications stunned her: if they'd been the ones to search that area, they could've lied about what was there. Recovering, she said, "My son is here. Althea Cooper is here. We're not safe."

"Do you know why he's there?"

"No. I mean . . . No."

"Just sit tight. Everything will be fine — help is on the way. The nearest trooper is just ten or eleven minutes away. I was afraid of this. I've been building a case around Garr, but I didn't have enough that was solid to say anything . . ."

She barely registered it. This whole time, Footman had been interested in Garr, not Abel. Or Abel, because of what he knew about Garr, maybe.

"Ten minutes," Footman repeated. "That's all. When police come, act like it's a follow-up to today. Make it about Harper. That he's not pressing charges, something like that."

It might've been a good idea, she just felt panicked. "Okay," she said to Footman.

"Hang in there, Callie. We're coming. Okay? We're coming . . ."

Her hand was shaking so bad she almost dropped the phone. She ended the call and looked around Cormac's room. Everything would be fine? Then why was Garr here?

She searched for a weapon, something to protect herself with. Cormac had a couple of sports trophies. Track. She stood on rubber legs and crossed the room. They were too lightweight, made of plastic.

She kept searching. Garr knew she'd been heading out to the Marsh house with Althea. Maybe he'd stopped by to hear about it.

He could've called.

Well, who knew why he was here, then? But one thing was certain, if she stayed up here avoiding him, then he *would* be alerted.

There was no weapon in here, anyway. There were clothes and old yearbooks and some Lego toys, which Cormac had never let her sell, boxed under the bed. Mac had been a video games kid; there likely wasn't so much as a Swiss army knife around.

Go talk to him. Footman said ten minutes.

Her movements clunky, she left Cormac's bedroom and headed back down the hallway. She told herself to act natural. Subterfuge wasn't her strong suit, though; she'd always been told she wore her heart on her sleeve.

But she had to try.

CHAPTER FIFTY-ONE

Garr could hear the shower. He pointed up. "That the kid?"

Callie nodded, attempting a smile. "Yeah."

Garr frowned. "He on break or something?"

"No. He should be in school. But he's got it in his head that he's going to drop out and start working. He's worried about the hospital bills."

They were in the kitchen. Garr stood where Cormac had stood not long before. Althea sat at the table. The young woman was many things, but she was not a gifted performer. Callie could sense the fear radiating from her. Her face betrayed it. Garr turned to her.

"So you're Althea," he said. He neared the table with his hand out. "Garr Sanderson. Nice to meet you."

She held out her hand like she was afraid of electric shock. *Come on, kid*, Callie thought. *Do better.*

At the same time, she checked the clock on the stove. Two more minutes had passed. In five, the police should be arriving. That was all she had to do — get through five more minutes.

Garr shook Althea's hand, then seemed to regard her for a moment. She gave him a pathetic smile, barely able to make eye contact. He seemed to rear back a little, taking her in. Callie had to make a move.

"I think Althea and I just had the scariest day of our fucking lives."

That got him. He turned to Callie and lifted his thick eyebrows. "Yeah? I saw the busted taillight on the Chevy."

"Well, that was earlier . . ." She blushed just the same.

"Wow, yeah. Right, so tell me all about it." He pulled out the chair opposite Althea and sat down at the table. He wore stained jeans and a flannel shirt. Blond work boots on his feet. Callie could see his hands were dirty, black grime under the nails.

She told him they'd driven there so that Althea could get a look at the place. "I was scared shitless," Callie said. "Especially as Althea was having all kinds of feelings about it. About Abel being chased."

Garr looked at Althea a moment. Callie could tell he wanted to ask her questions. It was on the tip of his tongue: *So what's your deal, anyway?* But he returned his attention to Callie.

She skipped ahead and told him about the cabin, and the snowmobile coming. When she described the time in the outhouse and the key, Garr let out an involuntary laugh and clapped his hands. "Oh my God. Sorry. It sounds terrifying. But you two are badasses! It's like one of your books, Cal! So what did the cops say about Harper?"

"They're investigating."

Garr sort of tipped his head forward and his eyebrows climbed even higher. "Really?"

"Yeah."

"But I mean, there was nothing there, right? In the inner room, or whatever?"

"No. But he has several cabins," she lied. "And he was in the snowsuit. And they said he had a record." The lies kept coming. "In fact, someone is on their way to talk to us a little more, and update us on the investigation into Harper."

Garr tensed. His eyes darted around. "Tonight? Coming here?"

"Yeah." Callie nodded and tried not to look at Althea. The honesty on the girl's face was too much.

Garr rose quickly, catching her off guard. "I'm right in the driveway," he said.

"I'm sure it's all right."

He looked worried. "Well, Lynn is sitting out there."

Another surprise. "Lynn is out there . . . in your car?"

He shrugged. "She's just looking at her phone. She's fine. I wanted to come in and make sure everyone was decent, you know. Didn't want to just barge in on you. But I wanted you to meet her, yeah."

It really threw Callie. She checked the time — her telling the story had eaten up the last few minutes. The cops were going to be here literally any second.

Now it felt like things had shifted. Mostly she still wished Garr gone, but she also wanted this whole thing to be over, resolved. She wanted the police to close in around him. But he was striding toward the door, his boots thumping across the wood floor. "Let me just warn her, anyway," he said. "So that the cops don't just roll up and freak her out."

Callie followed him. Did he mean it? Was he worried? Had he bought her story about why the police were coming? Or was he going to jump in the car and hightail it out of there?

"I talked to Louise Mullins," she blurted.

Garr stopped, his hand on the doorknob. He slowly turned. "Yeah, I know."

"I just, you know . . ."

He looked at her, and his eyes seemed to darken. Her stomach sank. Had she just blown it? She was hoping that curiosity about Mullins — namely, whether the woman had mentioned him or not — would hook him to stay. But instead it seemed to tip him off. She was trying to manipulate him, and now he knew it.

"I'll just go warn Lynn," he said. He opened the door.

Wait! She almost called it out. But why? Better to let the chips fall. If he ran, the cops could find him. He had that rented blue Jeep. His girlfriend's family lived nearby. There was no hiding in the modern age.

Callie went to the door and held it as he let it go and stepped out into the wintry night. She looked across the dark, snowy landscape at the figure in the front seat of the car, which was still idling, headlights on. The lights framed Garr's silhouette as he moved toward the vehicle, his large size, his broad back.

Lynn.

What did she know? How much was she in on it? She'd helped search her own property, possibly to cover up her own boyfriend's tracks . . .

Oh God, Callie thought again. Was this really her life?

And then, in the distance, sirens.

CHAPTER FIFTY-TWO

The sirens were welcome but worrying. It would've been better for the police to approach with stealth. But that was her fault, maybe — she'd called 911.

Callie watched Garr react. He stood with his hand on the car door. Lynn, inside the car, seemed to be peering out at him. He stared off toward the sound. Then he looked into the vehicle. Finally, his head swiveled this way. Across the distance, Callie knew he was looking at her.

Then he started running toward her.

"Oh no," Callie said. She shut the door and locked it. Backing away, she called to Althea.

"Get back upstairs," she said. "Get Cormac — get my son. Lock yourself in the bedroom." Callie glanced over her shoulder to see if she'd been heard. Althea stood at the bottom of the stairs. White as a ghost, she nodded, said, "Okay," and then ran up the steps.

Callie thought she heard the water turn off in the shower. Straining to listen, she jumped when Garr pounded on the door. "Callie! Let me in!"

No way.

She continued to retreat, slowly at first, until she remembered the back door. Turning, she hurried through the kitchen and through a door with a step down to a combination pantry and mudroom. The exterior door was there. She drew the deadbolt across and attached the chain for extra security.

There was a third door; the basement was a walkout. She hurried back into the living room. Beside the front door was a window. A shadow crossed in front. Then the glass exploded inward. Callie shrieked and rounded the corner to the flight of stairs down. She closed the door behind her — pointless, since it didn't lock from the inside — and took the stairs two at a time.

As soon as she landed in the basement, she heard the thumping of Garr's footsteps above her. His weight shook the dust from the floor joists.

She ran to the walkout door, her heart in her throat — it had been locked. But he was already inside the house. Now she unlocked the basement door, her mind clearing: *get outside, get to the police.* Hopefully, Lynn was innocent. Hopefully, she wouldn't cause any trouble out there. She could wait while the cop went inside and dealt with Garr.

But: Cormac. Althea.

They were upstairs. Vulnerable.

"Down here, Garr!" Callie studied Abel's office in the finished corner at the other end of the basement. His desk, those filing towers, and the wooden cabinet where he kept his hunting rifles.

She hurried to it in a breathless rush.

The cabinet was locked and she didn't know the combination. *Damn!* She searched Abel's desk, remembering the password book she'd found yesterday. What had she done with it? Was it upstairs?

"Callie!" Garr's muffled voice.

"Down here! In the basement!" She kept looking. There — it was on the roll-top desk, partly hidden beneath some papers she'd printed out. She grabbed it and flipped through. It was alphabetized — which letter? G for gun cabinet? This time, she was lucky, and got it on the first try.

The police sirens suddenly stopped. Callie wondered what the trooper — or troopers; at night, they usually worked in pairs — would do first. Talk to Lynn, maybe? One of them, while the other approached the house?

Or maybe they'd wait for backup.

"All right, Cal . . ." Garr's words were muffled, but loud enough to understand. "I'm coming . . ."

Despite the lack of heat in the partly finished basement, she was sweating.

The combination: 10-5-35. She dropped the password book, grabbed the padlock, and started dialing in the code.

Garr's footsteps clomped across the floor above her. A moment later, she heard the door creak open. She finished dialing in the numbers and popped the lock. Opening the cabinet doors, something fluttered out and landed on the ground. An envelope with her name on it. It looked like Abel's handwriting. She didn't have time for that now.

Three guns hung vertically: two deer rifles and a shotgun. Abel had taught her how to use one of the rifles; she'd gone hunting with him a couple of times. Both to be with him and to learn how to use the gun.

It was a simple Winchester, lever action. A .30-30. The cartridges were in a box above the hanging rifles.

But Garr was already coming down the stairs. There was no time.

Still, she needed to protect herself. To protect Cormac and Althea. Where were the troopers? Why had the siren stopped? Why weren't they coming in?

Callie grabbed the box of cartridges. It fell from her grip, ammunition spilling. Garr stopped halfway down the stairs — she glanced up and could see just the lower half of him. "Callie? What are you doing?"

She crouched and scrabbled through the loose ammo, grabbed a cartridge and pushed it into the gun. She racked the lever. Now the cartridge was loaded into the chamber. Ready to fire. She stood just as Garr stepped into view.

He looked at her. He looked at the gun. He raised his hands. But he kept walking. "Jesus, Callie, listen . . ."

"Don't come any closer."

"Listen to me," he said, but he stopped. "It really was an accident."

She aimed the rifle at him. Her body shook, but he was close enough that if she fired, she'd hit him.

He winced. His eyes shone with emotion. But his forehead was furrowed, pensive. "The thing with his head. It really was an accident."

"You hurt him."

"Callie. *Listen*. Things got heated that day. There's a lot of things you don't know . . ."

"Why? Why did you hurt him?" Quaking with adrenaline, she managed to keep the gun steady. "Did he catch you doing something?"

Garr's lower jaw started to shiver. His mouth turned so low at the corners, he got that boyish look again. Like something had polarized in him long ago, some trauma had gotten him stuck.

Before he answered, Callie heard a man's voice from upstairs. Maybe outside. Barely discernible. "Garr Sanderson! This is the New York State Police. Come on out of the house with your hands up!"

Some commotion followed — hard to say what. Were multiple cops surrounding the house? Had Footman sent the cavalry?

Staring at her, Garr lowered his hands some, but kept his palms out in a *let's stay calm* gesture. "Callie, I didn't mean for it to happen . . ."

"Did you know Kerry Mullins?"

His mouth hung open like he wasn't sure how to answer. Then, "Yes. I grew up with Stan. He sometimes shacks up with Louise, her mom."

"What did you do to Abel?"

"We had an argument. He's been helping me. Well, we've been helping each other. That's what you do. You try to forgive. He was trying to forgive me. For when we were kids . . ."

"But he found out. He found out what you were doing. And then you hurt him. Right?"

Garr looked up when footfalls crossed above them. Callie thought they'd come from the stairs to the front door. *Cormac?* God, he had to be careful. If there were cops out there with guns . . .

She heard his voice. It was lower than the trooper's, almost inaudible. But a moment later, multiple footsteps came through the house, and Callie guessed what had happened: Cormac had figured out that she and Garr were in the basement and told the police. Now they were coming in.

"What did you do?" Callie yelled at Garr. She was feeling bolder now, knowing that help was here, and her voice gave direction. She took a step toward Garr, keeping the rifle aimed.

"We fought," Garr said. "I told him too much."

"Where are they? What did you do with them?"

Garr seemed not to hear her, lost in memory. "We fought and he fell. He hit his head. Then he got in the truck and left. He left me there — I was on foot. I was in the woods, hiding, when all the police were there. I can't get in trouble, Cal . . . I don't want to go to jail . . ."

"Sanderson!" There was a trooper right at the top of the stairs. Garr was still at the bottom. He looked up that way — the light from the kitchen shone down on his face. And he lifted a hand.

Now he had one palm up toward Callie, one toward the cop upstairs.

"Stay right there," the cop said. "Keep your hands where I can see them. Keep them on the—"

But Garr, slowly raising his hands to his head, stopped doing so, and ran.

He ran toward Callie. She cried out and squeezed the trigger. The sound was deafening in the enclosed space. There was a puff of smoke from the old Winchester. Garr jerked back but kept running past her. He reached the walk-out door and undid the lock.

The state trooper came cautiously down the steps. By the time he reached the bottom and told Callie to drop the weapon, Garr was gone.

Callie set the rifle down. The trooper aimed his weapon at her, but he understood who she was. His radio squawked. A voice said that Garr was outside. He was trying for his car. He was trying to get away.

Callie tensed when she heard a gunshot. Then another and another in quick succession.

On the radio, a cop said, "He's down, he's down. The suspect is down."

Callie slowly sank to her knees.

CHAPTER FIFTY-THREE

Callie watched from the front stoop as the paramedic zipped up the black bag. Garr's face disappeared.

Lynn saw it, too. Callie could tell, from the back of Footman's car, where she'd been sitting for almost an hour. It had all happened so fast, Callie was still processing it. They had just been in the basement. Garr had been opening up to her. Then he'd run.

Footman was next to Callie on the stoop. Thinking of Lynn, her mind settled into the present. She asked Footman, "Do you think she wants to come in for a while?"

"I don't think so."

"What does she know?"

"Not much. She seems to be in the dark about what Garr was doing. She can verify the dates he was here in the area. He's been here quite a lot. But we'll get more in a formal interview."

"Does she know how much he and Abel were together?"

"Not really."

"What about the night of the crash?"

Footman nodded. They both watched as the stretcher with the black bag containing Garr was lifted into the ambulance. The state trooper who'd shot him was also in a vehicle nearby, a trooper car, just visible, talking on the phone. His journey down the road of an officer-involved shooting was just beginning.

Other troopers milled around the driveway. One was in the basement, securing the scene. There would be evidence techs down there soon, reconstructing the events of an hour ago. Callie firing at Garr. She had only grazed his arm.

"She thinks Garr could've been with Abel," Footman said. "The night of the crash. He said he was delivering furniture. She was back in Telluride. She heard from him two days later, when he came back. I've compiled a lot of his movements, though. He was here in the region for each of the girl's disappearances."

Callie gazed across the distance at Lynn in the backseat. Her face was ghostly behind the glass. She might've been looking back. "What does she say about the trailer?"

"Well, there'll be troopers headed there at first light. She says she hasn't been there in months."

"Did she search it when Naomi Bannon went missing?"

"She searched the property. But she didn't go into the trailer. It creeped her out, she says. It was Garr who went in."

Callie lowered her head and closed her eyes. There was too much to take in at once. If anything, there was one over-riding sensation that seemed to transcend all else: she was hungry. Famished, really. Like she hadn't had a proper meal in weeks.

Footman said, "So, accompanying the troopers will be another body retrieval unit. If there's anything there . . ."

He didn't need to finish. There was no chance girls kept in a trailer in the woods in the middle of a North Country winter would still be alive.

"So sad," Callie said. "Two beautiful young women, their lives ahead of them . . ."

"Three," said Footman, holding up fingers. He stepped off the porch, toward the driveway.

"Three?" Callie felt a fresh alarm pulse at the back of her neck.

He nodded woefully. "Could be. A girl was just reported missing yesterday. From Bakerton."

Callie knew roughly where it was — not far from Glass Lake. Sort of between there and Speculator.

"He was down there," Callie said. "Garr was just right in that area." The nausea was returning, wiping out her appetite.

Footman nodded. "That's why I'm not waiting until morning," he said. "I'm going to have her take me out to the trailer right now."

It had to be going on midnight. But yes, he was right to do it. If a girl was just taken, *she* could be alive.

"Good luck," Callie told him. What else was there to say?

Footman nodded at her. "We'll take good care of you. Just keep answering all the questions as best as you can, and I'll be back around to see you."

She raised her hand at him. "I will."

She stayed on the stoop and watched as Footman returned to his car, got in. He maneuvered out of the driveway, then drove off into the night, Lynn McNamara with him.

Callie watched the dark road for a moment, considering that any second now, there might be some intrepid reporters showing up. And wouldn't that be grand.

"Mom?"

She turned. Cormac leaned out of the door. "The officer in here is wondering if she could finish getting your statement."

"Sure, honey. Tell her I'll be right in."

CHAPTER FIFTY-FOUR

The way it had gone down: Garr had run out of the base-ment. He'd tried to return to his vehicle and leave with Lynn. But by then, a second and third trooper car had arrived, each with a pair of officers. Footman had not only alerted his fellow state police, he'd told them Garr Sanderson could be dangerous. He'd put together the timeline that showed Garr in place to abduct the girls. Garr had a record, too — a domestic abuse charge. Not only that, he was wanted in Utah for assault; he'd nearly killed a man in a bar fight weeks before. He had a history of violence with young women, and of domestic battery. When Callie called, it was enough for Footman to act with prejudice. All the cops present had been on high alert.

Garr had gone for his vehicle. The troopers had given several commands for Garr to stop. He didn't; he'd almost reached the vehicle. Judging that the woman inside the car could be in jeopardy, the trooper fired a warning shot. Still, Garr kept going. The two final shots put him down, one having severed his femoral artery. Despite paramedics being close by — they'd been advised to hold in place just a half-mile away in case there was an active shooting — Garr had quickly bled out and died.

Callie gave her statement three times. Once, briefly, to one of the troopers first on scene, then once more to Footman when he arrived. Then at her own kitchen table, hand-written this time. By the time she was done, it was almost two in the morning. Callie set down the pen, flexed her hand and took a drink of water.

"Thank you," the female trooper said. Trooper Washburn was pretty and young. She'd also taken statements from Althea and Cormac. Cormac was up in his room. Althea had been examined by paramedics and released — mild shock and low-level dehydration, but otherwise okay, and neurologically sound. She'd called Casey and updated him, told him everything was okay, but that was it. After that, she'd gone upstairs to rest.

Washburn hung around a while longer, relieving the trooper in the basement. She would secure the scene until morning, when techs would arrive to take pictures and dust everything. Callie understood police procedure, but it did seem a little pointless when Garr was dead, and determining blood spatter and ballistics from the Winchester wouldn't help any missing girls. But it was the way.

Mostly, she thought about Abel, and what he knew about Garr, and what he hadn't said to her — and then she remembered the envelope in the basement.

"I'm sorry," Washburn said. "Really need to keep everything exactly as it is down there. Not for much longer."

Callie pressed the issue. "There could be helpful information in there."

Washburn set her jaw.

"My husband's brother might've confessed to him. There could be other details. Things you need to know."

Washburn's jaw relaxed. "Okay," she said. "I'll call my supervisor. Maybe I can get a look at it."

"Good," Callie said.

In the meantime, she made a couple of sandwiches — she only had peanut butter and jelly on rye, but God, it sounded good. She took them upstairs to her bedroom.

Althea was still awake, lying on Callie's bed. Callie sat beside her. "How you doing?"

"I'm okay." She seemed to wake up a little and see Callie anew.

"Here," Callie said. "That spaghetti was a long time ago."

Althea took a plate and a bite of the sandwich. They chewed in silence.

"I feel wide awake," Callie said, after swallowing some sticky peanut butter. "But that's probably the adrenaline."

"You'll crash soon."

"Yeah."

They ate a little more.

"What a night," Althea said.

"What a night."

Finished eating, Callie decided to stretch out. She did so beside Althea. "This okay?"

"Yeah, totally."

They both stared up at the ceiling. It did seem to take a while for the crash, but when it came, Callie welcomed it.

Unconsciousness is such a funny thing, she thought.

And then she slept.

CHAPTER FIFTY-FIVE

WEDNESDAY, FEBRUARY 29

Footman called in the morning. Callie felt like she'd been hit by a truck, she was so tired. But his words cut through the fog. "No girls at the trailer."

She sat up straighter, listening.

"We had fifty searchers by nine this morning. Checking for any buried bodies, signs of anything." He sighed, sounding exhausted. "There's nothing."

"Were they ever there?"

A pause. "I don't know."

"What's Lynn saying?"

There was noise in the background, people talking. Footman was distracted. "Sorry — looks like I gotta go."

"Did you find something?"

"An ATV just got stuck crossing a creek. Lots of little creeks out here threading through. The snowpack is thick. It's been tough going."

"There was an envelope in the basement addressed to me. It could be what Garr told him. It could be the location of the victims. I asked—"

"It's not. I talked to Washburn a couple of hours ago, at her shift change. She told me about it. There's nothing in there about the location of the victims."

It was a letdown. "Okay."

"It's for you," Footman said cryptically. "It's dated. From a month before the crash. But I'm not going to sum it up; it's best you read it. I'll get it to you soon."

"Okay."

They didn't speak for a couple of seconds — just the background voices, men calling to each other. Then Footman said, "Gotta go."

"All right." For some reason Callie added, "Thank you."

She hung up, feeling empty. Perched on the edge of the bed, she thought about the letter for a moment. What had Abel written to her? If it was unrelated to the case, then what?

She tried to relax, watching the trees outside sway in a gentle wind. Birch and maple, pine and spruce. The master bedroom overlooked the woods behind the house. The steep bank down to the burbling creek. The sun was out fully; it was late morning. If it were any other day, she might take a walk down there, between the creek and cairns of giant boulders.

Her thoughts swung to the missing girls.

Where are you?

"They didn't find anything?"

Callie startled. For a minute, she'd forgotten Althea was in the room with her. The young woman was still on her back, her hands folded over her chest. Almost like a corpse. Her gaze fell on Callie as she waited for an answer.

"No. Not so far."

Althea went back to studying the ceiling. Callie could see the pulse working in her neck.

Last night felt almost like a dream. Callie could still feel the shape of the rifle in her hand, the kick as she fired at Garr. The guilt had been all over his face. A kind of volatility coming off him in waves. Like he might do anything to escape. Or to prolong the inevitable.

What did you do with those girls?

262

He'd been busy here, flying beneath the radar. Her radar, at least. But Cynthia Marsh had seen him. And he knew the Mullins girl, and Naomi Bannon. Bakerton wasn't far from Glass Lake — for all Callie knew, this new girl was friends with Naomi. Perhaps they went to school together.

She pictured Garr hanging out at a high school, watching the girls. Then she pulled out her phone and searched for information. Several papers had picked up the story.

The latest missing girl was named Alyssa Kitsch. Sixteen years old. She was pretty, like they all were. An impressive volume of wavy hair, red lips, sparkling eyes full of life. She resembled the other two in a general way, but more than that, she resembled Althea, really. That same kind of natural beauty, no makeup required; she would age well. Garr wasn't just kidnapping anyone; he had an eye for talent.

Callie shuddered. Those poor girls. What they'd had to go through, their families. Kerry Mullins was six months ago. Callie hated to think it, but she didn't expect Mullins was still alive. Or Naomi Bannon, taken just after Christmas. But there was a chance with Alyssa Kitsch. Wasn't there? Garr had been disrupted in the middle of things . . .

"What's up?" Althea was watching Callie pace.

But Callie didn't answer. She was thinking more and more about a girl stashed away somewhere that only Garr had known. With him gone, her life could be hanging in the balance. She might be somewhere without food and water. With no one coming, she could have only days to live. Maybe less.

It was just speculation. Callie really had no idea why Garr had run or what he might've done to any of the girls. They could all be alive; they could all be dead. But still. What if . . .

"Did Detective Footman mention if Lynn said anything?" Althea asked.

"He didn't. That's what I wanted to know."

"Yeah."

"Lynn was with detectives all night. Sacony, Footman's BCI partner." Callie thought about calling Sacony directly.

But that was probably unnecessary. The police would eventually let her know what she needed to.

When Callie turned back to Althea, the young woman was squinting again, touching her forehead.

"You okay? Can I get you something?"

Althea was quiet a moment longer, seeming deep in thought. "No, I'm fine."

"Just let me know." Callie turned back toward the window. Last night kept returning to her in pieces.

We fought.

Those had been Garr's words, sounding somewhat remorseful. Talking about what precipitated the confrontation with his brother. The one that led to Abel swerving into a frozen lake.

I told him too much.

The memory resonated. Just because the letter didn't contain any specifics — and it was from a month before the crash — didn't mean Garr hadn't told Abel important things. Like the victims' locations. It would've been the night they delivered the hutch to Cynthia Marsh. At some point, Garr had unburdened himself. He'd regretted it too late. Then he'd hurt Abel, trying to stop him from leaving, maybe trying to kill him for what he now knew.

Callie felt her skin break out in goosebumps. She stood, paced over to the window, then turned and stared at Althea. It just felt right. She could picture it. Imagine it, almost like it had happened to her and she was remembering.

Althea sat up on the bed. The way she looked at Callie, it was as if she intuited what Callie was feeling. Experiencing.

This *knowing*.

"*I told him too much*," Callie recited.

Althea's eyes shone with understanding. "Garr said that?"

"If he'd told Abel what he'd done — what if he told him everything? What if he told him where he took them?"

The women watched each other. The more she considered it, the more it made sense. Garr had said something, at any rate, that was so bad Abel tried to get away, and Garr tried to stop him. That much was clear. And if it *was* in fact the details of the kidnappings, then Abel could be lying in a hospital bed right now with that information locked in his brain.

The way Althea looked back at Callie, it was like she was thinking the same thing.

You make your decision in an instant . . .

Maybe she'd known what she was going to do from the moment she'd gotten off the phone with Footman. Now she was just coming to terms with it.

I think I have to get close to the person.

Althea had said it about Marsh. That coming into contact with him had been the catalyst for everything.

I have to be near them. And then something . . . transfers to me.

There was skepticism in Althea's eyes, yes. Doubt. Callie saw that. But it was okay.

They both knew exactly where they were going next.

CHAPTER FIFTY-SIX

Three news vans crowded the road at the end of the driveway. A reporter in a long black winter coat, golden curls flowing, spoke to the camera. When Cormac drove through, Callie riding shotgun and Althea in back, the cameraman lifted his camera off the tripod and tracked their movements.

As they headed down the road, Callie watched the mirrors: two of the vans, plus another vehicle, pulled out and followed. Cormac reached the first stop sign and made a left turn.

"Easy, not too fast," Callie warned. But they zipped through the small downtown area of Hawkins. It was midday, mid-week, not much going on under an overcast sky. Which was good. Cormac handled the driving like a pro, and by the time they'd left the town limits, Callie didn't think anyone was still following.

Still, she checked the mirrors again when Cormac parked near the front of the ferry. Just two vehicles separated them from the prow of the boat as it cut through the chunks of ice; most of the cars were behind them.

"You see anything?" Cormac asked. She hadn't wanted to bring him, but she hadn't wanted to lie, either. *Oh, I'm just taking Althea to see Dad for the heck of it.* Nor did she want to leave him alone after so much had happened. He did seem to be taking it in stride, but still. He was nineteen.

"I'm not sure." She kept watching as the ferry went up over the swells of Lake Champlain. She thought she saw a figure moving between the cars. A winter hat pulled low, a thick red parka. Coming her way.

"Okay. Yup. Here we go," she said.

The figure reached the Chevy and stopped at Callie's window. He was young, maybe not that much older than Cormac. Clean-cut, somewhat baby-faced. He smiled and gave a little wave.

"Just ignore him," Cormac suggested.

"It's okay. Let me get the window down."

"You sure?"

"Yeah."

Cormac turned the key so she could roll down the window. The young man's breath plumed out. He rubbed his gloved hands together. "Hi, sorry to bother you. But you're Callie Sanderson, correct?"

"Yes, I am."

He glanced around the vehicle quickly, then his eyes came back to her. "I'm Mason Hubbard with Spike TV News." He stuck his hand into the cab for her.

She gave it a quick shake. So he wasn't local. At least, it didn't sound like it.

"I've been following your story since January, after your husband's accident. Please let me offer my heartfelt sympathy. I understand he's at Pearl Medical Center — are you going to see him? And is this his son? And who are you? Hi, Mason Hubbard . . ." He reached his hand back toward Althea.

Callie interrupted. "Thanks, Mr Hubbard — we really need our privacy right now."

"Oh. Sure, yeah. Here, let me leave you my card. Whenever you want to talk about your story, I'd love to hear it."

"Thank you." She took the card and rolled the window back up.

* * *

More media swarmed outside the hospital. Nurse Brie let Callie in, but she didn't seem happy about it. Callie thanked her profusely, then shut the door.

She entered the room with Cormac and Althea. Cormac went right to his father — he'd gotten used to it by now. He put his head on his dad's chest and murmured some silent words. Althea was much more timid. Callie realized it was the first time she was seeing someone in the flesh she may have only seen on a screen. Or in her own dreams. *He won't bite* came to Callie's mind, but she withheld the words.

After Cormac moved away, Althea got close enough to touch Abel. Instantly, she jerked her hand back as if she'd received a mild shock. Then she touched him again, just a light grip on his wrist, almost as if she were taking his pulse.

Her eyes closed. Her pursed mouth opened slightly, and a soft breath escaped her.

Callie went to the window and looked out. Two news vans in view. One cameraman setting up a shot. As she peered out the window, a reporter saw her and pointed. The camera then aimed her way. Callie closed the curtain and retreated from the window.

Althea was in the same spot. Her eyes moved beneath their lids. Back and forth, like she was in REM sleep.

Callie saw her skepticism reflected back in her son's blue eyes. What in the hell were they doing?

The words of Louise Mullins leapt to mind: *I was willing to try anything. I thought if I saw words in my alphabet soup, I'd follow the signs.*

Hallelujah, sister.

Althea's eyes fluttered open. She looked at Callie, and Callie waited, but the young woman shook her head, as if disappointed. "I just . . . I don't feel anything. Or see anything. Except all the same memories."

Callie exhaled.

There were things about Althea that discredited her as a clairvoyant; she'd been to see Marsh as a potential patient, for one thing. But that didn't explain how she'd known about

Kerry Mullins. There were just too many coincidences to write her off completely.

There was something there. Even if it wasn't ESP, Althea knew something. She just needed to come out with it.

Callie moved near. "Maybe it just happens so subtly that you don't notice? Or maybe it will come to you later?"

Althea didn't answer.

Callie said, "You might need to be closer to him."

She stayed silent so long Callie wasn't sure she'd heard. But then the young woman removed her snowy winter parka and pulled off her boots.

Callie avoided Cormac's gaze as Althea Cooper climbed into bed with his father. It was absurd, it was weird. But it also made some kind of sense. Given everything that'd happened in the past few days . . . yeah, it felt exactly right.

Abel, covered in the fleece blanket, had a clairvoyant woman lying next to him, snow still melting in her hair. Callie couldn't wait to tell him someday.

Althea curled into a fetal position beside his supine body and lay one tentative hand across his chest. Abel liked to sleep on his back, and Callie had spent many nights in a similar arrangement. The sight of it choked her up and she bit back the tears.

"No," Althea murmured. Her eyes were closed, but she said, "Let yourself feel everything."

And so, Callie did. She reached for Cormac, who moved next to her, and she put her arm around him. Not sobbing, the tears still slipped down her cheeks. She brushed them away, and waited.

And then it happened.

CHAPTER FIFTY-SEVEN

Footman met them back at Callie's home. He was accompanied by several state troopers. They didn't need many — Callie's property wasn't that big. Just ten acres. And Althea had been pretty sure where they needed to start looking.

"For your own safety," Footman said to Althea, "we're going to take you into custody, okay? Trooper Bennett here will take good care of you."

Once more, Althea sat in the back of a state police car. Callie was starting to think there was a natural look to it.

Her head was spinning. Althea's revelation back at the hospital had been stunning. And it was as if a certain kind of rationalization of the whole thing was trying to get into her thoughts, but she was blocking it out.

She'd *seen* Althea with Abel. The young woman had lain beside him and not moved for twenty-five minutes. Then her eyes had opened, she'd moved to the corner chair, and finally, after an eternity of silence, had spoken.

I know where they are.

"I hope to God this is it," Footman said to Callie as they walked down the switchback trail. He wore his long black coat, but instead of the usual dress shoes, he had on deep boots. And black gloves.

Where? Callie had asked.

And Althea had slowly lifted her face, and her eyes were glassy and pained. She looked deeply wounded, as if she'd seen more than she ought to have seen.

They're in the rocks.

They'd been clearer to her than ever before, she'd said. In a deep, dark place. But not a cabin. Rather, in the cave formed by two particularly large boulders on Callie's own property.

Callie felt some nerves — it was her property, after all, hers and Abel's — but this was obviously Garr's doing. Cormac had seen him here at the house. God, Cormac might've even caught him after Garr had brought Naomi Bannon here.

The thought was just too terrible.

But it tempered by another. A persistent doubt, one that threaded through everything that had happened since Althea's first phone call.

The first state trooper found a body. The victim was wrapped in cellophane, or something like it, but still nevertheless badly decomposed. And it was alone, no other victims in proximity.

The troopers worked the area, checking every nook and cranny between every rock and boulder.

After twenty minutes, the searchers recovered two more bodies. It would take a pathologist to formally determine identities, but no one doubted it was Kerry Mullins and Alyssa Kitsch, with the first being Naomi Bannon.

Callie was arrested. Cormac, who was a legal adult, was also arrested. Their home soon crawled with more emergency personnel and evidence technicians than Callie had ever seen in one place. The evening was a blur, and became night. Callie was questioned for hours.

She answered everything and cooperated, understanding it was all a formality.

She hadn't done anything to those girls, and neither had Abel. He couldn't have — not Alyssa, anyway; he was in a coma.

It had to be Garr.

But Callie's question persisted: aside from magic, how could Althea have known?

CHAPTER FIFTY-EIGHT

At the state police barracks in Ray Brook, it was late, nearly two in the morning.

Footman sat across from Callie at a table in the otherwise empty cafeteria. Each had a cup of coffee.

The anticipation was getting to be too much to take. It crawled along her skin like tight packs of termites.

"I was wrong," Footman said.

"About?"

"About your brother-in-law. Garr."

Footman just looked at her. He seemed to be paying this out in small bits. Like it would overwhelm her to hear all at once. Maybe explode her head. She could take it. If there was one thing that was clear from the past several days, she was stronger than she ever would've given herself credit for.

"What about him?"

"Well," Footman said, and shifted his weight. "Garr had issues. No question. Anger management problems, trouble with the law, and he definitely made some irresponsible choices. With women in particular." Footman swallowed some coffee. "But he's not a killer."

"He's *not?*"

She tried on the idea. Things had seemed to fall into place near the end which placed Garr in the role. But she'd had a hard time reconciling it with her feeling for him. He'd seemed genuine about his brother. His remorse. His earnestness. She'd swept all of that aside and assumed it was him, because Footman had talked about building a case.

Footman shook his head. "We can put him in place around the time of the abductions, but we can put someone else there, too."

She was confused. And felt a spike of fear.

"Not Abel," Footman said, picking up on her thoughts. And then he was quiet, seeming to wait for her to put it together.

She thought it through some more. There was only one other person that fit the bill. And the more she considered it, the more sense it made.

"Casey?"

Footman pursed his lips and slowly sat back. Then he nodded.

"Casey Cooper," she repeated. "Althea's brother."

Footman took a sip of his coffee, then nodded again. "He confessed. To everything."

"How. What did he . . . ?"

She needed a moment to process. The thoughts kept bubbling up. She recalled the almost piercingly friendly expression he'd given her at the market.

She went back to those early phone calls with Althea — worrying that Althea was under duress, maybe threatened by someone in the background. And the way she seemed to have no life but to follow her brother around. How they'd been foster kids together, moving from house to house.

And how Red's Market, of which Casey was co-owner, was in Speculator, near the center of the region where all these missing girls lived. A place that thousands passed through each week . . .

His demeanor there, while surely meant to put her at ease, had actually made her a bit uncomfortable. And then there was the odd way he'd cleaned up Althea's spilled coffee, like he was her caregiver.

But why would he have let Althea go off with Callie? Why let his sister call people and give them these pieces of information?

"He's methodical and patient, first of all," Footman said. "He waited months after first noticing Kerry Mullins before making a move. He first saw her at Red's Market on her way to visit a college downstate."

"Why did he confess?" She felt like she was trying to catch up.

"Well, because of Althea. That's the big thing, I think. It was late last night, and she really came out with a lot of stuff. She talked for hours."

Callie closed her eyes a moment. "But he knew she was doing this. It doesn't make sense . . ."

"The other reason he confessed is because of Tim Watkins."

She opened her eyes. "The private investigator? The one the Bannons hired?"

"According to Watkins, Naomi had been to Red's Market before, too. But it's a very popular spot, so we weren't looking too hard at it. Watkins, though, has only one case at a time to deal with. He looked a little harder."

"He asked Louise Mullins about it," Callie remembered. "About Kerry looking at colleges downstate."

"That's right."

"Why was Watkins coming around my house? Was that him?"

"Yeah, it was. Watkins has some friends in the department and found out that Garr and Abel were persons of interest. So he started with them. And since Garr wasn't around, and your husband was in the coma, it was just you. He checked you out, followed you around a few times."

"He was on the property. Did he guess that the . . ." She had a hard time saying it. "That the girls might be there? The bodies?"

"Well, we're still getting ahead of things . . ."

But she had so many questions. "So was Nathan Marsh Althea's doctor?"

Footman shook his head. "No. She does this sort of doctor-shopping. She doesn't have a neurological problem. She's a malingerer."

Callie knew the word; it meant someone who made up medical problems.

"Marsh probably knew there was nothing wrong with her and sent her on her way. When Casey needed a distraction — when Watkins was getting too close, staking out Red's Market, watching him — Althea threw the suspicion on Marsh to protect her brother."

Callie felt leveled. She hadn't ever fully bought the psychic thing, but she'd been taken in by Althea. "She seemed so determined something was there, on the property. The Harper property."

"She didn't know everything about Casey, about what he was doing. I believe Althea wanted her brother caught, but she has a complicated relationship with him. So she used this 'clairvoyant' thing. Which works with her malingering, in a weird way."

"I mean . . ."

Footman nodded, like he knew what Callie was wondering without her having to ask. "To be honest, I can't be exactly sure about her. But she's holding to it, that she's psychic. Whether that's because she's convinced herself, or her brother has, or both . . . She talked about visions and alternative memories during her childhood. I told her, you know, when she was filling out her statement, go ahead and write about it. And she did." Footman mulled it all over a moment. "If it's an act, she's gifted."

Callie had thought similarly more than once.

Footman said, "Anyway, whether it's a delusion, a way of coping, or whether she's just trying to protect herself . . . that's for a psychiatrist to evaluate at this point."

Callie could imagine Althea drawing attention to pain she couldn't show the world directly.

"But how does any of it involve Garr and Abel?"

"Here," Footman said. "I want to show you something . . ."

He brought out his phone, tapped a few items on the screen, then looked around, as if to see the cafeteria was clear. He handed it to her.

"I'll let Casey explain," he said.

CHAPTER FIFTY-NINE

The camera angled down on Casey Cooper from the corner of an interview room. Footman's back was visible, the silver sides of his hair. Cooper looked relaxed, typically friendly and alert. The same man she'd met at Red's Market, despite the drastically different situation.

Footman said, "So, Casey. We have pictures of you leaving Red's the other night, following Alyssa Kitsch back to Bakerton. A private investigator has been watching you for weeks and turned everything over to us. Is that how you usually did it? Just follow the girls from the store?"

"I'm sorry — I'm happy to cooperate, but I don't know what you're asking," Casey said.

"We have all the bodies. All the evidence. And we have a log of your activity for weeks, thanks to the private investigator. We know everything you did, Casey. Now the question is, how bad and hard do you want things to fall on Althea?"

That got him, Callie saw. Even on the small screen of Footman's phone, the low-quality video of the interview room camera, she could see it in his posture, his body language.

Footman drove the point home. "There is no question that you're going to prison for the kidnapping and murder of these three young women. The only variable left is her. Your sister. Your story will let me know how to proceed with her, do you understand?"

Casey finally answered. "Yes."

"Let's start with Kerry Mullins. After first seeing her at the market, then what?"

"I used her debit card information to track her to Shelter Falls." He said it with the same cordial tone of voice she remembered from the store. *You sure I can't get you anything for the road?*

"Okay," Footman said. "You found out where she lived, and you went up there. Pretty far away, huh?"

"About three hours. I almost scrapped it. But she was . . . she liked to stay in this little bunkhouse out back. She drank and she smoked. She was unsupervised."

"That's kind of nice, right?"

For the first time, Casey switched. The happy-salesman facade seemed to drop. "I know what you're doing. The whole 'take the morality out of it' routine."

"Morality doesn't factor into it," Footman said. "We're adducing facts. You liked that she drank and smoked and was unsupervised. And how she looked. Are those facts we can agree on?"

"Sure."

"Okay. Then what happened?"

"The day I was going to introduce myself, some guy came around who seemed to know the family. He knew the man who sometimes stayed there, Stan, and the mother, Louise."

Callie felt an invisible hand take her heart. She knew who Casey was talking about.

"You're referring to Garr Sanderson," Footman said on the recording.

"Yes. But I didn't know that yet. When I came back two days later, there was another guy with him. They were doing construction, building a deck."

Gooseflesh on her arms and neck; now he was referring to Abel. To hear her husband described by this man was surreal and unsettling.

"So I used it."

"It gave you a way in," Footman clarified. "A jumping-off point with Kerry Mullins."

"Right. I think that's one way to put it." Casey sounded chipper again.

"When you approached Kerry Mullins that August evening, you told her you were looking for your buddies."

"Exactly. I'd looked them up by then. Two brothers."

"She might've known otherwise, might've suspected you were full of shit, but it worked. Because she went with you."

"Yes."

Callie took a deep breath, let it out. Footman had Casey explain what happened from there, and he did.

After he was finished with the Mullins girl, a couple of months had passed. Casey was watching Garr Sanderson online, ogling his young girlfriend, Lynn. And Lynn's cousin, named Naomi. Who was even younger, and more perfect.

Looking up from the phone, Footman said, "Something I learned about Casey just recently — he had a pattern of this in foster care. He'd be with some new family, and he'd start to mimic the behavior of one of the kids living there. He'd dress like them, try to take their friends, things of that nature. So he was studying Garr and Lynn McNamara, and found out she had property in the Glass Lake area. They liked to show it off on social media, and Naomi liked to ski, so Casey figured out his next move."

By the time Abel Sanderson got the furniture job with Cynthia Marsh, Casey had captured Naomi. He'd pretended to be a skier himself, lost — could she give him a hand? She'd been a little more challenging than Kerry Mullins, but still doable.

Then Footman asked about Althea.

"I told her," Casey said.

"What does that mean? Everything?"

He shrugged. "I told her that I'd found some people. A couple of brothers. And I was having fun with their lives. And the people they encountered."

He thought she'd understand it — they were twins, after all, and they'd been through a lot together.

But she hadn't understood. Not quite.

And so she'd tried to work against him without directly *going* against him.

Casey said, "Thea called the Mullins woman and gave her hints about where to find her daughter. That was on her own. She just made that up. I was suspicious, and I made her tell me. They weren't even very good hints, if you asked me. Not in a place like the Adirondacks, which is all deep woods and dark places. So I didn't worry about it too much. If anything, it added nicely to the drama."

He was right. The cops had searched and found nothing.

Casey had by then decided to use Abel's ten-acre property to dispose of the remains. To hide the victims in the caves formed by the glacial boulders.

But then the Bannons had hired that damn private investigator, Watkins. And Watkins started coming around Red's Market before long.

"That's when I started to worry a little bit. Because I saw him. He was there a couple of times in that gray car. But I was still getting past him, getting around without him following."

The next time he followed Abel and Garr, the brothers had been offloading some furniture at the Marsh place. Which was outstanding, because Casey thought he recognized the name.

It was the one true coincidence of the whole thing. A doctor who'd briefly seen Althea owned a second home in the North Country.

After delivering the hutch, Abel and Garr had had a confrontation. Casey said, "I was out on the main road. I saw them turn in the driveway, both of them, furniture in the back of the truck. But only one drove out. The other guy came out on foot ten minutes later. After that, there were sirens. I didn't know what was going on. I bolted."

The next day, it was in the paper. Abel had suffered a terrible auto wreck. And Garr was conspicuously silent. In the news, on social media, everywhere. He disappeared back to Telluride.

For Casey, it was a situation ripe for exploitation.

He encouraged Althea to keep doing what she'd been doing. But this time, he'd control the narrative. "I said, 'Call the Sanderson woman. Put her on Marsh's scent.' I figured it would sic the state police on Marsh too. Or even Abel — you might think he was guilty after all. Or the brother! It didn't matter. It was the perfect swirling of chaos," he said. "It would throw everybody off."

He laughed, then he sobered.

"When Althea told me the Sanderson woman wanted to meet, I thought, okay. You can even go up there. Check out the Marsh place with her. I kind of played it like I could've left one of the bodies there. She didn't really know which end was up, Thea. I messed with her head pretty good."

"Did you ever tell her the actual location of the victims?" Footman asked.

Casey smiled a little, and nodded. "I did. After the whole Marsh place fiasco."

"After I talked to you on the phone?"

"Yeah. When I spoke to her next, I told her. She wasn't very happy with me." He looked off into a corner for a moment, seeming mildly amused. "I don't really know why I told her, I just . . . She's clever, my sister, I'll tell you that. Everyone thought it was Garr Sanderson, and that he must've told his brother the location of the bodies, and she used that. To go get it from him, you know, psychically. She wanted to help those girls, she wanted to stop me, but right to the end, she wanted to protect me, too. That's love."

CHAPTER SIXTY

Callie slowly came out of the shock of the video. While watching, Footman had refreshed their coffees. Neither of them was drinking any, though. "When did Casey bring the victims to my place? When did he bring Kerry Mullins there?"

"Pretty soon after he fixed on her," Footman said. "The deck took your husband and Garr three days to complete. At the end of that, Casey abducted Mullins. By then, he'd scoped out your house and decided that's where he would stash her when he was done."

"God." Callie would have cried, but there was nothing left. "It's horrible."

"It is."

The worst thought of all: had her actions led to Garr's death? Callie thought she was going to be sick.

Footman seemed to intuit what she was feeling. "Hey, I got something else." He rose from the table. He'd taken off his suit jacket and draped it on a nearby chair; now he pulled an evidence bag from the inner breast pocket.

And then, out of the bag, an envelope.

Callie's name was on it. In Abel's handwriting.

"Go ahead," Footman said.

Eager for relief, she hastily opened it and read.

Callie,

My brother Garr started coming around early this summer. He doesn't have the best way with words, but I can tell he's sorry for the things in our past. Sorry for what happened between him and me, even stuff that has to do with Leila, our sister. And he's in some trouble. I'm not sure what, exactly. But he's contrite, and really seems like he wants to start over. So, I'm going to help him.

But it's a tough subject. And I don't know how to tell you. We've got so much going on. You're in a new book, Mac is going to school — I want our lives to be as stress-free as possible. So I'm not telling you. Not right now. I'm just writing it down, haha. It feels less bad this way. It feels like I'm talking to you.

And I will. Soon.

Maybe I'm just writing this because, you know, in case. By the way, that reminds me — we don't have a will or anything. We probably should. What if something happens? We need to decide about DNRs and all of that.

Someday, maybe.

Anyway, I'm going to stick this away for now.

You'll never see it, hopefully. But if for some reason you do, know that I love you. No matter what happens, the bumps we have along the way, I'm yours forever.

I love you, baby.

Abel

The tears she'd thought were gone came flooding back. She brushed them away and folded up the envelope.

Even Footman's eyes were shining. "Keep it," he said, crumpling up the evidence bag. "I've got my copy." And he smiled.

She laughed and, for a moment, felt lighter.

Footman said, "Garr was in all kinds of trouble, like I said. He and Lynn McNamara financed that property with money he'd embezzled from two different companies. And he confided that in your husband, and your husband wasn't pleased. They fought. And Abel fell and hit his head."

She blew out air, steadying herself. "How do you know all this?"

"Lynn McNamara has cut a deal. So what I'm saying all comes from her." Footman shook his head, as if in disbelief. "It just happened to take place out there, in Lake Clear. If it hadn't — if your husband and his brother had fought somewhere else, if Abel had crashed somewhere else — we might never have found those girls."

"Well, Althea seemed pretty intent on getting the message across."

"She did — she was — but she had basically tried. And we'd failed."

Footman leaned back from the table. He rubbed his face. When his phone rang, he checked the number, then excused himself. "Sorry, just need to take this."

Callie sat there, processing it all. Her mind drifted. For a moment, she eavesdropped on Footman, who was standing a few feet away. Callie could hear a man's voice on the other end.

Footman said, "All right, I'll be home when I can," and ended the call. He sat back down.

Callie said, "Well, it's late. We should get some sleep."

He grimaced and shook his head. "Too much paperwork. I'll be here all night." His gaze found her. "You should go, though. Take your son and go home."

"Yeah."

She stood up. Footman, a bit wearily, got to his feet as well. Callie stuck out her hand. "Thank you, Mr Footman."

"Mike," he said, shaking her hand.

She felt herself smile. "Okay. Callie."

His eyes were kind. "Thank you, Callie," he said.

CHAPTER SIXTY-ONE

On March 29, ten weeks after he'd slipped into a coma, Abel Sanderson woke up.

He had lost a total of twenty-seven pounds. It took another three weeks in the hospital before he regained the ability to walk.

Words were slow to come. He didn't seem to have any cognitive impairment but often complained of headaches and mental fog. But by late that April, on a balmy day just reaching the seventies, birdsong in the trees, Cormac turned into the driveway of their home, his mother and father sitting together in the back of the car.

Cameras tracked their progress. Reporters called out. Callie didn't feel the same disdain; because of all the media coverage, support had poured in from all over the region — all over the world, really, with people as far away as Singapore donating to the GoFundMe page for Abel's hospital bills and recovery.

The bill had reached over three hundred thousand dollars. Garr was dead, Lynn was broke, and Casey Cooper was in prison, so there really wasn't anyone to sue for damages. If it hadn't been for all the support, Callie would have sold the house. Which would have been fine; they could have started over. But this way, they had options.

"The first thing we're going to do is completely remodel," Abel said as he hobbled toward the house. He still required either a cane or help from someone. In this case, Callie and Cormac flanked him, his arms over their shoulders.

"Honey," Callie said. "Let's not overdo it."

But he was only responding to what she'd told him — that, as much as they loved their home, it had become tainted by Callie's time alone there, and the terrible events of that night two months before.

Garr was gone, and Abel had mourned him in his own way. Mostly, Abel felt he had a new lease on life. He didn't remember much of the accident or the events leading up to it. Not at first. But over the next few days, the reporters stopped coming, and Abel began to share what he could remember about his brother, and the moments leading up to the crash.

After delivering the furniture to the Marsh home, Garr had gotten suddenly emotional. He'd unloaded all his misdeeds, all of his guilt. He'd taken money from two different guiding companies where he'd worked in Colorado. He'd used some to pay fines to avoid jail for an assault charge, and the rest he'd given to Lynn.

"I don't remember exactly what I said," Abel told Callie. "But I told him he needed to get help. For his anger. And that he should turn himself in about the money. It wasn't what he wanted to hear. We were leaving the Marshes', driving down that long road, and he said, 'Let me out.' I did. And I should have left it there. Should've left *him* there. I should've come straight home to you. If I had done that, none of this would've happened. You wouldn't have had to go through any of this."

Sitting beside him on their bed, Callie rubbed his back. "Shhh, it's all right."

"But I didn't. I got out of the truck. I always think I can fix things. Take care of everything. So I went around to him and he just hit me. I mean, just out of nowhere. He yelled at me: 'Get away from me, Abel,' and I didn't. It happened fast — he hit me, and I hit the truck. Bam. Bashed my head against the side of it. Or the ground, I don't know. And that was it. He walked off up the road. I recovered, got in the driver's seat, and left. Almost ran him over. I just drove, got to the end of the road, and kept driving. I figured I'd never see him again." Abel took a slow deep breath. "And there were some snowmobilers out, I remember that. Buzzing along in the background. And one zipped across the road, and I pumped the brakes. And the back end slid out. I tried to correct for it, but it only got worse, and I went right off the road, I guess. That's it. That's all I knew until I saw your face."

Callie remembered the moment he'd awakened. She'd been skeptical at first, thinking it was something that could happen — an involuntary opening of the eyes — but his gaze had fixed on her, and he'd smiled a dry-lipped smile. And he'd murmured, "Hey."

It had turned into the best day of her life.

Now, she brought him downstairs and made him something to eat. He needed to put that weight back on. They talked about Cormac, who had finally returned to school the morning before. And they talked more about renovating, but her heart wasn't in it. Neither was his. After all that had happened, those poor girls, they were going to have to let this place go. They were just getting comfortable with a decision they'd already made.

You make your choice in an instant.

It would be tough — there were good memories here, too. The bulk of their lives as a family. The cat, Meister, and their beloved Breezy had lived and died here.

But there were too many bad memories now, hunkered in the shadows.

* * *

It was midday the next day when Callie's phone rang. Had she dozed off? She was on the couch. Abel was in his recliner, the one he never used to sit in before, with the TV on. He was dozing, too. They'd had a big lunch of roast chicken with a side of mac and cheese. It was from a box — she was still getting her groove back in the kitchen.

The incoming number on the phone said UNLISTED. "Hello?"

An automated voice told her an inmate from the Cold Brook women's prison was calling — would she accept the charges?

Callie briefly hesitated. "Yes."

A moment later, after a few clicks on the line, a familiar voice: "Hi, Callie."

"Althea . . . how are you doing?"

"I'm okay." The young woman sounded the same. Intelligent but cautious, full of doubt about the world in general. "How are you?"

Callie left the living room, so as not to disturb Abel. "I'm good. What can I do for you, Althea?"

"I heard he woke up."

"Yes, he did." Callie debated whether to say more. "It's amazing. It's great."

"Yeah, I mean, that's incredible. It's wonderful. I'm happy for you."

There was a lull, just the clicking of the line as the call was recorded.

Callie began, "So, is everything . . . ?"

"I just wanted to explain. I mean, at least a little. I can't explain everything. Not perfectly."

Callie was skeptical, but compassionate. Clairvoyant or not, she'd eventually given up her brother by directing Callie and the police to the actual locations of the victims. She'd played a significant role in events that led to Callie being here, being safe, with Abel again.

"I just want you to know, it's not like I was messing with you. It probably seems like that. Like I was jerking everybody around."

Callie made no comment.

"I told you it doesn't work perfectly. They're memories like anybody else's memories. They can be wrong. And then on top of that, Casey found out what I was doing and tried to get me to lie. Just lie and get everyone looking in the wrong places. But I was trying. I was trying to make him think I was on his side, and work around him at the same time."

"Althea, I can't imagine being in the position you were in . . ."

"You think he just told me things and I pretended I knew them in other ways, but it wasn't like that. It's not like that. I'm not trying to get sympathy. I just . . . It's important to me you understand."

"I do understand."

More silence, more clicking. Althea might've been assessing whether Callie meant it. And did she? She understood that Althea had had a hard life. Being given up by your birth parents couldn't be easy. Why hadn't she and her brother been adopted? Maybe because they wanted to keep the kids together. Maybe because there had been problems. Casey had been a budding psychopath. Althea thought she could have other people's memories.

It could've been that her malingering, her fantasies, were born out of that very hardship. If your only blood family was your brother and he was a serial killer in the making, a sexual predator, your coping mechanisms might get pretty wild.

"I'm sorry," Callie said.

"For what?"

"For all of it. For all of us."

Althea breathed like she was getting emotional. "Me too."

Callie watched Abel in the other room. She thought the conversation might be over and prepared to say goodbye.

Then Althea said, "I still see things."

"I know," Callie said, without much conviction.

"I still have memories. In fact, when I was with him, when I was with Abel, I got other memories, too."

"Okay . . ."

"I know what happened to his sister."

Callie started to respond, but her mouth went dry.

"I know what happened to Leila. How she died."

After a few more seconds in shock, something switched in Callie. This felt like the beginning, back to the start of it all, when Althea had first called with her information about Abel.

But there was no need to go down that road again.

"Maybe you do," Callie said. "Or maybe you think you do. But you need to understand something. My brother-in-law is dead. Garr is gone, and I'd be lying if I said there wasn't a part of me that faults you for that. If you'd just been straightforward. So there's no more. No more time for games."

It was something Callie had been feeling since her talk with Footman but hadn't fully verbalized until now.

"I'm sorry about Garr," Althea said. "I am. I never wanted that to happen. But you have to believe me."

"No, Althea, I don't. I don't have to believe you."

But then something hit her, and Callie doubted her own words.

The snowmobiles.

Abel had swerved to avoid a snowmobile in the road and gone into the lake; he'd said so himself. And Althea had known that; she'd told Callie on their drive up from Speculator. But Casey couldn't have told her. In his confession to Footman, he claimed to never have seen the wreck occur.

So how could Althea have known?

No, Callie told herself. *Althea doesn't know anything about how Leila died. And whatever you need to know, you can get it from Abel directly, not a stranger.*

That's how life works.

She was done with Althea Cooper.

"Callie? Are you there?"

Callie made no response. The line hummed and clicked. She held on for one more second, then ended the call. After stuffing the phone in her pocket, she wandered back into the living room and sat down on the couch.

Abel stirred and looked around, as if alerted by her presence. His eyes were glassy with sleep. "Everything okay, honey?"

She looked at him, and then she smiled. "Everything is fine."

She almost said, *Go back to sleep*. But honestly, she preferred him awake.

THE END

ACKNOWLEDGMENTS

When it's been just me and a book for months, the first people to look at it are like my rescuers, come to save me from the deserted island. My deepest gratitude to Veronika Jordan and Sara McLachlan, two readers who provided absolutely brilliant feedback at a critical time — whether it led me to clarify a plot point, sharpen a character's motivation, or just gave me the confidence to continue the process.

Thanks to my editor, Jodi Compton, for her wisdom, steady hand, and sense of humor. A good editor is like a colleague, a teacher, and a therapist all rolled into one. And Jodi is *great* editor, so imagine how lucky I am.

Thanks to Emma Grundy Haigh and Jasper Joffe for taking this story into their capable hands, for giving it a life outside my head, for bringing it to readers. And for making it possible that I — at least for a short time — can relax and enjoy the fact of having written a book.

ALSO BY T.J. BREARTON

THE NORTH COUNTRY SERIES
Book 1: DARK WEB
Book 2: DARK KILLS
Book 3: GONE

THE TITAN SERIES
Book 1: HABIT
Book 2: SURVIVORS
Book 3: DAYBREAK
Book 4: BLACK SOUL

SPECIAL AGENT TOM LANGE
Book 1: DEAD GONE
Book 2: TRUTH OR DEAD
Book 3: DEAD OR ALIVE

STANDALONE NOVELS
HER HUSBAND'S LIES
HER PERFECT SECRET
HIGH WATER
THE HUSBANDS
WHEN HE VANISHED

Thank you for reading this book.

If you enjoyed it please leave feedback on Amazon or Goodreads, and if there is anything we missed or you have a question about, then please get in touch. We appreciate you choosing our book.

Founded in 2014 in Shoreditch, London, we at Joffe Books pride ourselves on our history of innovative publishing. We were thrilled to be shortlisted for Independent Publisher of the Year at the British Book Awards.

www.joffebooks.com

We're very grateful to eagle-eyed readers who take the time to contact us. Please send any errors you find to corrections@joffebooks.com. We'll get them fixed ASAP.